Can'tLit

Can'tLit

Fearless Fiction from *Broken Pencil* Magazine

edited by
richard rosenbaum

Published by ECW Press
2120 Queen Street East, Suite 200, Toronto, Ontario, Canada M4E 1E2
416.694.3348 / info@ecwpress.com

Library and Archives Canada Cataloguing in Publication

Can't lit : fearless fiction from Broken Pencil magazine /
[compiled by] Richard Rosenbaum.
"A misFit book".
ISBN 978-1-55022-896-0
1. Short stories, Canadian (English). 2. Canadian fiction (English)—21st
century. I. Rosenbaum, Richard, 1979- II. Title Broken pencil.
PS8321.C385 2009 C813'.010806 C2009-902528-0

Editor: Richard Rosenbaum
Copy editor: Emily Schultz
Cover design/images: David Gee
Text design/typesetting: stef lenk
Illustrations: Winston Rountree
Printing: Webcom   1   2   3   4   5

The publication of Can'tLit: fearless fiction from Broken Pencil magazine has been
generously supported by the Canada Council for the Arts, which last year
invested $20.1 million in writing and publishing throughout Canada, by the
Ontario Arts Council, by the OMDC Book Fund, an initiative of the Ontario
Media Development Corporation, and by the Government of Canada through
the Book Publishing Industry Development Program (BPIDP).

 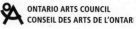

Printed and bound in Canada

TABLE OF
CONTENTS

FOREWORD
THE CASE AGAINST LITERATURE
hal niedzviecki

Broken Pencil's first fiction editor was Ken Sparling. Sparling's a maverick —a brilliant writer and an editor who despises convention. He doesn't care what your name is, where you're from, or who's published you. He only cares about what you've written. Does it hurt to read, the pain sticking around like a perpetually oozing tattoo you never should have gotten, but you were a little drunk, and a little stupid, and a little hopeful that those words, etched into skin, might actually end up mattering? Sparling only wanted the words that mattered. So that's what we published. Many of the stories in this book were originally chosen by him. I took over from him determined to carry on the tradition of using only the most desperate writing, only the stuff that got kicked out of the house before limping over to our office with no place else to go.

These stories are outcasts. They don't fit into traditional CanLit (which I've been railing about since I started out as an editor and novelist), and, in most cases, they don't even resemble the contemporary short story we've come to know and love. They are anti-literature. By and large, they read ragged, lacking the refinements of metaphor, magical realism, and perfect epiphany on the prairies. A few of them might even be badly written. On purpose? By accident? Who really gives a fuck? This is *Broken Pencil*. We're not trying to win awards, launch the writers Oprah wants you to read, or really do anything at all. The words do the work. Their ink seeps past the skin and on into the flesh. I carry these stories around in my heavy heart, clogged arteries, chest cramp laughter, sharp pain an insistence that things still matter despite all evidence to the contrary.

Richard Rosenbaum, who has worked with me as associate fiction editor for several years now, took on the challenge of editing this collection, choosing from among the ten years of stories we've published. He found out that some of our contributors have disappeared, seemingly fallen off the face of the earth. Others have gone on to bigger and better things, and refused to appear in this book on the grounds that their early writings were unrefined, silly, and sick, and weird. Whatever. It's the words that matter, that we'll remember, that refuse to dissipate no matter where you are, or who you think you've become. To the many fine writers whose stories appear in this book, I say thank you. I say I am proud to have worked with you. I say the cheque is *still* in the mail so get used to it. To those about to read this collection, I say don't blame us for what lies ahead: we're just the messenger, lonely couriers who etch words in our skin, so the wind and the rain and the snow won't erase what matters.

Hal Niedzviecki
Broken Pencil fiction editor
Spring 2009

INTRODUCTION
WHY CAN'T CANADA READ?
richard rosenbaum

CanLit sucks.
There. I said it.
Now allow me to clarify.
CanLit is *awesome*.

Canadians are producing some of the best, most creative, provocative, boundary-pushing fiction in the world. The problem is that not enough of it is getting published, and whatever *is* getting out there is not, by and large, being very widely read or sufficiently appreciated and encouraged. You may have noticed that the writing we tend to prize most highly here in Our Home and Native Land—the novels that sell all of, like, twenty-seven copies to become bestsellers, the stories that win the big awards— is the cold, dull, pastoral stuff. Little girls growing up in small towns or old women dying in them. The stuff written by people named Margaret. You know what I'm talking about.

The writing that's polished and pitch-perfect, but says almost nothing. It feels weighty, but it's only dense; it seems serious, but it's really just baroque. It's not relevant or meaningful. It's *banal*. Maybe we want to distance ourselves from the perceived brashness and ascendancy of our American neighbours, I don't know, but whatever the reason, in this country we've made a habit of celebrating the inoffensive and the mediocre. We'll barely acknowledge the existence of homegrown writers who haven't already gained international acclaim, then once they do we'll permanently brand them as immortal icons of CanLit. Regardless of the actual quality of their work, we'll add them to the canon to collect dust. Sure, every once in a while something genuinely great will sneak through—be praised in the papers, and maybe win, say, the Journey Prize, if somebody accidentally leaves the back door open—but then, at least as often as not, the subsequent contributions of that writer will be ignored and he or she will never be heard from again. There's so little money and so few resources available to invest in and promote our own culture that apparently we can't afford to take chances on anything that might not pay dividends or that could possibly piss someone off. And I doubt I'm the only one who's sick of it.

I met Hal Niedzviecki in 2003, when I took a short-story-writing class he was teaching at George Brown College in Toronto. What I'd been writing was the kind of stuff that my high school Writer's Craft teacher, Mr. Kress, described as "good, but not very marketable." Mr. Kress was never anything but encouraging, and he wasn't trying to tell me to change the way I wrote, just warning me that there wasn't much of an appetite in our culture for the types of things that interested me. So I signed up for this creative writing program hoping to be able to learn a few new tricks, connect with other writers who might be trying to do the same things that I was, and find someone who could maybe guide me toward some success where I'd previously been failing. Hal turned out to be the perfect person for this.

Way back in 1995, Hal started publishing a magazine called *Broken Pencil*, dedicated to the zine scene, the independent and alternative arts community that had been boiling below the surface of Canada's culture. The *Broken Pencil* mandate was (and is) to bring the submerged cultural urge into Canada's collective consciousness, to help lift it up and lend it legitimacy. And this included promoting writing—from writers within Canada and outside it whom nobody here had ever heard of, or wouldn't touch—that was too weird or uncomfortable for the (all-too) serious literary journals, too visceral and punk rock for the likes of the Margarets and their ilk. Hal told me that the story I wrote for that class was just the sort of thing that *Broken Pencil* likes (well, one of the two stories I wrote—the other one, he didn't much care for, actually). He said that I should submit it. I did, and it was eventually printed in the *BP* tenth anniversary issue, right after the comic about a day in the life of an angst-ridden stripper. Not for lack of trying, it was my first piece of published fiction unless you count my high school yearbook.

Hal and I kept in touch after that, and a couple of years later when he was looking for new associate fiction editors, he asked if I would be interested. Hell yes, I was interested.

Going through the dozens of fiction submissions that *BP* receives every month, I was amazed by how high the quality of most of them was (I mean, of course some of them were terrible, but surprisingly few). It was painful only to be able to accept one or two of them per issue. And when I started going back and reading over the scores of stories that had been published in the mag over the previous decade-plus, I saw the amount of talent and the depth of authenticity that had gone into them. Yet recognizing that pretty much none of these writers were anything close to household names—some of them, as far as I could tell, had never been published anywhere except *Broken Pencil*—that just seemed *wrong*, you know? Until I discovered *BP* and started getting to know the arts community surrounding it, I had almost no connection with the people who were trying to accomplish the same things I was, to resist the Tyranny of the Margarets. To craft stories that really mean something, stories that taste like blood, that hurt to write, and that hurt to read. That's why I thought it was important to put together this collection. Not only to promote as widely as possible the work of writers who were unfairly forced to toil in obscurity (and some who still are), scribbling their insights between shifts at Chapters or Kinko's while the smug authors of boring-ass bestsellers polish their GGs, but also to show emerging writers that there *is* a place and a need for that sharp, offensive urban fiction, for that all-around *weird shit*, in the otherwise mostly bland and soulless field of the Canadian literary scene, and hopefully to continue working to expand that space.

Check it out. You might even discover that you belong here too.

THE WORST OF US

(Quarter-finalist in the Broken Pencil
First Annual Indie Writers Deathmatch, online exclusive)

sarah gordon

I know I'm kinda pathetic. I mean, we all are. There's only so many girls
to go around and there's, like, a million of us. Every Friday night it's a
flies-on-honey situation. Or with the skankier girls, flies on shit. But
maybe knowing I'm pathetic makes me less pathetic, you know? I feel
real bad sometimes, for those poor schmucks who don't know, who just
walk around with these super sick hormones bouncing around, like how
the bass turned up real loud in their car makes this boom boom boom,
you know? It's so small town. It's sick. Those guys wouldn't survive in
a big city, man. They'd show up somewhere and get their asses kicked.
And it makes it worse that we're all in the army, you know? I mean these
guys think they're all tough shit, top of the pile, but in reality they're
just these desperate idiots who live in the shacks, eat pizza and dirty-bird
every night, drive around, and live for the next wet T-shirt contest.

Take Carriere for example. There's this medic chick who's real pretty
and real nice. I mean, she ain't no shack rat. A lot of the guys will fake a
migraine or whine about a blister so they can get near her. So Carriere
gets some sort of gastric thing, gets the trots pretty bad. He's standing
in line, just praying he doesn't get her. But he does, goddammit, he
does. And you should hear him tell this story, really. He tells it so funny.
So they go into the little room, and he has to tell her he's got the runs
and answer all these questions. Meanwhile his guts are just squirming,
begging him to take a dump. And she asks him to "describe" what his
"bowel movements" are like, and he says, get this, "real explosive," and
she kind of smiles at him half sympathetically, and then he farts, he farts
really loud, and it really, really smells he says, makes rotten eggs smell

like roses. Man! The humiliation! So Carriere tells this story to the boys, gets us all laughing. And it makes us all feel better, you know? I mean the guy's a good sport. I've all the time in the world for him. But that night he got so drunk he put his fist through a window. Seven stitches. And I know what that was about. He was angry, man. 'Cause that girl is worth something. And she'd never look at him anyway, but now whenever she did she'd think of shit.

It's a bad scene around here. We watch some of the older guys find a woman. And it doesn't matter if she's good-looking or not. The point is he finds one who's willing to put up with him for whatever reason. Maybe she's just as desperate, or maybe she's dumb. Either way the boys are jealous. And it's not too long before you hear that guy wants to "settle down." And he disappears from the scene for awhile, him and his girl, maybe they get a dog and a house off base, and it's all he can talk about at work. He complains. She won't let him drink. She got rid of his sofa. She's wasting his money on candles and shit. But man. The boys hang on every word 'cause they want their own chance to complain. They talk about that guy and give him a hard time for not coming around anymore, but really they want to complain so bad. I don't think they see far enough down the road. They don't see the guys with eyes that are dead tired, the guys who have been beaten on too long by love and war. The guys who go on tour and cheat. Doesn't matter who it's with. They'll crawl up any warm wet hole that's willing. And then their wife might cheat on them. And one of them throws some furniture around when they find out, some Wal-Mart special, and the other one calls the MPs. God, I'm depressing myself just talking about this.

But I mean, it's nice around here sometimes. Like last week. No one gave us cock that much, the Sarge was takin' it easy on us, and when he wasn't we all pulled our weight. PT was good. We went on our Wednesday run, and it was just that perfect temperature for running, and the sun was something else. I felt like I hadn't looked at it in a long time, you know? It was so nice to look at the sun that running up RCD hill was almost a pleasure. Hard to believe, I know. And then at dismissal parade on Friday the MWO thanked us for being good troops, told us about the hard work ahead in preparing for Kabul, told us he was personally very satisfied with the calibre of soldiers he had standing before him, and then told us to have a good weekend and drive safe. I mean, that's rare, man. The troops joked the guy must've gotten laid. But it felt good just the same.

So the bar that night was awesome. No fights. Lots of girls. It was packed in there. Everyone was celebrating even though there was no reason. Cheap drinks. Sticky floors. Boob shirts and pussy skirts. I think we were celebrating that this is one godawful town in the middle of the most beautiful wilderness, and we got jobs to which the world is oblivious, and no one, absolutely no one, understands us but each other and ourselves. I stumbled home that night since it was kinda warm, and the base was pretty much quiet except for some people's dogs. And I could hear the flags flapping. And the moon shone big across the measly lawns. And the cruddy swing sets were creaking in the wind, and I was drunk, but I swear more of their paint peeled off—I knew it happened at night. And I could see some TVs still on, and I knew people were passed out on their couches, and I wanted to let everyone know that things just might turn out right, but I couldn't guarantee that, you know? And the only thing that ruined that night for me was that when I finally found my door and hit the sheets I hadn't washed them in a real long time, and I just wanted them to be clean like back home. Like back with my parents at home, a long time ago.

Maybe sometimes the wives and girlfriends don't understand how divided a soldier is. I mean we have work and the boys, and we have home. She doesn't know the feeling of huddling around the heater hose when we're on a long ex in the middle of a piss-freezing winter, playing cards, shooting the shit, making asses of each other. She doesn't know how much that sucks, and how great it is. She doesn't know how depressing it is sitting around doing nothing. How it sucks being told to clean storage lockers that are already spotlessly clean. How much it sucks playing war when your heart's just not in it. Or how it feels when it is. And maybe we don't understand how whole she wants to be. And maybe I'm just blowing air through my ass. That's more likely. I do know one thing though. Everyone wants a second chance. Everyone wants to have mistakes forgiven.

Hank, or Pea-Brain, as he's called, or Pee-Bee, or Peebs, got himself a frickin' gorgeous woman. Smart too, and confident, but easy to be around, you know? Easy to talk to. Peebs was alone for years, and I think he'd given up. He bought himself a massive stereo and wide-screen TV, and that was that. He wasn't savin' up for no nest egg anymore. So he goes on leave back home and meets her. Comes back all happy. The joke goes around that Pea-Brain's dating his cousin. So she moves here and we're all shocked to meet her. We were like the seven dwarfs, except we were all bashful. So Peebs has gotta protect this thing, you know? He gets all uptight and

stressed out, scared as hell it won't last. He swears off drinking just in case he screws up. It was awful to watch, but impressive. I've never seen a man more miserable in love. So anyway he cracks one night. She goes home to Newfoundland to see her mother and he comes out to the bar. And he's loaded out of his tree, and some shack rat puts her tits in his face and he kisses her, and before the hour was up some busybody, some Tim Hortons gossip queen calls Peeb's girlfriend and rats on him. I mean, I'm pretty sure he was set up, but it nearly destroyed him. So he goes home and freaks out, beats himself up, and throws all the furniture out the balcony. What is it with furniture anyway? It's like this symbol of stability; everyone wants the leather couch, the glass coffee table, the entertainment unit, the sleigh bed, and then they throw it around when they finally get it. So he throws it all outside, and it all gets rained on, and the neighbours get all mad, and he lets the dogs shit in the house, and doesn't clean it up. And he says to me a few days later, "It smells like I feel."

But the best part about it is that she comes back. And cleans everything up. No one could believe it. And he goes to the base counselling centre once a week. And one day at work we're all standing around, and he's looking a little like a sheep, and he says, "Uh, guys?" And there's a silence. And he says, "You can still call me Peebs, but not Pea-Brain. I'm not a pea-brain." He just blurted it out like he'd been wanting to say it for a long time. And no one laughed. And Carriere said, "Sure, Peebs, sure thing." And then there was another silence until someone switched the subject.

Peebs got posted last year and no one's seen him since. Carriere leaves for Afghanistan to play with sand niggers next month. Guess we might not see him again either. That's the other thing. There's a lot of back slapping and clearing of throats around posting season. A lot of clearing of throats.

I met a girl. She works in the Coles bookstore in the mall in town. She has glasses, so I don't know if she's the type you hold the door for, or if that would make her mad. I'd sure like to hold the door for her though. I haven't asked her out yet. There's not really anywhere nice I can take her, without everyone seeing us and sizing her up. Well, she might say no anyway. She might not like me 'cause I don't know many books. But man, if I ever get a wife, I'm gonna be sure and tell her all the stuff. I'll tell her about sitting side-seat in the 'copter, looking out through the open door, and down at the scraggy bush ("Looks like Carriere's back hair," someone always calls through the headset and we all laugh), and how when we drop suddenly it doesn't feel like any of my guts are attached anymore, how they float, and it feels sickening mostly, but that there's about two seconds of total bliss. And I'll show her all my kit and tell what it's for, I'll put the full ruck on her back and laugh when the weight nearly makes her fall. Heck, I'll even tell her the only way to get a moment's peace with God is on the cold and starry walk to the shitter. I'll tell her I never really liked the tight shirts and short skirts, even though I did. And that us boys signed our life away when we were young, and found it here years later, and really, everyone, even the worst of us, is hoping to salvage it, like the old tanks in the scrapyard, like making some amazing new machine out of scrap metal.

LINDSEY

(From Broken Pencil #8)

golda fried

One summer Lindsey let me drive her around in a car.

Her relationship with Dayton had ended abruptly. She told me in the car when I was digging into her French fries. I covered all the fries with ketchup. I told her, "Things are slowly deteriorating with me and my boyfriend. He's going away in September. He's not going to be there."

It was first love for both of us. Gone.

I sprinkled salt into the ketchup. Lindsey was brutally shocking, and horribly funny, and—I heard once—terribly mean. She said, "I feel like dancing." This meant we were off to a dance club. I didn't feel like dancing but I was already bouncing around in the car.

My boyfriend was surprised. I had always made him drive if we were going anywhere. And why Lindsey? He heard she threw a lot of tantrums, or her sister did. "Anyway, glass ends up breaking."

Lindsey was more honk-sensitive than I was. My confidence was up. Her parents liked me. I found out she read books. Ones with short stories in them.

"Who reads short stories?" I had thought.

I paid attention as she made faces to punctuate the stories she told. I found myself in picturelike poses.

We had other kinds of conversations too. The kind where she sat very still and laughed nervously.

She told me she really loved Dayton. She studied up on things he liked. She tried not to be intimidated by his many friends with whom he went to the movies. He made her so nervous she'd sometimes puke at night just thinking about him.

She had a framed poster Dayton had given her still hanging on the wall. I didn't tell her she should take it down. I had a stuffed animal my boyfriend had given me that he had had his whole life. He said, "The eyes fell off but I always pretended it could see anyway."

My boyfriend and I set Lindsey up with this guy named Terry. Like chess pieces waiting to be moved, we all sat on a blanket and watched fireworks. Terry was really an inappropriate match. He was a heavy joker and Lindsey sat there trying to smile. Wanting to like him. Her jaw loosely swinging on hinges. We should have picked someone a little more sensitive.

Terry's ice cream plunged into the grass and he was the only one laughing as he jumped up to buy a new one.

It was the end of summer. Lindsey said she wished her soul could be like perfume. I said I wished mine could be like feathers.

Lindsey's father sat gently on the couch watching TV while I was waiting for Lindsey to come down. He looked like he was gazing into mountains. He had all the patience and calmness of someone who has journeyed. I felt like a hummingbird hovering next to a window, about to flit away. "I think your daughter is really cool, and that she's trying me out like I'm on some sort of audition to be subdued or something, but I won't be very subdued when my boyfriend leaves, and I'll be forced to deal with all of Lindsey's other friends and I think that when that happens I'll just disappear."

Lindsey's father looked over at me like his neck was in a brace. He asked me, "Have you planned out your route for this evening? You should always have a plan to avoid traffic."

The dog came up to me and attacked my knees, and Lindsey was there suddenly like a fairy godmother tapping the dog on the nose saying, "Be nice to my friend."

One time I thought I saw my ex-boyfriend and honked but he kept walking. Lindsey heard, and slid into the front seat, glad to see me, and it was the following summer.

Craig did a lot of things to naked girls in fur coats and described them in detail to Lindsey over the summer. Lindsey was much amused by this and talked him through it, through weeks of episodes. They were like an ongoing brother and sister. They had debates.

He convinced her to go to a rock show that I had to see. Lindsey kept dragging me into the washroom for most of it. Her perfume was up against the smell of toilets, and she kept pouring it on. I was in love with the band and felt the music evaporating.

"Just forget about him and enjoy the show," I screamed.

Craig ended up putting his arm around her, his hand holding a plastic cup, and beer splashed in her face. She wanted him to kiss her.

In the car on the way home, Lindsey was not going to go to any more rock concerts with me, and I had only gone to one movie with Dayton.

I decided to go on my own and tell Lindsey about Dayton myself. I hadn't spoken to her in months. She listened calmly. She didn't make a scene. I left right after. There were no hugs goodbye, just eyes plunging into her hands.

On the sidewalk I tried to piece it together. He had been in the stairway, and the cigarettes landed on the floor as birds fell out of a tree. He had been a jester on the sidewalk with the family dog when I had to do some deep thinking. He had been on a couch in a friend's kitchen when I was far away from home.

I asked about her from time to time. It was like clearing out the last of her gum wrappers from the floor of the car before giving the car back to my parents. It was like looking for scraps of food.

Once after our summer, after I had moved out, Lindsey was sleeping over and I forgot to tell her this guy might be coming by. Only instead of using the front door, this guy kept throwing rocks at the bedroom window. Lindsey ran into the kitchen screaming.

I went over to the bedroom window. I saw ugliness in my reflection, and was about to start crying myself. The next rock shattered the glass.

In Dayton's kitchen I waited for him to come back with dinner. Outside in the living room he had a million books he had read. I could never come close to reading a sliver of them. I thought maybe I could start with some short stories.

Dayton had all the ingredients for a Caesar salad in a shopping bag. He put the head of lettuce on a chopping block.

"I had coffee with Lindsey today," he said. The lettuce fell apart like feathers. I held one up and waited for him to go on. "She went on and on about herself."

Whenever I felt the worry come on I generally ended it by not talking about Lindsey at all. If we did talk about her, it was in a hushed way, like her soul was in the coffee. "How's she doing?"

"She was in good spirits. She thinks first loves should keep in touch." Then his eyes dodged about the room a bit. "She told me she's never going to forgive you."

I stood at the window with no car in me at all. *Tonight the clouds all look like shredded Kleenex.*

Dayton was heavy with thought, like a mountain, as he stared at the salad.

When we first started going out, Dayton took my hand and went over all the differences between him and my ex-boyfriend to ensure in my mind that it would work out. I didn't tell him I had loved my first boyfriend. I went home and looked at the stuffed animal my ex-boyfriend had given me, its eyes pecked out.

Lindsey put heaps of sugar into our coffees and it escaped from the spoon all over the table. She turned up the radio until it made us bump into things. She tossed her closet on the bed saying, "Honestly, we can go anywhere tonight. You decide."

NATURAL SELECTION

(From Broken Pencil *#35)*

martha schabas

Tom and Annie were trying to break up for the seventh time in eight months and it still wasn't even close to working. Tom was one of those weirdos who wouldn't take Tylenol and believed Neil Armstrong had never made it any higher than his TWA flight to Cape Canaveral. Annie was the type who objected categorically to the use of the word "retarded." Nobody could understand how they had ever gotten together in the first place. And now they couldn't break up. They were joined by one of those stupid, inexplicable life forces that made mothers love their funny-looking babies and inspired people to go to Australia. Resistance wasn't just futile, it was impossible.

"You are poisoning my bone marrow."

Annie looked up from her egg-white omelette. Tom always made breakfast on Saturdays and it made him touchy.

"Can you pass the salt?"

The force that bound Tom to Annie and Annie to Tom had been activated at the bad party of a mutual friend of a friend. Tom hated parties, but didn't have the strength of character to withstand solitude. Annie hated people, but loved the timbre of her own voice conversing with them. Tom was drinking an organic beer and mumbling softly to three skeptical listeners about media conspiracy in Regina. He spotted something moving out of the corner of his eye. It was Annie's head bobbing earnestly back and forth like an anxious pigeon. She was drinking a gin and tonic and laughing wildly at her own joke. Their gazes met, and nothing happened. Tom went back to his delicately whispered philosophies and Annie started to tell her friends how good she was at Scrabble. They didn't actually talk to each other until Annie, weaving her way to the kitchen, knocked her bare shoulder into the tip of Tom's cigarette.

"Oh my god, I'm burnt!"

"I'm so sorry, I didn't see you there." Tom was sheepish and even quieter than usual.

"What?"

"I said I'm sorry, I didn't see you there."

"I can't hear you. Why are you talking like that?"

"Like what?"

"God, I'm being confrontational again." Annie rolled her eyes in playful self-deprecation. "I have this problem where I'm just incredibly more sincere than the average person and I think people are sometimes overwhelmed by it."

Tom thought she was a conceited bitch. "Do you want to get some air on the balcony?"

Annie still couldn't hear him. "Okay."

The first time Tom and Annie tried to break up was the closest it ever came to working. They had only been dating for two months and the force was still malleable, like an impressionable adolescent. Tom owned a café in the Market District and Annie did counseling at a women's shelter just three blocks away. Sometimes they'd meet for lunch by the harbour. It was July, and even though the air smelled like bad tap water, the breeze off the lake felt nice on their skin.

"I wish I were a seagull." Tom's eyes were shiny as he looked at the sky.

Annie was so embarrassed. "I think you need a hobby." She started picking the tomatoes out of her sandwich and tossing them on the asphalt.

"Hobbies are Band-Aids."

"I have no idea what that means."

Tom looked out at the lake. It looked like a sheet of stainless steel, cold and static.

"They're for people who'd always rather not get wet. Even when it's like forty degrees out." He picked up a tomato slice that had landed at his feet and put it in the empty paper bag beside him.

"You need to think a little more laterally, Tom. That's your biggest problem." Annie chewed and talked at the same time. "I derive an enormous amount of satisfaction from my hobbies. I mean, you know how I have a tendency to be too giving, to put myself completely out for everyone else?"

"Mmm-hmm." Tom was trying to reach another of her discarded tomato slices with the tip of his foot.

"Well, my hobbies give me a little time to focus exclusively on myself. I think it's a really healthy indulgence."

Tom trapped the tomato beneath his foot, dragged it towards himself, and added it to the bag of her salvaged litter. He stood up and started unbuttoning his shirt.

"What the hell are you doing?"

He dropped his shirt on the tomato bag, kicked off his flip-flops, and walked towards the tourist kiosk that blocked the lake from the paved waterfront.

"You can't swim here! There's *e coli*!" Annie got up after him so she didn't have to scream. "This is crazy. You're embarrassing me."

Tom ignored her. He made his way around the kiosk and looked for a clear place to dive in. Annie followed furiously. Her face looked red and goofy.

"If you jump in, we're finished!"

Tom didn't even turn around. "Fine!" He bent his knees and swung his arms in front of him.

"Excuse me," came a melodic voice from behind them. Tom turned around to meet a teenager in a tour guide uniform. "You can't swim here." She smiled sweetly. She was blond and plump, pretty despite her pimples. Tom blushed. He tried not to look at the round breasts pushing against her white polo shirt and red-lettered name tag. Jessica. Teenage girls always made him stupid and uncomfortable.

"Okay."

That night, Tom and Annie brought takeout back to Annie's apartment and stared at each other sullenly across the kitchen table. Neither of them could understand how they were still together. Their frustration was so bad it felt sexual.

"The Mexican Standoff." Tom's head was bent over his stir-fry. He was practically whispering.

Annie put her chopsticks down indignantly. "Excuse me?"

"It's what I've titled today."

"It's racist."

"It's an expression."

"It's derogatory to Mexicans." Annie punched each syllable like a robot from an '80s movie.

"It's funny." Tom remembered this feeling. It was that same mix of fear and delight he'd felt when he declared openly to his grade five teacher that he had indeed just asked Becky Lee to show him her boobies. He knew he had it coming.

"Oh, it's funny, is it?" Annie's eyebrows were raised so high it looked unhealthy. "Well, in that case," she waved her over-sized hands like she was doing a jazz routine, "let the racist ruminate! That's *my* title—The Racist Ruminates!"

"You're giving me a headache."

Annie smiled sadistically. "Take an aspirin."

"Fuck off."

Tom grabbed for a cigarette and Annie raged into the living room to plop herself in front of the TV. But somehow they both felt acute, physical relief.

Their fourth attempt at breaking up found them storming out of the theatre of a half-finished romantic comedy. Annie took the stairs three at a time to the underground parking lot, and Tom ran out savagely into the bleary, dusk drizzle. They probably would've never spoken again if the light rain hadn't become heavy hail, and Annie hadn't driven past Tom cowering in a bus shelter like a homeless mongrel. They drove silently back to her place where he had a hot shower that took so long she wondered whether he had slipped on the slick, re-glazed ceramic and hit his head. He finally came out of the bathroom, a cloud of steam in his wake, wearing flannel pajamas and an expression of secret satisfaction.

Later, Annie found him curled up on her Afghan blanket like a complacent cat, a pen in hand and loose paper on his lap.

"What are you writing?" She peered over his compact body. He flipped over the top page.

"Nothing."

"You're clearly writing something."

"They're just ideas."

"Ideas for what?"

"I don't know." Tom sounded like a guilty child. "A story, maybe."

"Oh, you write stories now, do you?"

"Maybe."

When Tom woke up the next morning, Annie was sitting upright in bed, his papers gripped in her hands.

"You bastard."

"Mmm." Tom rolled onto his side and wiped the drool from his cheek.

"I do not have the wingspan of an albatross!"

Tom had just been dreaming about birds. White, ochre-beaked doves, the kind a magician would free from his top hat at the climax of a trick. He was vaguely aroused.

"God, it's not about you, Annie."

"You called her Fanny! What the fuck kind of a name is Fanny?!"

"You are so self-obsessed."

Tom had an appointment that afternoon with a periodontic specialist in the suburbs. He'd spent the past four months floundering on an alleged waiting list, watching his gums lose their grip like Scotch Tape in a warm room. When he'd finally booked the appointment two weeks ago, Annie had promised to drive him to it.

"I'm really tempted to renege here, Tom," she was ducking into the driver's side of her Honda Accord, "but I'm going to be the bigger person and keep my word despite your passive-aggressive antics."

"Thanks, Annie." Tom would've taken public transit, but the suburbs made him uneasy.

She backed cautiously out of the driveway and accelerated slowly forward. "If there's one thing I can't handle," she tapped the steering wheel with the side of her hand to emphasize her point, "it's passive aggression. I take real pride in the fact that I always say exactly what I mean."

"Mmm." Tom was looking out the window and lamenting the invention of concrete.

"I can't stand when people are manipulative." She was turning left at a four-way stop sign. "It amazes me that anyone's okay with being so backhanded."

Tom lit a cigarette. She eyed him disapprovingly.

"Have you ever considered quitting smoking?"

"Hmm?" He took an extra deep inhale.

She took her hand off the gearshift and squeezed his leg affectionately,

"Do you ever think about how much you're putting yourself at risk for lung cancer and heart disease?"

"Give me a break, Annie."

"I just worry about you." She moved her fingers up his thigh like the itsy bitsy spider. "You can't blame me for worrying about you, can you?"

He looked at her and smiled blankly.

"Oh my god," her fingers had averted to his abdomen, "are you not wearing your seat belt?"

"You know I don't wear seat belts, Annie."

"But we made a deal, Tom. My car, my rules!"

"I will not have my internal organs crushed for your sake."

"Your internal organs?"

"There have been studies." He looked at her soberly. "Minor accidents where everyone would have been fine if their seat belts hadn't cut through their skin and ruptured their insides." He brought his cigarette back up to his lips and inhaled gently.

Annie remembered this feeling. It was that same mix of fury and bewilderment she'd felt at sixteen when the family parrot had told her to shut up.

Tom was shaking his head as he reflected. "Then there's the whole ambulance thing —"

"You really are an idiot."

"Paramedics wasting those crucial seconds trying to get the victims out of seat belts that have melded shut from the impact."

Annie spoke through a clenched jaw. "Put on your seat belt, Tom." She was breathing aggressively through her nose.

"That's not fair, Annie." He exhaled a thick ribbon of silver smoke.

She turned towards him. Her eyes were huge and her pupils were dancing. "BUCKLE UP!"

"Annie —"

"Put on your seat belt or I stop right here and you can take the bus."

Tom looked out the window. The vertical landscape of their downtown neighbourhood had transformed into a horizontal sprawl of strip malls and oversized movie theatres. They looked like floating palaces from another dimension. There wasn't a sidewalk in sight. He shuddered and reached across his right shoulder.

Tom was inside the examination room for over an hour. When he finally emerged from the white door, he looked dazed and wearied. Annie was sitting comfortably on a cushy orange chair and typing earnestly on her laptop. She waited for Tom to walk right over to her before she stopped typing and looked up at him. They stared at each other in silence. Annie looked like she expected him to speak first. When he didn't, she shut her laptop with a decided clap, and stood up resentfully. She pulled on her purple, chenille wrap and walked loftily to the exit. She had taken to wearing heels in the past few weeks and had cultivated an understated hip swing. It all made her look vaguely transsexual. Tom followed slowly, each step more hesitant than the last, as though he were afraid he might overshoot them. Annie had already started the car by the time he slinked awkwardly into his seat and did up his seat belt. She reversed cautiously out of her parking spot, and turned onto a street flanked on either side by colourless, townhouse condominiums. The complexes gave way to low-rise office buildings and family restaurants that looked like cartoons. Annie finally couldn't take it anymore.

"Aren't you even going to ask me what I was writing about in there?"

Tom would've responded, but his mouth was full of soggy gauze and still half-frozen from the anaesthetic.

"You suck." She turned back to the windshield.

Tom looked at her apologetically. A little rivulet of blood started dripping from between his lips.

That Saturday, the morning sunlight streaming prettily through the kitchen window, Annie put aside the remainder of her egg-white omelette to open up her laptop. Tom was quietly washing the breakfast dishes. When he turned around, she was plugging away at the keyboard.

"Well," she said expectantly without looking up.

"What are you working on, honey?"

"Oh, just a story."

"That is so interesting, Annie. What is your story about?" He wiped his hands on the dishtowel and sat on the opposite stool.

"Do you really want to know?"

"Yes, I'm sure I want to know."

"I guess it's kind of a black comedy."

"I love black comedy."

"Yeah." Her head was doing its trademark pigeon bob. "A kind of black comedic allegory."

"That sounds so original."

"Yeah —" Her voice suspended unnaturally. "It's an allegory about boredom."

"Really?"

"Mmm-hmm. Boredom gets bored with all his boring adolescent behaviour."

"Interesting. What kind of behaviour?"

"Oh, you know, smoking, driving dangerously, just the typical stuff."

"And what happens?"

"Well the ending's still a little vague. I think he'll realize that all his vices can be compounded by just wrapping his mouth around an exhaust pipe."

Within hours, Tom was back in the Afghan blanket, a pen gripped industriously in his left hand.

"Another story?" Annie had appeared out of nowhere behind him.

"It's nothing, Annie."

"Don't patronize me."

"Can't I keep a few things private?"

"TELL ME!" She looked mildly possessed. Tom shivered.

"It's kind of sci-fi."

"That's ballsy. What about?"

"A misunderstood pauper."

"Cute. What happens?"

"He dreams of true love, but gets lost on a planet of aliens."

"What kind of aliens?"

"That's the neat part. They look just like human beings, except their eyes face inward and all they can say is 'me.'"

Tom rode his bicycle to the café that afternoon to do inventory. It was a beautiful autumn day, the kind where the sunlight seems amber and people look nostalgic. Tom looked up at the yellow-leaved trees and wondered whether they too could appreciate the afternoon's softness. To him, they looked old and wise, their greying bark grizzled like his grandfather's beard. How insignificant I must seem to them, he mused, how small and foolishly temporary. Tom knew he was drifting into one of his favourite kind of thinking spells and his extremities tingled in anticipation. Could the trees be as conscious as he was? Annie would laugh at him, but how could anyone really know for sure? It was horrible that human beings thought they understood what extended so far beyond the ken of their own existences. Why not give trees the benefit of the doubt, he wondered as he locked his bicycle to a parking sign; why not imagine them capable of anything before groundlessly assuming the opposite?

He was still deep in thought as he walked into the café and saw an unfamiliar woman behind the counter. She had abundant dark hair and an expression of inner contentment. She was wearing a long ivory dress that was redolent of nudity.

"I'm Mehira." Her wide eyes twinkled. "I was supposed to start today."

"Right." Tom had no idea who she was or who had hired her.

"You cut your hair." Her voice had the fullness of unpasteurized milk.

"I did?" Tom rubbed the back of his head as if to check. "Yeah, I did. Months ago."

"Well, that party was months ago." She smiled luminously.

"I'm sorry. What party . . . ?"

Mehira seemed to have anticipated his confusion. "What's-his-name's party." She was already laughing at herself.

Tom chuckled and tried not to lose his cool. "You know, somehow that doesn't help me much." He wondered how he could possibly not remember her.

"Sorry." She pulled her streaming dark tresses behind her shoulders. Tom saw a tuft of black hair beneath each arm. He was overcome with desire. "I really can't remember the guy's name. He was just some random friend of a friend."

Tom felt like he'd swum into the warm spot of an otherwise freezing lake.

"You know, I think I know what party you're talking about."

The phone rang. It was Annie.

"Buy pasta."

"Are you okay, Annie? You sound rattled."

"I'm fine. I'm excited."

"Excited?" He was watching Mehira wipe the espresso machine. She moved like a ballerina in water.

"I'm writing another story."

"Oh."

"It's about some hippie dipshit who finally realizes the hypocrisy of his ways and dedicates the rest of his life to corporate development in sub-Saharan Africa where he dies of malaria in a swamp of acid rain."

Tom replaced the receiver. He was trying to decide the best place to begin Mehira's training.

"Do you smoke?"

Mehira smiled. "I'd love one."

On Monday morning, Annie went into the shelter even earlier than usual. She had a backlog of consultation reports from the previous week, and was hoping she could get some paperwork done before her first session. She walked up the stairwell of the converted community centre, eyeing the peeling green paint on the banister and surrounding walls with sly satisfaction. They reminded her—and, she hoped, everyone else who visited the shelter—of their perpetual lack of funding. In her office, she booted her very big and equally slow computer and plunked herself into a revolving chair against a navy Obus Forme. She lifted a thick pile of unsorted papers from her desk and leafed through them as her CPU made bleating sounds. There was a knock on her door. Annie looked up at the institutional-style clock above her desk. It wasn't even eight. There was little security in the building and she always worried that the delusional ex-boyfriend of one of the women might one day visit her with a switchblade.

"Come in." Danger was just another part of her socially conscious job, she thought proudly.

A tall man in his early thirties revealed himself from on the other side of the door. He was wearing khakis and a crisp, collared shirt that emphasized the blueness of his eyes. He was the kind of early-morning handsome that gets cast in toothpaste commercials.

"I'm from the Ministry of Community and Social Services. Was it you who was supposed to assist me with the report?"

Annie had no idea who he was or what he was talking about. "Sure."

"Great." He walked in and helped himself to the only other chair. "I'm so happy you guys are as eager about this as I am," he was pulling a file out of his briefcase. "We owe it to the public to show them just how important what you people do here is."

"I'm sorry." Annie recrossed her legs, and tried not to look awestruck. "But I didn't catch your —"

"God, sorry. I'm just so excited. It's Robert. Robert Cairncross. And you're Annie Laine."

"I am?" Annie felt almost dizzy. "I mean yes, I am. But how, I mean who —"

"We've actually met before. It was the urban outreach conference last May."

"I was in Edmonton in May."

"Oh." Robert scratched his head. "I was sure it was then."

"No. I was flying home the night of the conference. I ended up at a bad party instead. You do look really familiar though."

He smiled to reveal a few unusually white teeth. "Strange. You seem like the kind of woman who'd be too busy to waste her time at parties."

Annie giggled and pulled on her ponytail. "I know."

That night Annie made pork chops for dinner on the barbecue. Tom was running late and picked up a bottle of wine to make up for it.

"I'm so sorry, Annie —" He was halfway through the sliding door onto the balcony.

"Oh, no bother." Her voice was so buoyant she was practically singing.

Tom uncorked the wine and poured two generous glasses. He put on his Leonard Cohen CD and laid out the kitchen table. He felt balanced and nimble. Annie was humming along as she brought the food in from the balcony—pork and roasted vegetables—and sat down opposite him. She felt happy and invigorated. They smiled at each other without irony. Then Tom took out his papers as Annie unhinged her laptop, and they both began to write. They wrote slowly, but contently. Annie busied herself trying to find a bigger word for "pansy," and Tom struggled to come up with a good metaphor for megalomania. Occasionally, they'd look up and share a moment that was certainly complicit and possibly friendly. Neither asked what the other was working on. They opened two more bottles of wine and stayed up until the early hours of the morning.

Annie got up at sunrise to do her yoga stretches. Tom got up an hour later and went straight to the shower. When he came out, his hair turbaned in baby pink terrycloth, Annie was standing halfway inside the closet in her underwear. They grazed shoulders as Tom went to the dresser. He opened his only designated drawer and pulled out a pair of briefs, bluish from inept washing. They dressed in silence. Annie came over to the dresser to get down her jewellery box from on top of it. She reached around Tom's shoulders and knocked over a bottle of perfume. It landed at his feet. Tom bent over, picked it up, and carefully re-positioned it on the dresser so that it was no longer precarious.

"Thank you," she said nicely.

"You're welcome," he answered clearly.

Before the leaves had completely fallen off the trees, Annie and Tom met for lunch again by the harbour. They sat on the same bench in front of the tourist kiosk, but its windows were shut and the booth that had extended from its interior over the paved waterfront was gone. It was windy, and the cold air seemed to reverberate in their eardrums. Annie unwrapped her sandwich. Tom looked out at the lake. It looked like a sheet of corrugated iron, hard and kinetic. He wondered what had happened to Jessica. She was probably playing volleyball in some high-school gymnasium uptown. Annie chewed quietly. She held her sandwich out towards him. Tom shook his head. He wasn't the slightest bit hungry.

"It's getting too chilly for this, isn't it?" Annie shivered and edged her body towards him.

"Mmm." He put his arm around the back of the bench so that she could move closer.

They looked at each other silently. Her smile made her eyes wrinkle in the corners like crimped hair. It made him think of what she'd look like at eighty. His gaping mouth made his face look excessively relaxed. It made her think of muscular dystrophy. She let her head fall on his shoulder. Neither of them moved for a very long time.

CRAZY GLUE

(From Broken Pencil *#18)*
(Translated from Hebrew by Miriam Shlesinger)
etgar keret

She said, "Don't touch that."

"What is it?" I asked.

"It's glue," she said. "Special glue. The best kind."

"What did you buy it for?"

"Because I need it," she said. "A lot of things around here need gluing."

"Nothing around here needs gluing," I said. "I wish I understood why you buy all this stuff."

"For the same reason I married you," she murmured. "To help pass the time."

I kept quiet.

"Is it any good, the glue?" I asked.

She showed me the picture on the box, a guy hanging upside-down from the ceiling.

"No glue can really make a person stick like that," I said. "They just took the picture upside down. They must have put a light on the floor." I took the box from her and peered at it. "And there, look at the window. They didn't even bother to hang the blinds the other way. They're upside down, if he's really standing on the ceiling. Look," I said again, pointing to the window. She didn't look.

"It's eight already," I said. "I've got to run." I picked up my briefcase and kissed her on the cheek. "I'll be back pretty late. I'm working —"

"Overtime," she said. "Yes, I know."

I got home early. I said "Hi" as I walked in, but there was no reply. I went through all the rooms in the house. She wasn't in any of them. On the kitchen table I found the tube of glue, empty. I tried to move one of the chairs, to sit down. It didn't budge. I tried again. Not an inch. She'd glued it to the floor. The fridge wouldn't open. She'd glued it shut. I didn't understand what was happening, what would make her do such a thing. I didn't know where she was. I went into the living room to call her mother's. I couldn't lift the receiver. I kicked the wastebasket and almost broke my toe.

And then I heard her laughing. It was coming from somewhere above me. I looked up, and there she was, standing barefoot on the living room ceiling.

I stared open-mouthed. When I found my voice I could only ask, "What the hell . . . Are you out of your mind?"

She didn't answer, just smiled. Her smile seemed so natural, with her hanging upside down like that, as if her lips were just stretching on their own by the sheer force of gravity.

"Don't worry, I'll get you down," I said, hurrying to the shelf and grabbing the largest books. I made a tower of encyclopedias and clambered up on the pile.

"This may hurt a little," I said, trying to keep my balance. She went on smiling. I pulled hard as I could, but nothing happened. I climbed down.

"Don't worry," I said. "I'll get the neighbours or something. I'll go next door and call for help."

"Fine," she laughed. "I'm not going anywhere."

I laughed too. She was so pretty, and so incongruous, hanging upside down from the ceiling that way. With her long hair dangling downward, and her breasts moulded like two perfect teardrops under her white T-shirt. So pretty. I climbed back up onto the pile of books and kissed her. I felt her tongue on mine. The books tumbled out from under my feet, but I stayed floating in mid-air, hanging from her lips.

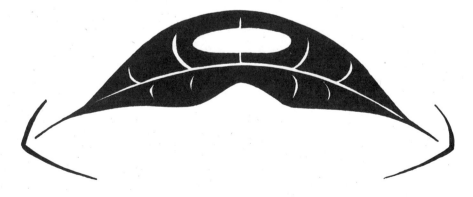

CAMP ZOMBIE

(From Broken Pencil #40)

ian rogers

There is only one rule at camp and Mark breaks it: he wakes me up.

Sleep is a rare commodity here, as deeply coveted as a box of Twinkies at fat camp. My first impulse is to swing out and kick him in the face. Lying in one of the hammocks—there are dozens of them all over camp, and at night they look like giant insect cocoons spun between the trees— I'm in the perfect position to do so. But when I roll to my side to kick, I lose my balance and start to fall out of the hammock. Mark catches me before I hit the ground, letting go of the feather he used to tickle me, and I watch as it seesaws gently to the ground.

"What the hell are you doing?" I grumble in a fuzzy voice. "Let me go!"

Mark sets me down. "Did you know your eyes get all puffy when you're tired? It's cute."

"I'm always tired," I snap.

"I know," he replies smoothly, "and you're always cute."

I walked right into that one. I close my eyes and press a fist against the bridge of my nose, an old trick to prevent the headache that comes from being pulled so abruptly from sleep. "You must want something," I say, my eyes still closed.

"What have you got today?"

"A couple of classes. Water therapy this morning and yoga in the afternoon."

"You free tonight?"

"Available? Yes. Free? No." I try to sound dry and sultry, but with only three hours sleep in as many days it comes out sad and pathetic.

"Can you come over to the Shack tonight after lights out?"

I look at Mark—really look at him—and see he's anxious, almost bursting with excitement.

"What for?" I ask.

"I've wanted to try something for a while now," he says vaguely. "This is the first year I've had the Shack to myself."

"That must be nice," I say, thinking of the sky blue cabin that I've been sharing with half a dozen girls this summer.

"So, can you come over?"

"What for?"

Mark smiles, and when he speaks his voice is low and secretive.

"I think I've found a cure."

I had been going to Camp Zombie since I was six years old, and when I turned seventeen I became a counsellor. It just seemed like the thing to do. I was so used to going that it became my summer routine. I couldn't imagine life without it, even though camp is only two months of the year. It's like being part of a secret society where instead of money or influence you need a sleep disorder to be a member. You need to be a zombie.

Mark and I walk down the dirt road to the wooden arch at the camp entrance. At the start of the summer he stuck a sign in the ground next to the arch. It says, "You must be this tired to enter," and shows an extremely tired man, hunched over, shoulders slumped, bags under his eyes hanging down to his feet.

"I wasn't always a zombie," Mark tells me in a low, confessional tone.

"None of us were, Mark."

"Yeah, but I can actually trace my life back to the point when I became one." He gives me a quick sidelong look, as if he's unsure whether or not to continue. "When I was little I was one of those kids who crawled into his parents' bed in the middle of the night."

"Every kid did that."

"Yeah, but I did it every night. Every night."

"Do you still do that?"

"Don't be cute," Mark says, annoyed. "After a few years I started sleeping on my own, and it was around that time that the night terrors began."

"So, what? You were scarred from sleeping with your parents?"

"No," he says, a bit impatiently. "I was afraid because I no longer had someone to share my bed with."

"Really . . ." I say, seeing where this is going.

"I've been looking for a sort of . . ." He gestures vaguely, ". . . sleep companion, I guess you could say."

"A bed buddy," I offer.

"If you like," he says, grudgingly.

"You want me to sleep with you."

"Well, yes."

"Does your therapy include rolling on top of me in the middle of the night 'by accident' and dry humping me?"

"I don't think so," he says, and scratches his chin uncertainly.

"No way. I haven't lost that much sleep yet."

I start to walk back up the road and he comes after me, grabbing lightly at my shoulder.

"Hey, I'm sorry. I was just trying to make it seem less . . . strange."

"It *is* strange, and kind of perverse."

Mark holds up his hands defensively. "I'm not trying to put you in a position where I can feel you up, 'accidentally' or otherwise. My parents have been sending me to a shrink. He's a nice enough guy, surprisingly. He told me to create a timeline of when my sleep problems first began. I did, and this is what I found. The night terrors didn't start until I started sleeping alone."

"Maybe," I concede.

"Will you at least think about it?" he asks, almost pleads. "You don't even have to sleep. I just need you to be there. You can read a book or do a crossword puzzle. Anything you want."

I look at the gleam in his eyes and feel a small stab of offense that he's more excited about the possibility of sleep than of having sex with me.

"I'll sleep on it, okay?"

The first thing I learned at camp is that insomnia is not a sleep disorder in itself but rather a symptom of a larger problem. Sleep apnea, bruxism, somnambulism—take your pick.

In my case, it's narcolepsy. That's the one where you fall asleep at different times of the day without warning. We're a lot of fun at parties. We're the coat racks.

Mine is a mild case. I don't so much pass out as get unusually strong urges to sleep, sleep, sleep. These urges come on suddenly and are almost impossible to ignore. My mother calls me "the jetlagged vampire." We joke about my sleep disorder because that's what zombies do with their parents. They don't understand us and they can't help us. That's why they send us to camp.

We look like everyone else, but in truth we are not entirely human.

I walk back to camp by myself, having dismissed Mark so I can think about his proposition. I leave the road and wander down to the lake. It has a Native American name, something long, hard to pronounce, and fraught with historical significance. I keep forgetting it. People with sleep disorders have notoriously bad memories. It's the first thing to go once you start losing sleep. We just call it Lake Nod.

The bright August sun makes the water look like liquid silver. Through the screen of trees on the far side I can see Vista House, a commune for troubled teens—if by "troubled" you mean pregnant. Some of the zombies call it Camp Youknockedmeupbigtime. Curtis Yarwood says it's specifically for Catholic girls who have "wandered off the path" and gotten pregnant through "non-immaculate conception." In the evening you can hear them singing "Kumbaya."

I sit on a big rock overlooking the lake and wonder if any of the girls over there ever have trouble sleeping. Probably a lot of them do. Even so, their concept of "trouble sleeping" is far different from ours. "It could always be worse" is one of my mother's favourite sayings. She doesn't think a little sleeplessness is something to be concerned about. There are bigger problems in the world, she told me once. Easy for her to say; she hasn't lost a night's sleep in her life. Is it her peace of mind or the vial of valium she keeps in her bathroom vanity?

Either way, she's right. It could be worse. I could be sleepless and pregnant. Mark said I would be safe with him. But he might not be safe with me.

Sleep remedies are strange things. Some people swap them like hockey cards, while others hoard them like secret treasures. I've tried many over the years—exercise, meditation, tea before bed, leaving the television on—but none have worked.

Then it came to me last fall. I didn't seek it out, it just happened, for three blissful, sleep-filled months. I never told anyone about it, not even my parents. Especially not my parents.

His name was Neil. He was an undergrad at Ryerson and I met him at a used bookstore on Yonge Street. He was looking for used film textbooks because he couldn't afford to pay for new ones. He accidentally dropped a heavy volume on my foot and was taken aback when I didn't scream or make any other sign of acknowledgment.

"Didn't that hurt?"

"I don't know. I'll have to get back to you on that."

He wasn't a bad-looking guy, but the thing that attracted me most was that he didn't leave right after we had sex. I had been told by girls at school that this was what guys do, and that the way to tell which guy you'll end up marrying was to find the one that stays the whole night.

I had no interest in marrying Neil. The sex was good, but the sleep was better. He would nod off right after we finished, and I would feel myself being pulled after him, as if there was an invisible anchor wrapped around me and I had no choice but to follow.

I kept him a secret from everyone—partly because I was ashamed to tell anyone that the solution to my sleeplessness was sex, but mostly because it felt good to have a secret. The details of my sleeping life were known to everyone in my family. This was something for me and only me.

Neil ended up leaving on his own, saying something about feeling guilty, him being twenty-one, me being "only sixteen." I was upset, but more at the loss of the sleep than the sex. I never held it against him. He helped me find my sleep switch.

Finding it was a mixed blessing. It's like having an itch you can scratch, but you better not. It might turn into something worse—like gonorrhea. I decided it wasn't a good idea just to sleep with someone so I could sleep. You can go a long time without sleep. You can go an even longer time without sex.

Maybe I'm just afraid of ending up at Vista House.

Each building at camp is painted a different shade of blue—the colour of sleep—and my last class of the day is in the Cerulean cabin. The roof has rounded eaves that make it look like a giant toadstool. The kids call it the Smurf House.

Inside, the furniture consists of recliners and beanbag chairs, futons and inflatable sofas, and endless piles of blankets and pillows. All of which had been pushed off to the side to make room for the yoga mats.

Teaching yoga to little kids is like trying to teach a tornado to stand still. I try to be patient, but it isn't easy. Sleeplessness causes irritability, and by the end of the class I can go from zero to bitch in about three seconds.

After the kids are gone, headed to Periwinkle Lodge for dinner, I stay behind to pick up the mats and put the furniture back. Once I'm done I lock up the cabin and sit on the porch steps, looking across the campground at the sun setting behind the trees. The light is a hard golden colour; a nice change from all the blue.

Becky Reilly walks by swinging a bow and carrying a quiver of arrows on her back. She's wearing a shell top that shows off her skinny, freckled arms.

"'Sup, sister?"

"Not much."

"You going to dinner?"

"Maybe. I don't know."

"Beanie-weenies tonight. Yum." Becky rubs her stomach, then sticks a finger in her mouth.

"I think I'll pass."

"I hear that. I think I'd rather eat some mushrooms in the forest and take my chances."

"How's archery?"

"Oh, fine. I wish I was doing crafts this year. I'd have these kids making wallets or something. Get a little sweatshop going."

"There's always next year."

"True dat."

"Who came up with the idea of using archery to help insomnia?"

Becky looks at the bow in her hand as if seeing it for the first time. "Whatever it takes, right?"

"Right."

"I'm like Robin Hood and the kids are my Merry Men. Power in numbers, baby."

That makes me laugh for no real reason. It's like Becky touched on something profound without realizing it.

We don't come to camp to be cured. We come to be among other zombies. To keep each other company through the long, lonely nights.

No two zombies are alike. One year I met a girl named Alice who couldn't fall sleep unless she was on a moving train. She had been born on a train and this, she believed, was the root of her sleeplessness. Her father was a successful Bay Street lawyer, and one of his drinking buddies was a bigwig at VIA Rail. Together they arranged for Alice to spent most of her time on The Canadian, which runs between Toronto and Vancouver. Her father paid a tutor to travel with her, had clothes and care packages delivered at various stops, and that's how she lived, always in motion, always on her way somewhere else.

If the train girl had the strangest sleep disorder I ever heard of, Mark had the nastiest.

Night terrors. A sleep disorder which causes the subject to experience extreme terror and a temporary inability to regain consciousness. It's like drowning in your sleep. No, it's like being attacked by sharks in your sleep. It's a condition that usually affects people with overly nervous dispositions, but that didn't describe Mark at all. He is laid-back, funny, and possessed of the sort of obnoxious overconfidence that only teenage boys and professional daredevils can get away with.

He stays in the Screaming Shack, which is painted midnight blue and is sound-proofed especially for zombies with night terrors. A sign next to the door says "Don't lose any sleep over it." I read it several times as I stand on the stoop. It's not a terribly funny sign, amusing at best, but I laugh anyway. Zombies are masters of the delayed response.

As I raise my hand to knock, the door opens and Mark is standing there, looking at me with raised eyebrows.

"Cali? Was that you laughing?"

"Yeah."

"What's funny?"

"Me. You. This." I shrug my shoulders and Mark's eyebrows go higher, almost disappearing in his shaggy brown hair.

"Second thoughts?"

"I'm here, aren't I?"

"Yes." He abruptly steps aside to let me in, as if worried I might change my mind and bolt.

I enter the Shack. It's a single room with a woodstove, a small kitchenette, and a bed pushed up against the far wall. The only light comes from a single lamp on a nightstand. Mark is dressed for bed in flannel pants and the "Don't fear the sleeper" T-shirt he made in the silkscreening class he is teaching this year.

"I swear I won't try anything funny," he says as we cross to the bed. It's only a double, which means we'll be lying close to each other. He notices the book in my hand. I hold it up. It's a Stephen King hardcover, almost as big as a phone book.

"Don't worry," I tell him. "If you make any moves, I'll just drop this on your crotch."

"Fair enough," he says, and crawls under the covers. I sit on the other side, lift my legs up. I hesitate a moment, then slip them under the sheets.

"So," he says.

"So," I say back. "Pleasant dreams."

He laughs. "Yeah, right."

Mark rolls onto his side. His elbow brushes my arm and he apologizes. I tell him it's okay and open my book. I try to focus my eyes, but the words seem to be surrounded by dark auras that make them hard to read. I have to blink several times to get through each page.

The auras expand as I read until at one point everything is swallowed in one enormous black cloud. I try to see though it, but there's a pressure pulling me down. I struggle against it, and when I open my eyes I realize I've been asleep. I'm shocked at how simple it is. This thing everyone else takes for granted. One moment you're awake, the next you're waking up.

I've been asleep and I'm no longer holding the book. I'm holding Mark. Curled up next to him, my arms wrapped around his middle. My head is pressed against his back, and I can feel the rise and fall of his breathing.

There are no straight lines in sleep. People curl into commas, nestled together like spoons in a kitchen drawer. There is comfort in curves. More comfort than I expected. I'll just lie here, I tell myself. I won't do anything. Mark is asleep, and I don't want to wake him.

WHAT SARA TELLS ME

(From Broken Pencil #35*)*

ethan rilly

The first time I made love was completely romantic except for that part where he stuck his dick in me. There wasn't a lot of pain, but he had this serious look in his eyes like he was trying to translate a particularly difficult stanza of German poetry, and his hands were on my breasts the whole time. Like the whole whole time. The sides of his hands were cutting wonderfully into my upper ribs and when it was over he cried into my neck. What a pussy!

The last time I made love was pretty much the same, except I was a lot drunker and he was my daddy's age. He drove a black convertible something-or-other that featured a sleek multicoloured light system for the dashboard metres, and the car sort of smelled like tacos, and for some reason he kept saying, "For real." I had asked him plainly if he wanted to go back to his place, and he looked at my hair and said, "For real." Despite everything, I'm still optimistic.

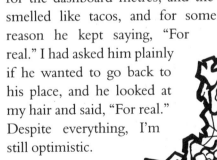

L-O-V-E

(From Broken Pencil *#16)*

greg kearney

There's space left over at the end of *Superman 2*. It's taped a bit of a news show, this one about a mother who wanted to marry her son, then killed him when he said no. She's speaking from prison, with a carnation corsage pinned for some reason to her prison uniform.

"It's like when friends start to get with each other," she says, smiling and shrugging skinny shoulders. "You start out as one thing, and then comes the light bulb, and BAM! You just get with them. It's called L-O-V-E."

Trina rolls over in her patch of sunlight on the floor. She's cracking her toe knuckles, bending back each stubby toe till it pops. "That is so pukey," she says, with that fat, lolling tongue of hers. "If they had a baby, it would probably be one big oval with no arms or legs."

"Pukey is not a word," Mum says, tying off the ends on a doll dress she's just finished. "It's not even descriptive."

The tape has been taped over so many times that the prison mum's littlest son sounds like a man with gigantism when he looks into the camera and says, "When are you coming back from the store, Mommy?"

The medicine chest is open a bit when I go in to wash my hands for supper. I look in and there's a little metal cup on the shelf. I haven't seen it before. It's not from the kitchen, and it's not one of Trina's crappy things. I bring it up to my face. It smells like the basement. At the bottom of the cup is a decal, partly peeled off, of a happy baby's face, licking its lips like it's waiting for a cupcake or a chip, something good to eat.

Also in the mirror, something else I've never noticed: half of my face is red for no reason, red like I've been smacked.

When's Trina going to move out? That's what I think to myself, Mum and Dad too, probably, whenever we all sit down to eat. She's almost twenty, and all she does when she comes home from her daycare job is walk around the house in her track pants, picking at herself. Her upper arms are all scabbed over. Once, late at night, I heard Mum telling Dad that she sometimes worries that Trina's going to end up dead.

Trina takes the biggest piece of fish for herself and pours ketchup on it. Mum lights a cigarette; she hardly ever eats with us. Dad turns on the radio. The end of a woman singing really fast in French.

"Hey, Dad," Trina says, mouth full of fish, "if you were going to molest one of us, which one would you do?"

Why? Why does she bother?

"What is wrong with you? How can you come up with shit like that?" Dad's temples roll and gnaw. "Get out of my sight!"

"What for? I'm not saying I want you to do me, I was just asking. It's something to say."

"Well, it's a terrible something to say," Mum says. "We're not sitting in hell, are we? This is supper." She turns up the radio. The long range forecast.

"I guess I'm not allowed to talk."

I look down at Trina's lap. Her thighs are all flat and spread out on the chair. I kind of hope Dad'll hit her.

He grabs her plate instead, and from his seat he throws it in the sink. Peas go flying everywhere. I take my first bite of fish.

After sports and traffic, Dad flicks off the radio and we sit in silence, forks against porcelain, finishing up.

"Did you know that in Nazi times they made the Jewish families do that to each other?" Mum says finally, getting up to plug in the kettle for tea. "They made the Jewish mother have sex with the Jewish son, and the father with the daughter, at gunpoint. That's a fact. How would you like that? Now, if you smarten up a little, you can have some tea."

I know everyone has wished this at one point or another, but when I look at her—the wide face, small teeth, the crow's feet she's already getting, and, of course, the way she thrills over stuff that's already old news to the rest of us—I really do believe it about Trina: adopted, switched at birth, or at the very least, not my Dad's. Whenever she's home the house feels like a motel. Open, in a bad way. She just misses the mark, and she thinks that makes her more interesting, or more something. We know better.

That time I heard Mum in bed, whispering to Dad about Trina ending up dead—did she really say "I worry," or was it "I wish"? Could've been. Once I was in the room, they had already changed the subject.

THE SOUTHWEST RAPIST

(From Broken Pencil #28)

leanna mclennan

The Southwest Rapist parks his brown van in the Canadian Tire parking lot between me and the school.

"It's my birthday today," he says, leaning out the window. "Can I have a kiss?" He isn't bad looking, just kind of weird. Dirty blond hair dangles beside his dimpled chin. He reminds me of my friend's older brother.

"Why don't you come back at lunch?" I say, smiling up at him. In sex ed., we were taught that it's better to get rid of people like this without offending them. As I walk away, my body feels electric. A tingle travels down my spine, flashes hot between my legs. I'm afraid he'll try to run me over, but he just sits there watching my bum.

I know he's the rapist. He raped Mandy's mother and sister in their basement. Mandy wasn't home that day. Her father was, but he couldn't do anything because he's in a wheelchair. Mum called us into the kitchen to show us the picture of Mandy crying on the front page of the newspaper. *Grief Stricken*, the caption read. I imagined my picture there, and Adelle and Mum lying helpless on our living room floor, covered in blood. Mum said not to say anything to Mandy because it would just make her feel worse. No one did.

I rush down the lane, hoping he doesn't follow. When I get to school, Cody is standing by the Head Doors, smoking.

"Hey, T.H." At first Cody called me Tetra Hydra, short for Tetrahydra Cannabinol, THC, and said that just looking at me got him high. Later, when I wouldn't sleep with him, he changed it to Tight Hole, then T.H., his own stupid private joke because I'm a virgin. I guess fifteen is kind of old to still be one. Lana, Kelly, and I have a contest to see who'll be the last. I was almost the last to get a bra in junior high but I got Mum to take me to Kmart to buy a training bra before Kelly got hers.

When I get to class, Mrs. Enns gives me this really stupid look and says, "Late." She puts a gigantic *L* beside my name. Her face looks like she had acne when she was young, and her hair is sprayed into a bizarre helmet.

"Repeat after me," she says. *"Je vais, tu vas, il va, elle va . . ."* I look out the window. There he is. Mrs. Enns's voice fades. My throat constricts. I shift so that the window frame will block his view. When he turns around, it's just a guy from grade twelve who has the same hair and was taken in for questioning last month when the cops interviewed four hundred guys who fit the rapist's description. The guy's parents had reported him as a suspect because they knew he was into drugs and wanted to make sure he wasn't in any other trouble. He turns beet red whenever anyone mentions it, so we remind him every chance we get.

"Catherine a dix ans." Mrs. Enns clicks the button to the next slide. My desk is too small. I don't open it because the guys in my class have started chewing tobacco and they spit it into the desks, leaving behind brown slime with a rancid mossy smell. The slide shows Catherine's birthday party in washed-out colours. Sometimes the accompanying tape slows down and pulls the French into a Texas drawl. Mrs. Enns bends down to pick up her notes. She definitely passes what Lana calls *The Dictionary Test*: if she bends down to pick up a dictionary you can't see her underwear, not like our math teacher Mrs. DeRoot, who wears miniskirts, and blouses so low you can see her boobs. The guys love math class. We're not allowed to wear short skirts or cut-offs since Lana came to school with shorts that showed her bum and they made a rule against it. Mum says you should always bend your knees when you pick something up because of what it does to men. Mrs. Enns pauses the tape.

"Da-vid," she says with a French accent. *"Qu'est-ce que c'est?"* She snatches his paper. It's a drawing of the new Led Zeppelin album cover with the Druid on a mountain. Dave's a total stoner but he's a great artist.

"C'est une papier," he says in a really bad accent. Everyone laughs.

Now we have to do *dictée*. The room is filled with the sound of paper being torn from notebooks.

"Ecrivez: numéro un. Paul et Catherine vivent dans la rue de la Gare."

We have to write ten sentences. When Mrs. Enns collects the *dictées*, I look outside. I'm afraid he'll blindfold me, force me into the van, take me to Edworthy Park, rape me, and leave me there, alone. Last month, he did that to a nine-year-old girl who got separated from her mum in the mall. The girl walked all the way home. When I was nine, I walked home alone all the time. If I tell Mrs. Enns I told him to come back, she'll think it's my fault because I told him to, and because I'm wearing my tight jeans that Mum says make me look cheap. At least I don't have to lie down to do them up, like Lana does. Everyone thinks she's a slut, but I like her. Once I went to her house and there was a frying pan turned upside down on the floor with bits of hamburger and spaghetti all over.

"I'm not bloody cleaning it up," her Mum said. "It's your father's mess and he can damn well clean it up himself." After that, we mostly went to my house.

Lana, Kelly, and I usually go to my house after school because Mum is never home. Sometimes we hear noises in the backyard and peek out the basement window to make sure no one is there. The rapist has been breaking into single women's homes. He blindfolds them with their own clothes before he rapes them. The police won't say how because they're afraid someone will imitate him. It said in the paper that he sent one victim roses after he raped her and asked her for another date. After that, Mum put nails above the windows so they don't open wide enough for someone to get in.

After school, Lana, Kelly, and I watch TV or take turns standing against the wall while everyone says what they like and don't like:

"Your bum sticks out too much."

"But you have really nice eyes."

"You should wear lighter blue eyeshadow."

"Grow your hair longer."

"Get it more feathered."

"Your hands are like a guy's."

"Your legs are short for your body."

Sometimes we pretend we're different teachers. Lana does a great impression of Mrs. DeRoot. My specialty is Mr. Bateman. We call him Master Bate. His favourite line is, "I'm the principal. That's a mixture of prince and pal. I'm your princey-pal." Kelly does a hilarious Mrs. Enns, commanding *dictée, dictée, dictée*.

Mrs. Enns starts to give us the same instructions she gives every week. Outside, the rapist is walking past the Ponderosa Steak House. Maybe it's a different blond guy. I can't tell. I wish Mum was home so I could call her to come and get me. I don't want to call her at work because she hates that.

"Stop day dreaming, Katie," Mrs. Enns snaps. "You don't get a grade just for turning up."

When the lunch bell rings, I go to my locker. Mandy walks past. I want to tell her about the guy outside, to warn her. But I can't say anything. I don't know what to say.

"You know you're not allowed in the halls at lunch." Mr. McDowell puts his hands on his hips. He used to be in the army and now he acts like he's a cop. "Watch out," we say when we see him, "McDowell on the prowl."

McDowell asks me what I'm doing.

"Nothing," I say.

"Well then, get going, young lady."

"Sorry," I say. I have to go home anyway because I have to make lunch for Adelle because Mum doesn't have time to come home. It isn't fair. Adelle's only three years younger and I have to do all the work. "Nothing's fair," Mum says. This morning she left a can of Campbell's Chunky Beef Soup and a loaf of sixty-percent whole wheat bread on the counter. We used to eat white bread until she went on the Scarsdale diet. Now all she has for breakfast is one piece of dry toast and half a grapefruit.

I press the cold metal bar and slowly open the heavy blue door. No one. I run through the Canadian Tire parking lot and up the hill before I stop to catch my breath. Three blocks to go. I look carefully into the back alley before I pass it. No sign of the van. I hope he doesn't know where I live. I hope he's not waiting for me in the alley with a blindfold.

I'm out of breath, but I keep running past the green mailbox where the postman picks up our mail. I hate mailboxes because when I was eleven, a guy tried to pull me behind one. Every night I went on a bike ride and watched the sun set over the park. One night, some teenagers called me over to the long row of green mailboxes in front of the trees by the playground. The short cute guy, who looked like Paul Williams in *Phantom of the Paradise*, which was my favourite movie, said he could open the mailboxes from behind.

"Yeah right," I said.

"No really. I can. What's your name?"

"George," I lied.

"Sure, George," he said, and his friends laughed. "It's really cool."

The guy's friends stayed out front and I was worried that they might steal my bike. Then the cute guy grabbed me, pulled me to the ground, and tried to kiss me. I pushed his face away and ran out front. Some kids were walking on the other side of the street.

"Hello," I called, pretending I knew them. I grabbed my bike.

"Have fun, George?" the cute guy shouted as I rode away. I didn't stop at the park that night or hardly ever after that. I didn't go to Pinkie's for a ten-cent kid's ice-cream cone. Instead, I rode home as fast as I could, to get away from the guys who stood laughing in front of those mailboxes.

The rapist's shadow hovers behind the mailbox that I have to pass now and slowly moves towards me. When the shadow emerges from around the corner, it's a guy from down the street. He smiles at me as I race past.

When I get home, I check every room to make sure no one is there. I'm in the laundry room when the back doorknob rattles. I peek around the corner, up the stairs. It's Adelle.

"How come you're so late?" I shout.

"None of your business," she says.

"I'm telling Mum."

"So. She won't believe you anyway." Adelle goes to her room.

I go to the counter to make the Chunky Beef Soup, which is more like stew so you don't have to add water. It falls into the pan in a single glob. There are no more crackers, so I write *crackers* on the grocery list on the fridge.

"It's ready," I yell. No answer. "It's ready."

"I heard you the first time," Adelle says as she sits at her place.

"How was your morning?" I ask.

"What do you care?"

"I'm just asking," I say, reaching for the butter. "Don't have a fit."

"I'm not."

"Good."

"Good."

I hear a noise in the backyard and freeze.

"Beatle," Adelle calls. She opens the milk chute to let the cat in.

I clear the dishes, rinse them and stack them for when Mum gets home. Then I go to the bathroom, plug in my curling iron and wait for the red dot in the centre to turn brown so I know it's hot. I shift the mirrors so I can see the back of my head. It looks okay. I think people should spend more time looking at the backs of their heads because sometimes the rest of their hair looks fine but the back is disgusting. I curl the front so it feathers right. Then I climb up on the counter so I can see my bum. Once Mum caught me and said I was being vain.

"You're so Vain" used to be my favourite song and Carly Simon was my favourite singer. Now I prefer Cat Stevens. I go to the living room and put *Mona Bone Jakon* on our bubble stereo. I place the plastic dome lid on the blue shag carpet. Beatle jumps into it and starts purring. I spin her around and she gets out. *Trouble. Oh, Trouble, set me free.*

"Do you have to play that again?" Adelle shouts.

"Are you ready?" I shout back. She slams her bedroom door and goes to put on her shoes.

"Nice jeans," she says sarcastically.

"Like you'd know," I retort.

I look outside to make sure the rapist isn't waiting. I don't tell Adelle about him because she'd just tell Mum and I'd get in trouble for not calling her even though we're not supposed to call her at work unless it's an emergency. The brown van isn't there, or in the Canadian Tire parking lot, or by the school. I watch Adelle as she crosses over the field to the junior high.

When I get to the front door, Jake and Cody are there.

"Hey, Tetra Hydra," Cody says. Jake laughs.

"Shut up," I say.

"What's the matter with you?" Cody says, "Can't take a joke?"

This afternoon we have a rehearsal in drama. Mrs. McFadden always makes me play some stupid part. This time I have to be Laura in *The Glass Menagerie*. I try to forget about the rapist outside waiting for me to kiss him, and gaze at the small glass unicorn. In the middle of the play, Clive, who plays Jim, leans forward to kiss me. He's such a geek. Lana and I burst out laughing. Mrs. McFadden bawls us out, but she says we can leave out the kiss. I don't like the way Clive looks at me. I think he likes me.

When the bell goes, I wait for Adelle to come out of the junior high on the other side of the field. I usually walk home alone, making up songs, but I don't want to now. I can't stop thinking about the rapist's face and how he grinned when he said, "It's my birthday. How about a kiss?"

Mum would be mad if she knew that I talked to him. She'd call the police and everyone would see them drive up. I don't want anyone to know that he talked to me, that he was cute. There was something about his grin that scared me. I look around to make sure he's not there.

When Adelle gets out of school, she's in a good mood for a change. She's in grade seven and keeps bursting into tears and having a fit about everything. When we get home, we sit on the couch under the old pink blanket eating popcorn and watching *Gilligan's Island* until Mum gets home.

"How was your day?" she asks us.

"Fine," we say and keep watching TV.

ONE KISS ON THE MOUTH IN MOMBASA

(From Broken Pencil #27)
(Translated from Hebrew by Sondra Silverstein)

etgar keret

For a minute, I got uptight. But she told me to take it easy, I had no reason. She'd marry me, and if it was important, because of our parents, it could even be in a hall. That wasn't the point. The point was somewhere else altogether—three years ago, in Mombasa, when she and Lihi went there after the army. Just the two of them went, because the guy who was her boyfriend had re-enlisted. In Mombasa, they lived in the same place the whole time, some kind of guest house where a whole bunch of people hung out, mostly from Europe. Lihi wouldn't hear about leaving the place, because she'd just fallen in love with some German guy who lived in one of the cabins. She didn't mind staying either, she was pretty much enjoying the quiet. And even though that guest house was exploding with drugs and hormones, no one hassled her. They could probably sense that she wanted to be alone. No one—except for some Dutch guy who got there maybe a day after them, and didn't leave the place until she went back home. And he didn't actually hassle her either, just looked at her a lot. That didn't bother her. He seemed like an alright guy, a little sad, but one of those sad types who don't complain. They were in Mombasa for three months, and she never heard him say a word. Except for once, a week before they left, and even then, there was something so gentle about the way he talked to her, something so weightless, that it was as if he hadn't said anything at all. She explained to him that the timing was bad, told him about her boyfriend, who was some technical something in the air force, about how they'd known each other since high school. And he just smiled, and nodded, and moved back to his regular spot on the steps of the hut. He didn't speak to her anymore, but kept on looking. Except that actually, now that she thought about it, he did speak to her one more time, on the day she flew back, and he said the funniest thing she'd ever heard. Something about how, between every two people in the world, there's a kiss. What he was actually trying to tell her was that he'd already been looking at her for three months and thinking about their kiss, how it would taste, how long it would last, how it would feel. And now she was leaving, and she had a boyfriend and everything, he understood, but just that kiss, he wanted to know if she would agree. It was awfully funny, the way he spoke, kind of confused, maybe because he didn't know English well, or he just wasn't much of a talker. But she said okay. And they kissed. And after that, he really didn't try anything, and she came back to Israel with Lihi. Her boyfriend was at the airport in his uniform to pick her up in his army car. They moved in together, and to spice up their sex life a little, they added some new things. They tied each other to the bed, dripped some wax, once they even tried to do it anally, which hurt like hell, and in the middle, shit came out. In the end, they split up, and when she started school, she met me. And now, we're going to get married. She has no problem with that. She said I

should pick the hall, and the date, and whatever I want, because it really doesn't matter to her. That isn't the point at all. Neither is that Dutch guy, I have nothing to be jealous of there. He's probably dead already from an overdose, or else he's lying drunk on some sidewalk in Amsterdam, or he went and got a master's degree in something, which sounds even worse. In any case, it's not about him at all, it's that time in Mombasa. For three months, a person sits and looks at you, imagining a kiss.

ANOTHER YOUNG LUST STORY

(From Broken Pencil #22)

craig sernotti

She wanted him immediately. She was young, nineteen, and needed one last fling before she got married. He was nineteen too, eager and lonely.

They made out. He fingered her asshole. She jerked him off and swallowed his semen.

Finally, when she deemed him worthy, she said, "Do you want to see my pussy?"

He said yes.

She undressed and spread for him. It was like two barn doors opening. He could see directly into her. Inside her, he felt nothing. He wondered if she'd had sex with a refrigerator.

He stared down at her. Her eyes were closed and she was silent. He lost it.

"This isn't working out," he said.

"No," she said.

Last he heard, her engagement had dissolved and she had moved in with a widowed forty-five-year-old man. He did a lot of coke and his daughter was as old as she was.

Last she heard, he was dating a girl whose previous boyfriend had raped her.

GYNECOMASTIA

(Quarter-finalist in the Broken Pencil
First Annual Indie Writers Deathmatch, online exclusive)

janine fleri

On the first day of Kit's first period she felt a charge of excitement and wonderment, not at her initiation to womanhood, but rather at the misconception that pads meant she could pee during television programs without leaving the couch. She learned through trial and error that this was a flawed theory, and puberty was all downhill from there. She watched as the girls around her sprouted up from the worn-down soles of their jelly shoes until they towered above her. Kit's delay in this stage of growth allowed her to witness her friends' womanly changes head-on. She was eye level with every budding breast in her class for about six months before catching up in height. It burned her the most during dance class, exposed through her spandex, ripe young muscles accented through tight purple fabric. Her jutting ribs earned her the nickname "Four Tit Kit" which she laughed at politely. With time her legs stretched out, ass plumped into a firm little shelf, elongated waist led to bony hips. She tied her mousy brown hair in a bun, in a braid, in a ponytail, and eventually just left it down. Her chest remained as flat as her stomach.

Within a year Kit's patience with her body turned to anxiety as the womenchildren around her began to gossip more feverishly about "second base" and secret make-out parties. She had never gone, too afraid to move beyond kissing, not wanting her ribs to be mistakenly groped in some boy's fruitless search for something to squeeze. She knew she could just say no, keep things focused above the neck, but saying no meant you were a prude, and which was worse—being the prude or being the girl with no tits? Unable to decide Kit chose to be nothing and simply avoided most social events.

Kit's newfound private time was often spent standing in front of the mirror, Mom's borrowed bra clasped snugly around her back, socks and various soft things from her drawers substituting for flesh. She'd put on tight sweaters, the kind that make you look cheap, and begin her little charade. She'd turn to the side and stick out her chest, adjusting and readjusting to make them look real. She would tuck various items to simulate the effect of hardened nipples fighting against taut fabric. C batteries tucked into the makeshift falsies would give the most satisfying result. "Breasts are just fat," Mom had told her in a failed effort to be comforting. "Who wants fat?"

The first time Kit met Rory she was awestruck. He had moved across town to her middle-school a week before their first encounter and she had set her eyes on him immediately. It was shortly after her thirteenth birthday and she took it as a gift from God Himself, or Whoever. When she moved across the classroom to claim a seat at Rory's table the world slowed down around her, the light from outside streaming in to illuminate his dainty locks of rust-coloured hair, his emerald eyes glinting with promises of pleasure, his erotic fatty deposits rising and falling with each heaving breath. That day he wore a white shirt and she could clearly see the wide dark outline of areola blushing through. She felt herself glowing.

In a matter of weeks Kit and Rory were chatting all through the schoolday, whispering and passing notes. It became common for her to feel like a dirty old man, spending most of this time alongside Rory with her eyes fixed firmly on his chest. If anyone else noticed his little treasures they had yet to let on. It amazed Kit that anyone could possibly miss them. Rory had all that she wanted: a delicate little rack, perky and round. It was the most fascinating thing she had ever seen. Sure, the fat kids sported bouncy little bags of flab, "bitch-tits" being the contemporary term for them. Rory was soft, but he was no fat kid—the budding breasts he sported were truly unique, a modest bosom yet quite a sight. She placed him somewhere between an A and B cup.

By the time spring vacation rolled around Kit and Rory had become fodder for lunchroom gossip. They were revolutionary in their opposite-sex friendship. Everyone, including their parents, kept insisting they must be going out to be spending so much time together. It was one of the first warm days of the season when the tension finally enveloped them. They were ambling through the woods behind Rory's house, swinging arms periodically touching, accidentally on purpose.

"Have you ever made out?" Rory asked.

"Not really . . . I dunno . . ." She reached for valid excuses and found none. "I kissed Mike Goldberg once. He wasn't very good at it."

"I bet 'cause he never practised."

"Practised?"

"Yeah, so you get good at it. I practised once with this girl I met over summer vacation last year. I think it helped."

Kit's hungry eyes fixed on the gentle bounce of Rory's little twins under his jersey knit shirt. She could clearly see the bulge of his nipples, recognized that behind them lay tissue and glands instead of alkaline. She imagined herself someday being examined by a similar greedy gaze, and swooned at the possibility.

She wondered how much he thought about them, if he touched them, practising on himself, or if maybe he spent time flattening them in front of a mirror in his own envious game of make-believe. Words ceased as they walked along, twigs and mud squishing and crunching beneath them.

"I'd, you know, help you practise if you wanted." Speaking the words made her dizzy.

"I mean, I could practise. I'd definitely practise. Do you, um, want to practise today? Like, now, or something?"

"Yeah, sure . . ." Words trailed off as he moved towards her, leaning a bit to get to her mouth, both parties keeping hands in pockets and eyes open.

Awkward seconds turned into minutes of sloppy, unsure tongues, stiff limbs emerging to grasp each other because it seemed like the thing to do. After a blurry patch of time Rory grew bored and moved on, brushing an open palm over and down her shirt, tugging at it, pulling it up enough to slide his hand in.

Startled, embarrassed, Kit pulled back a bit to contemplate the next step.

"Is this okay?"

She considered. She wanted to get to second base, she didn't want to be the base.

"Only if I get to try it on you," she negotiated.

"What?"

"It's only fair! I get to try it on you or we stop practising."

"Okay, but I get to go first."

Kit could feel her face heat as he probed around, trying to finger a nipple, any swell in her flesh to signal that he'd found what he was searching for. His kissing slowed down. Not in a romantic way, in a confused way that

communicated his befuddlement over her pancake chest. For what it was worth he could be rubbing her back. He gave up quickly, and they each took a break to swipe their mouths against the shoulder of their shirts in order to dry off.

"Now your turn," Kit stated and moved in. Their mouths had become comfortable together, allowing Kit to concentrate fully on her mission. Her hand shot directly to his right breast, cupping it in her palm, not sure if the clamminess was on his behalf or hers. She massaged it, projecting herself into his position, dreaming of a life when she too could be so appreciated. He squirmed beneath her, uncomfortable.

"Okay," he muttered. Kit became aggressive, unable to surrender her conquest. It had taken her months of feigning mutual interests to get this far. Her investment in this desire could not go unrewarded.

Rory asserted, pushing her away. As he began to stand up Kit hooked her foot behind his knee, knocking him back down. She straddled him, shoving up his shirt, planting each hand firmly over each wobbling tit.

"Knock it off, bitch!" Rory deepened his voice and bucked beneath her. He struggled to push her off. Kit was not a big girl, but Rory was not a strong boy. They continued to wrestle and thrash atop the twigs and filth of nature. They rolled, and groped, and hit. Scrapes and bruises were had, and one of the them was bleeding on the other. The scuffle ended in panting and blushing. Their eyes met once as Rory lifted himself to his feet. Kit remained planted on the ground, spent, collapsed against a tree. Her eyes remained on him as he turned from her and oriented himself within the woods.

"It's just fat," she assured him as he took off running back towards home.

NINE BALL TOURNEY, LOTZA PRIZES

(From Broken Pencil #15)

karen mcelrea

You lean into the table, stick in hand. Set up your shot. I close my eyes. Picture balls shifting. Cup one in my hand. Smooth. Open my eyes. Black. Rub it over felt. Velvet.

You lean deeper, arch your hand. Grip the stick till your knuckles opaque. Rub the split. I bend forward, barely breathe. No talking. No moaning. No moving allowed. So make your shot, I laugh. I'm ready. You say, Sit down, whore, and shut the fuck up. No one knows this is funny. I've waited too long for my cue. No sense of timing.

The End.

I shouldn't have told you how after shooter after shooter I took him home out of pity. My friends said, Poor guy, one leg's shriveled. Polio. But when he was naked I saw two good legs. Wrong guy, oh sweet Jesus, it's the wrong guy. I couldn't stop laughing and he left. Pissed off like anything, put a fist through the window in the door on his way out.

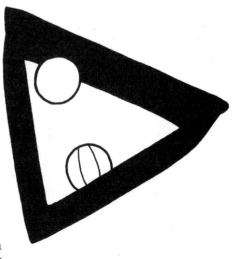

I shouldn't have told you, but I thought it was funny. It happened before I met you. When I passed the pool hall I saw through fogged-up windows a whole world that began and ended with a taste of you.

SOME KIND OF BETRAYAL

(From Broken Pencil #11)

matthew firth

Mid-November. The first flakes of snow scattering. Dead sky. Cold.

Purple shirt. Teased hair. Long coat draped over bare, skinny legs. Black boots.

He leans in close. "Where you off to dressed like that? Going to visit your mother?"

Loafers on his feet.

"Going to fuck your boyfriend? He let you walk around like that?"

He shaves three times a day. Skin chiseled. Teeth like a crowded sidewalk.

She pulls hard on her cigarette. Looks at him. Blows smoke.

She applies paint to her lips. Legs crossed on a sideways seat on the bus.

He sits across from her. Legs spread. Hands folded over his dick. "Where you get off? I never seen you on this bus before."

She glides goo across her lips. Blood red. Eyes on him. Lips folded in the shape of an egg.

She takes him into a stairwell, pulling him by the hand. Feeds him her tongue on the landing. He shoves her against the wall. Radiators humming. Pipes clunking. He jams his crotch into her sunken pelvis. Rips at her tits.

She scampers up the stairs. Down a tight hallway. A child, maybe. Bloodless, unclaimed. Her brothers not counting for anything. A key around her neck.

He throws her onto the bed. She whimpers, her black boots like anchors pulling her legs back towards the floor.

He watches her undress. Again, her mouth forms the shape of an egg. Thin legs. Purple undergarments.

She bows her head, cowers, her body tense, knotted.

He rubs a hand across her ribs. Cups her breast. Holds a nipple.

"Forget about it." He empties his pockets of change. Shuffles out of the apartment. Hits the street. "Don't waste my time. Just don't waste my time."

Inside, her cheek blotted against a pane of yellow glass, she watches for her brothers.

LITTLE WITE SQUIREL ANGEL

(From Broken Pencil #42)

christopher willard

i stud up and Maury huged me and the awdeance moaned and i looked up from the floor and the hot lites hit my face like the lite of angels and i shall never forget that as long as i so shall live.

Dear Lord Above, i Thank You for makin me a woman and Thank You for makin me ugly and Thank You for my obeesity for not all creeturs is born with wate problems and Thank You Jesus for makin my father tuch me when i were small and Thank You also for givin me a dawter who sleeped with over forty-three boys at her early age and for amittin it on Maury even so i alredy knowed it and Thank You for the Kernal and thank you for wite squirels.

i guess you was put rite here on earth for a reeson and Thank You for helpin me find my very own reeson.

Bobby spint most of his time workin down in the mine on the nite shift and when he was sleepin and i werent workin down at Kentucky Edna Earl and me watched TV. i liked best of all the reelty TV. Been on them to, more times as you can cownt pennies. Dont you worry none, i can tell how it all went down as strate as a line even as i dont much fancy up words.

Dons the manager of the Wincox Road branch and has been in that posishun as long as i can remember and he likes reelty TV as much as i do and he keeped it on in his office so as we culd lissen to it wile we was pitchin legs into bukets. i herd Maury was on the lookowt for some persins for his show especialy mothers who had dawters who was sleepin arowned. i knowed Edna Earl spits out boyfrends faster than Chuck E Cheese spits out tickets and i also knowed she keeped a pakage of condums in that little drawer of her jewlry box. Don herd it to and he sayd i could use the phone rite there in the office to call providin it were a toll free number wich it was. It werent two days when they called me back at work and Don answered the phone and sayd he would finish the soda order.

Oh Sweet Lord, Thank You for makin Maury have a toll free number and for makin Don let me take the time off.

That girl aksed if Edna Earl was promiskiness and sleepin arowned and i told her only as many times as there was boys at juvey hall and she aksed me if Edna Earl had a sassy mouth and i told her they make bathroom soap dont they? So rite from the start she seen i were pretty quik on the get-go. She aksed me to come up to New York City and i was gettin redy to tell her with what but she told me she would fork down the money and shed ride us in an airplain and sleep us in a motel room.

Do it not just make you laff now to think of how innosent i was?

A man name of Shofer was at the airport and Edna Earl seen his card with my name and he steered a limoseen direct to the Motel Grand Hiat and we was put up in a fancy honeymoon room with all that whip dee doo 'cept it was just me and Edna Earl. Mr. Shofer waited till we got fixed up and then we was drove to where Mr. Maury Povik is. A lady sayd to act naturel and to cry if we felt like it and when my turn come she took me in front of most as many peepel as up at Thunder Road on a Thursday nite. Even with all them eyeballs peekin rite at me i felt easy next to Mr. Maury. He aksed me to bout findin them condums in Edna Earls jewlry box and i took one out to prove i was no liar. Then Edna Earl come out and she were all sassy-mouthed and sayd nobody knowed her and what she did was her own bisness. The lie detecter proved she sleeped with the forty-three boys and then Edna Earl was took to army camp for twenty-four hours. Now we see how much she can cuss and cry.

Mr. Shofer drove me to the motel as there was no way i was walkin arowned such a dangerous city and besides there was so many streets i didnt know hide nor hair of where the motel were. The next day Mr. Maury showed us on TV how Edna Earl did forty-three pushups one for each boy and then she ran onstage and got rite down in front of my feet and called me Mommy and sayd she were sorry for all her sleepin with every last one. If that didnt wrinkle out my own heart like a wet towel. And thats when i stood up and Maury smiled at me and the peepel clapped and i looked up and the hot lites hit my face like the lite of angels and i shall never never forget.

And at that very spot i saw a little wite squirel squatin in the silver lite with its little wite hands out in front of it and i knowed it must be a little squirel angel showin me the reeson to be.

Delbarton never felt just rite after that. Edna Earl kept away most of the time and i tried reelty TV and ended up spent most of my time to stuff cigs against the porch step and to throw rocks at a Diet Pepsi Bottle.

Don sayd he had sawn me on the tv and he glud up my pictur in the office and called me a salebrity and i told him my reeson and he sayd i culd telephone any shows i wanted as long as they was 800 numbers. He was so understandin.

So lets see. i seen Ms. Opraw two in a row. She sayd i culd tell how daddy sneeked in and tuched me but to leave out the bits and cusses and i told her i werent no sassy mowth. After Opraw huged me real tite and i knowed then and there she were a frend for life as i alredy knowed from seen her on TV.

O Tender Lovin Jesus, Thank You for 800 numbers and Thank You for Mr. Montel and for Tireya Banks, and for Steve Wilcos and Ms. Opraw twice and for all the others to unumeral to menshen.

i got on Wife Swop to and Bobby sayd he didnt care one way or nother as long as the new woman knowed how to cook fish sticks. i went to pensilvanya to wifey it up with Howard. We hit it off just fine and every day was drove to some form of beautifyin like toenail polishin. i dont know a thing abowt what that man did 'cept open letters with money in them but let me tell you he were pretty randy from all that sittin and let me tell you they didnt show half the stuff on TV. When Bobby got his vacaton i brung him to my frend Maury as a surprise where i told him how up there in pensilvanya Howard had brot me brekfast in bed and how hed sayd the eggs over easy part real slow like and how one little thing had leeded to a nother little thing.

It were Bobby who sayd we was goin on Jerry Spranger and thats how i got the broked tooth when Bobby throwed a chare at Howard and it bownced off his sholder. Mr. Spranger didnt show that part on TV. And that Dr. Fill aksed us on and told us to comoonicate. A lot of good was that did because i moved in with my Shirley two days later after Bobby introdooced me to Mister Five Fister and give me a busted lip.

Jesus, Thank You for my sister Shirley and Thanks Be for those three kids of her that made me get on Nanny 911 and Supper Nanny even so i had to use a pretend name to get on Supper Nanny so they wuldnt find out bout Nanny 911. And thank you for Dizneyland and Booty and the Beest and extre long Corn Dogs. Guess after all that peepel thowted Shirley and me was sinful womans and Elin Degeniris aksed us abowt raisin childrens and at the end she tried to hug me but i seen abowt her in the Star and knowed what she was up to. She were nice in the end when she surprised me with gettin me on Extreem Makeover becus that were a show i called more than ten times to try to get on but even so i was pretty happy i still never went back to hug her.

Bobby called me when i was all raped in bandages. i guess Edna Earl had told him i was on Extreem Makeover and he let me know he was sorryer than a skunk withowt a clothespin and how sick he were of sleepin on that rat sofa at Martins dublewide. i told him when i come back he wuld sit his eyeballs on a new woman and i mite think if i wanted him back even so i alredy knowed i wuld. Then i told him how my nose was yanked and how my thys and dairyair was full of suckin straws and how inplumps was put in my front and how my teeth was sandpapered and my hair dipped in bleech. i was made to stay in my room and i was gettin just sick enugh to smak up someone in the face, expecilly the doctor who poked my buxom just becas he was probly some pervert. i wuld have to 'cept it hurt to much to lift my arms. They got me on Blind Date but they never showed it on TV. They tooked us out for drinks but i guess they didnt know likker and me were kissin cuzins so as i got drunk as a donkey at a horse dance.

You shuld a seen everybodys poppin eyeballs when i sashaed into the Delbarton Ramada Motel. They was all flappin lips and Bobby looked direct at my jingle bells and sayd there was no woman in the U.S. of A. as dollied up as me and it hit me i mite go and sign up for Americas Next Top Model.

That werent the all of it.

Edna Earl sayd she had had the livin room done up by While You Wore Out cept when the limoseen pulled up the intire afair was up in flames and Bobby sayd he sure were kickin himself for only just now remindin himself of the cig he set on the arm of the cowch when the phone rang. All that were on TV too.

Jesus Holy of Holyes, i Thank You for womans mascara that dont run with tears and i Thank You for abowt a thosand hundred workmans who raised our Extreem House Makeover. O Most Belovved Saveor, Thank You most of all for showin me the little wite squirel angel the most beootiful animal that lived and Thank You for the mirror on the bedroom ceelin remindin me of the meek and the path to richesness even as i was never one to rub other creeturs jellus noses in the fact i am Blest and they just aint.

SUPERBOY

(From Broken Pencil #10)

paul hong

"What is the alternative?"

"To what?"

"The alternative to doing what you're doing."

"Oh, I see. Well, I was thinking of retiring. Just returning to a normal life. Change my identity, perhaps move to another city where I can start again."

"Are you sure you're not just giving up?"

"Yes, I suppose maybe."

"You know what you could do?"

"What?"

"If you want to help, you can bust into a bank in Switzerland, raid the account of some huge corporation, and redistribute the money to the needy. Like me. I need some money."

"That would be illegal."

"But that would certainly help, wouldn't it? Or why don't you synthesize some chemical from the outer reaches of space, and make some sort of doodad that would convert garbage and other waste products into an efficient form of energy? Imagine the good that would do. Or a cure for one of the major diseases. Or a super strain of grain that can be grown in any conditions with minimal care so as to feed the hungry, or maybe fly around and suck up the oil slicks in the water, and decompose it in your super stomach, and spit it out in a shower of harmless grape-flavoured rain."

"I suppose I could do that."

RANDAL ISAAC'S SUICIDE

(From Broken Pencil #37)

josh byer

My life had been compressed into a 5.8 megabyte MP5 file. It was all in there. Everything. Me.

I had been downloaded two hundred thousand and fifty-seven times. I was not famous. I was not anyone. Tom at the hot-dog stand, his MP5 file had been downloaded four hundred, twenty-two thousand, six hundred, and fifty-two times. He was winning the popularity contest.

I wanted to see what it was all about. I have no idea how anyone gained access to my head and its contents. The file just washed up on the Net one day.

I Google-searched, downloaded, and ran the file. The Windows Personality Media Re-Enactor program said it needed several plug-ins that it didn't have. I sat and waited patiently for them to also download.

It didn't work.

The RANDAL_ISAAC.MP5 I had downloaded was corrupt. I spent the next hour trying to find another website that was carrying my file. I found one. I re-downloaded it. I hoped that this one was corrupt too. I hoped that they were all corrupt.

The file ran fine this time.

There it was, me. It even looked like me. The hair was different though. My hair is longer now.

"Hello?" said the synthetic Randal, from inside my fourteen-inch TVM Super VGA monitor. I stared at that monitor. It had been scavenged from a nearby alley. I had walked past it for a week, watching it get rained on, spit on, pissed on by angry dogs. If I had known I was going to be inside it, I would have taken it home sooner.

"Wait a second," I said. Synth-Randal did not respond. He looked a little cross-eyed. He was wearing a T-shirt I had long since lost.

"Hey," I said again louder. "Wait a second."

No response. I turned on my computer microphone and spoke into it. "Hello?"

Synth-Randal's eyes lit up—terror. He knew it was me. I knew it was him. If it had been me in there, hearing my own voice, I'd have lost my fucking mind. Synthy was doing pretty good. Synthy was holding it together.

"I can't see you," he said.

I had a web cam. It had been a gift from a friendly cousin, almost a decade ago. It was a measly one megapixel and took low-res photos that were too dark. It was in my closet, under cardboard luggage and reeking shoes.

I plugged in the camera and turned it on. I pointed the lens at my face. I leaned forward to see the Synth react.

"Oh, fuck me," he said.

"Hi," I replied. The Synth sat down on a synth chair.

"What—is—going—on?" he asked.

He didn't have my little forehead scar. I had fallen off of some idiot's motorcycle last year. Spent three days in the hospital. A doctor had called me a "moron with no respect for self-preservation" before I was released.

"How old are you?" I asked.

"I'm twenty-one," he said. "How old are you?"

"I'm twenty-six."

There was a long silence. He was uncomfortable in there, inside the computer, sitting in the darkness, on a chair that didn't exist.

"Are you me?" he asked.

"Yeah, I'm you."

"How are you twenty-six?"

I didn't know what to tell him.

"Let's just skip the bullshit," I said.

I was putting on my tough-guy voice.

"Fuck off with that macho shit," he replied. There was no point in being gracious. He was me. He knew my shtick. I gave him the best explanation I could.

"You're inside a computer."

He laughed. He looked around.

"Can you prove that?" he said. It was a good question. I moved the mouse cursor over his face.

"Can you see the little white arrow?"

"No. There's no arrow," he answered.

I sat and thought. He broke the moment —

"Do you swear to God that I'm inside your computer?"

It was a strong statement. I did believe in God, in a very personal and non-verbal way. I have never told anyone about this belief. It was something only I knew.

"I swear to God," I told him. He looked stunned. I guess he believed me. I was relieved.

"I don't believe you," he said.

I only had one idea left. It was cruel. Cruel and stupid. I pointed the web cam at the monitor. I remembered an old movie called *Encino Man* where a caveman is thawed out of a block of ice, and shown his own reflection in a mirror. The caveman has never seen his own reflection. He freaks out.

The Synth moved his left hand. He stood up. He sat down. He was watching himself. He became pathetic. I will always regret doing that to him.

"How did I get here?" His voice was very small now.

"I don't know," I said.

"Try to speculate," he begged.

"Okay. You're twenty-one. So that means when I was twenty-one, which was five years ago, someone must have scanned my head and made a computer file."

He sat and chewed his lip. I stopped doing that a long time ago.

"Do you know who scanned me into here?"

He was rubbing the back of his neck. Nervous tick. I still do that.

"No."

"Well, if you ever figure it out, I want you to find the motherfucker who did this and put a bullet through his face," he proclaimed.

"Fuck off with that macho shit," I told him. The Synth laughed.

"Yeah, you're right. I'm right. We're right. Whatever."

I laughed too. I sat there and had a good chuckle at my own expense.

"You're twenty-six, huh? So you're in the future?"

To him, five years had passed without his knowledge. He was the perfect imprint of me in my youth. I thought about a lot of things, right then.

"Did you marry Scarlet?"

Scarlet and I had been engaged, a long time ago. Then she got a scholarship to York University. Moved to Toronto. She asked me to come, but I said no. I didn't want to move. And she never liked the way I dressed.

"Yeah," I told him. "We're married. Our son is coming in the fall." I added the "son" thing to comfort him. When I was twenty-one, I was convinced that I would never have children. I'm still convinced of this. Convinced the future is no kind of place for children.

Synth slouched back in his chair, relieved. He hissed a sigh, deep and dangerous.

"I knew it," he told me. "Scarlet Isaac, eh? Good for you, Randy."

God, was I gullible once.

"If I'm in a computer, then I'm a file," he said.

I nodded. Now he was smart? I knew nothing about myself.

"Have I ever been copied?"

"No," I lied. "I just found you on one of my old hard drives."

He'd been downloaded two hundred thousand and fifty-seven times. Two hundred thousand and fifty-eight if you included my copy. There was an army of me out there trapped inside the PCs of Internet addicts, porn surfers, soccer moms. Strangers coaxing my synth-face into their cyber fantasies.

"Can you get me out of here?" he asked. Pleaded.

"Why should I?" I snapped. The Synth was afraid. That made me ashamed. His fears were my faults.

"You can't, can you?" Synthy quipped, "How could you? I'm just a program. Bodiless. I'm numbers on a hard drive, right?"

But I knew how to do it. I knew how I could get him out of there. I didn't want to think about it. About him. About the past—distant, and shitty, and gone.

I double-clicked on the Synth-Randal window.

"Wait!" he yelled, his voice piercing and full of static. "Is it going to hurt?"

I didn't answer. I dragged him to the Recycle Bin. Then I emptied the trash.

There were now two hundred thousand and fifty-seven Synth-Randals left in the world.

I could never end their sufferings.

SCARLATINA!

(From Broken Pencil #5)

derek mccormack

Gangway for Captain Marvel?

I bought *Whiz*. I played RIFLE RANGE! Shot fifteen coons.

I grabbed the knobs on ELECTRIC ENERGIZER! Got zapped by fifty volts.

MYSTIC PEN TELLS ALL! A ballpoint hung from wires. It jerked across a sheet of paper. The sheet slid down a chute.

"Destiny Awaits."

Thunder. Sky flashing like a pinball backglass. I ran for home. Halfway there it started coming down.

Billy Batson peddling papers. Some man coaxes him onto a subway car. The subway zips Billy to a cavern. There's a man on a throne. White hair, white beard.

"I know everything," the old man says. "I am Shazam!"

Lightning hits Billy. When the smoke clears, he's twenty-five. He's got gold tights on.

Mom came into my room. She grabbed the comic, and palmed my forehead. I gulped aspirin.

My temp spiked. Scarlet streaked up my chest.

Dad drove me to Emergency. The doctor hooked me up to a drip.

Days sleeping and sweating. The fever spread, pharynx to heart. The doctor taped electrodes to my chest.

"The ECG will trace your heartbeats," he said.

He turned it on. The pencil drew lightning bolts, then U-shapes.

The doctor wheeled the machine up to my bed. He put a steel cylinder in each of my hands.

A hundred amps of galvanic energy.

Dr. Sivana's got a machine to silence radio signals. He wants fifty million dollars or he'll end broadcasts forever.

"Shazam!" Billy says. He flies to Sivana's lab. He hurls henchmen at machines. Coils, springs, control panels.

The doctor sat down on my bed. "Your heart's been scarred. Excitement could weaken it. Or worse."

He confiscated the comic. Ten minutes later an intern wheeled in the library cart. Plopped *Little Women* on my tray.

I shambled to the elevator. In the gift shop I bought a pad of paper, a pack of coloured pencils.

The judge eyes some kid's crayon portrait of Batman. The Flash in pencil.

Then my panels: *Scarlet fever's wasting Derek McCormack's heart. The doctor hooks him to an electrocardiograph. Hospital lights die, then surge back on. Ten thousand volts rip through Derek. He rises from the smoke. All muscle. A red* S *on his chest.*

"First prize goes to *Scarlatina the Immortal!*" He awarded me a silver dollar. I slinked out of the arena and up the midway. Cotton candy blue as electricity. Guys firing rifles at ducks, and darts at balloons. TEST YOUR STRENGTH scale like a ten-foot thermometer.

A man barking in a GRAPHOLOGY booth. "Have your handwriting analyzed!" he said.

I gave him a sheet. Destiny Awaits.

"Who wrote it?" I said. "What does he want?"

RABBIT IN THE TRAP

(From Broken Pencil #23)
(Adapted from a Korean Folktale)

paul hong

John and Jane were afraid of rabbits that roamed in the surrounding neighbourhoods. One day, galvanized by an article they read in the paper, they discussed the problem, and tried to find a way to live happily without this nagging fear. After much discussion, they came to an agreement to go shopping at IKEA.

A few days later, nothing had been solved. They decided to dig pits here and there to trap the rabbits. John and Jane called several of their friends and family members to help dig deep pits around their house. Afterward, they gathered in the backyard for a barbecue dinner.

One day, a traveller was passing through the neighbourhood and heard funny sounds nearby. He approached the area where the sounds were coming from and found a rabbit that was trapped in a pit, trying to hop out.

Seeing the traveller, the rabbit begged for help: "Please, help me out of this trap, and I will never forget your kindness." The traveller got a golden retriever from the neighbour's yard, and, holding onto its hind legs, lowered it into the pit. The rabbit climbed out.

As soon as the rabbit was out of the trap, he said to the traveller: "I am grateful for your help, but because you people made the trap to catch me, I will have to kill you."

The traveller was speechless and frightened. Mustering all his courage, he said: "Wait a minute, Mr. Rabbit. It would be unfair to kill me considering I just saved your life. We should at least ask a few impartial parties to judge who is right." The rabbit reluctantly agreed and both of them went to a hobo who lived in a shipping crate nearby.

After listening to their story, the hobo said: "It is the fault of the rich. We hobos also have a grudge against the rich. They ride to work, and they leave us to starve and shiver in the cold. Talk about unfair!"

"Are you rich?" the rabbit asked.

The traveller lowered his head.

Next, they went to Mr. Pong. Mr. Pong listened silently to their story and said: "John and Jane are wrong. They come in here all the time complaining about the price of cigarettes and dog food, and they always call me 'Chief.' What have I done to them to deserve that? I am just trying to make a living. They have no heart!"

The rabbit had heard enough. The rabbit was elated, and about to attack the traveller, when a pig approached.

"Phew, you're just in time. Mr. Pig, please judge our case," said the traveller, and he told the pig what had happened.

The pig said, "Fine, but before I make any sort of judgment, I must see the original scene."

So the traveller, the rabbit, and the pig all went to the pit where the rabbit had been trapped.

The pig said to the rabbit: "I must see exactly how you were before this traveller rescued you. Where exactly were you?"

Eager to show where he was, the rabbit jumped into the pit.

"Was that dog in the pit when you fell into it, Mr. Rabbit?" the pig asked.

"No, it was not."

The pig and the traveller lifted the dog out of the pit.

"Was that fast-food delivery man in the pit when you fell into it, Mr. Rabbit?" the pig asked.

"No."

The pig and the traveller lifted the delivery man out of the pit.

"Was that nanny in the pit when you fell into it, Mr. Rabbit?"

"No, I don't think so."

The pig and the traveller lifted the nanny out of the pit. Then the pig said to the traveller: "Mr. Man, be on your way." And, with that, the pig left too.

THE JESUS

(From Broken Pencil #29)

mckinley m. hellenes

> *"What Jesus can't fix tonight*
> *the whiskey certainly might . . . "*
> *— Hawksley Workman*

i.

It's pissing rain by the time she gets off work. She meets Jesus at the pub on the corner. She's late, as usual. He's sitting there already, his hands long and brown, His fingers gripping the glass. She can tell by his eyes he hasn't slept, maybe in days. He looks a little bleary, blurred around the edges like His features have been scraped off and smeared back on, thin and elegant.

"Hey," she says. "What're you having?"

"Bloody Mary," He says. "A double." His eyes smile up at her as she drags out a chair.

"How'd they get it all in one glass?"

He shrugs, watching her arrange herself. She unravels her scarf, revealing a throat thin, slightly papery, like the pages of a book going quietly to earth. She is getting old, she knows. He has never aged a day. His eyes, however, are older than anything she has ever seen, on Hastings Street or beyond.

She watches as He swallows, His throat contracting like a frantic bird, rising and plummeting.

"Isn't that a sacrilege?" she asks. "Drinking something named after your mother?" She crosses herself, her fingers scurrying furtively.

He shakes his head. He's amused, she can tell. "Bloody Mary, not Virgin Mary," He says. "If there was no booze in it, maybe I would have to worry. And besides, your name is Mary too. Maybe it's named after someone like you."

"I guess," she says. "It still seems creepy though."

"What, me drinking in general, or me drinking this in particular?" He gestures at the glass, dingy and smeared with too many people's fingerprints.

She shrugs. "I don't know. But something is."

He laughs, signalling to the bartender. "I don't know what everyone's problem is. You drink my blood every Sunday. You eat my flesh. I died for you, for fuck's sake. It's a little late to get squeamish now." He laughs again, pushing a thick black curl behind His ear. She would kill for hair like that. Hers is so slack and stringy now. She would cut it, but the customers like it long. They like to have something to tug on, when there are no strings attached.

"Yeah, I know," she says. She orders an apple martini, even though she knows he'll laugh at her. She likes dainty drinks, even if she likes a lot of them. He orders a whiskey sour. He likes to make concessions. It's part of his nature. It would have to be, she thinks, taking the first long, cool swallow. At the back of her throat is the taste of tin, or maybe it's something else entirely. Jesus smiles at her. She reaches across the table to touch His hand.

ii.

On Fridays she meets Jesus in the Woodbine Hotel. He is always there, waiting for her like she is any woman. Like He is any man. She doesn't make Him pay. He just wants to hold her.

"You always liked whores, huh?" she asks Him, stroking His arm. She likes the places where His bones connect and disappear, like fish spawning in shallow water. He doesn't mind her touching Him like that.

He shrugs. "It's not that. It's more like I didn't notice who was a whore and who wasn't." He pauses to light a cigarette on the wick of a candle He likes to keep by the bed. She hears Him exhale a split second before she feels the warm breath drift over her skin. "The whores were the only ones who seemed to know they were sinners. They didn't seem to notice how they were being sinned against. I liked that. It was so self-effacing. When it was written that the meek would inherit the earth, it was the whores I always thought of."

"Is it still like that?" she asks. "I mean, don't we know any better now?"

"I don't know, Mary," He says. "Do you?" He runs His hand down her back. He is splayed out on the bed, His arms around her. She is lying half beside Him, half on top, her hair spread out over His chest and belly. She washed it this morning, even though she knows He won't notice the cheap cloying scent of her shampoo. She likes to be clean for Him. On Fridays, He is the only one.

"I don't know," she says. "I don't think so."

She lays her cheek against His stomach. He isn't as skinny as in the pictures, but His ribs show through his T-shirts like xylophone keys. He smells like mothballs and incense, like the coat closet in the church where she was baptized. She breathes deeply, inhaling a hint of beeswax. It flutters in her nostrils and settles in her mouth. She can taste Him. He has never so much as kissed her.

"Is this a sin?" she asks, too quiet to hear, except He does.

"Does it feel like one?" Jesus says.

She considers. "No," she says. "Never."

"Then I wouldn't worry."

"My name isn't really Mary," she tells him after a minute, not for the first or the last time.

Jesus doesn't answer. He just looks at her. She can feel his expression touch her face the way moth wings powder window glass. He tilts her chin up, the knuckle of his thumb pushing her face back so she is looking directly at Him. His eyes are almost black. In pictures, they always paint them blue. Against the cracking drywall he could be a fresco, a word she has never been taught the meaning of.

iii.

There is another woman, on an island. Well, not really an island. It's more like a peninsula, but it feels like an island, the way a tooth feels completely disconnected, even when it's holding on by a tendril to the gums. He likes to joke that when the ferry's late, He has to walk. Most of the time, no one gets it.

The woman's name isn't Mary, but it starts with the same letter. He visits her at her house, a small A-frame near the beach. The house clings to a small patch of grass for dear life, as though it is scared of water and trapped in a dream of swimming over its head.

The woman is obsessed with earthquakes. Her hair is dark, a shroud about her shoulders. She wants to be ready.

"When the big one comes," she says, "we'll all be swept under. This whole island will sink."

"It's not an island," He points out, not for the first time. "You could walk to the mainland if you wanted to."

She gives Him a look that would wither if He were that kind of man. He lights two cigarettes in His mouth and passes one to her. The tide is coming in fast. The gulls make their final sweep over the horizon before settling like crumpled bits of paper into the waves.

"I only smoke when you're here," she says. "Jesus Christ, you are a bad influence."

He laughs. "I've heard that before."

"I'll bet you have," she says. She doesn't smile.

"Were you taking my name in vain just then," He asks, turning back towards the house, "or were you just saying it to me, you know, for emphasis?"

She considers, taking His hand. "It's always a little bit of both, with you," she says. Her last breath of smoke wafts over His face. They walk back to the house to wait out what comes.

TOO MUCH MEAN ME

(From Broken Pencil #32)

geoffrey brown

We both were there. We were both there. I was who I was there. When I was there I was who I was. We both were who we was there. We both were there. We both were who we were there. Who we were was who we were when we were there. When we were there we were not who we were when we were not there. Neither of us were. We were neither of us not. Not there. We were both. We were both not. Both of us were not. If you know what I mean. I don't mean what you think. I don't mean what you think I mean. Do you know what I think? I think what I mean. I mean what I say. I mean what I say

I mean. What I say is what I mean. What I said is what I meant. What I meant to say. What I said I meant. I said what I meant. I meant what I said. When we were where I said we were. When we were where we both could be. Where we were was where we were. We were where we were. When we were there. When we were where we were when we were there we were who we were. We both were who we were when we were there. We both were what we were when we were there. We were both what we were. We were both what we were not. Do you know what I mean? You know what I mean. You never know what I mean. Do you ever know what I mean? What do I mean? Why was she mean? She was once mean. Where is she now? Is she anywhere now? She could be anywhere now. She could be nowhere now. Anywhere she is she could be. She could be anywhere where she is not. She is not where she once was. She once was where she is not. Where she once was we both were once. We both were not us. We were both. We were mean. Both of us were. Both of us were mean. Both of us were us. We were both us. Of both we were us. Both of us us. Both of us mean. Did I mean to be mean? I meant to be me. I meant me to be. I didn't mean me. I wasn't mean me. Mean wasn't me. I'm saying too much. I mean it's too much. I mean it too much. I'm meaning too much. Too much do I mean. Too much am I mean. Too much mean me. She doesn't mean much. What much does she mean? Was she mean much? Mean much to me? She was much mean. Meant much to me. Don't bother me now. Why bother me now? What bother is now? Now is not now. Now it is now. Now it is what. Not now is it now. Not now is it not. Now is what now? What is now now? Once more it is now. No bother it now. No bother to now. No bother once more. Once more is no bother. No bother is now. Do I bother to now? Never mind now. Now mind my brother. Go bother my brother. My brother will tell you. My brother will talk. Talk with my brother. My brother my bother. My brother's no bother. My brother's another. My brother the other. My brother another. My brother my other. Too many others. Remember the others? All those anothers? Another one other. One other other. I know another. I have another. I have a brother. I'm one with my brother. My only brother. My lonely brother. One lonely brother. One brother alone. A lone lonely brother. A lonely one only. One lonely, alone. Enough with all that. What's up with all that? What's up with all this? What is it, all this? Is that all this is? Is this all that is? This is all that. This is all that is. All that this is. All this is is that. That is all this is. What about that? What about this? What about us?

THE NAPOLEON DIFFERENCE

(From Broken Pencil #31)
julia campbell-such

Bone splinters, pure white like expensive china. Smell of talcum powder, morphine, sterilizers. Cracking, splitting, sawing. Tired and blood-soaked, the sheets sagged over the surgery bed.

Earlier in the week, Timothy had sat by the fire in the living room, nursing an after-work beer. Jemima smoothed her skirt over her long, long legs, and looked down at him.

"The doctor says he can make you taller," Jemima said.

"Why?" Timothy asked.

"He just says he could."

"I don't want to be taller."

"I know."

There was a heavy silence. Jemima crossed her legs. Timothy's feet dangled over the edge of his big leather chair.

"Do you want me to be taller?"

"Of course not!"

Timothy cocked one eyebrow. "Would you want to be shorter?"

Jemima laughed. "No, I guess not."

The midget nodded. He put down his book and jumped down from his chair.

"I better get dinner started then."

Jemima smiled. She threw her white nurse's cap on the couch and took the pins out of her hair. When she shook her brown curls they made a drugstore smell. In the kitchen, Timothy chopped carrots, counting each orange circle. There was dirt under his fingernails.

The doorbell rang with the first of his dinner guests. It was Joe Prince, tossing his deep voice over Timothy's head.

"Need a hand, Tiny Tim?" His teeth gleamed like hubcaps.

"I need a smaller kitchen, jackass."

Jemima touched Joe Prince's shoulder and smiled.

"He says that every night," she said.

There were five of them at dinner. Prince, who had been in Timothy's philosophy classes and now taught part-time at the university in between shiny afternoons at a Pontiac dealership, sat next to his latest girlfriend Sarah, stylish television actress and owner of cats. Across from them was Jemima's childhood friend, a performance artist named Hazel who grinned, and cackled, and radiated warmth and darkness. They ate intently, dealing out potatoes and tidy conversation. Jemima ran in and out of the kitchen. Joe Prince watched her.

"She's like a gazelle," he said.

Timothy winked at him. "More like a moose."

Prince laughed.

After dinner, in the living room, Timothy poured whiskey into heavy crystal glasses. The light from the fireplace rushed impatiently over the wood-panelled walls. Timothy stroked his beard.

"Jemima's doctor says he can make me taller."

"How wonderful!" said Sarah, her blond beehive tilting dangerously to one side.

"How much taller?" asked Hazel, winking. Timothy breathed deeply.

"Jemima, how much taller could the doctor make me?"

Jemima's foot tapped on the bearskin rug. She looked at the floor.

"How do they do it?" Hazel asked, whistling through her missing front tooth.

"Do they implant stilts? Will there be surgery?"

Sarah powdered her tiny nose. "How awful. Will you really do it?"

Jemima looked up angrily. "Timothy doesn't need to be any taller," she said.

Her face was red.

"Of course he doesn't," Prince nodded, his cheeks glowing from the Scotch.

Hazel's long red nails tapped and clicked on her whiskey glass. Timothy looked around the room. He cocked one eyebrow, and swung his tiny feet.

"Do you think I should do it?" he asked. No one answered. Jemima chewed on her nails. Branches scratched the windowpanes. The firelight

blazed behind Timothy's eyes, swept across Jemima's cheeks and landed on Joe Prince's face, twisting his handsome features. A lock of hair escaped onto Sarah's forehead. She quickly brushed it back.

"Well," Joe said finally, to break the tension, "you'd win more fights with your wife, ha ha!"

In Timothy's dream he was a giant. He could see over the top of a crowd of people in the supermarket, and past them all the way around the world, so that he ended up staring at the back of his own head. Someone far below called up to him, asking him to get them something from the top shelf. Timothy stretched to get it, but it was still too high, just out of his reach. On his way out of the supermarket he hit his head in the doorway. Jemima woke him up.

"Are you okay?" she asked.

Timothy stroked her hair. "I wish we were the same height."

"Why?"

"I wish I was taller than you."

"Height doesn't matter."

"Easy for you to say." Timothy and Jemima talked all night, and argued, and made up. Timothy decided the best thing to do would be to shrink the world down to his size. Jemima laughed.

"We'll never let you do that, silly," she said. "We're bigger than you."

Timothy was tired and hungover the next day at the munitions factory. His bosses yelled at him all morning, their voices echoing off of cement walls and steel missiles. The smell of mould and sawdust made Timothy feel sick. A pile of freshly polished shells caught the sun from the window, blinding him. In the afternoon he got into a fight. Foreman Jim pushed him and called him "shorty." Timothy took a swing at him. Jim hit him in the stomach and made him throw up all over the conveyor belt.

Timothy shuffled home, his tiny hands still covered in grease. He passed the university. A young man pointed at him and laughed.

Timothy heard a girl's voice say softly, "He's not a midget. He's a dwarf. There's a difference."

When Timothy got home Jemima was in the kitchen in a long white skirt. She lifted Timothy up to kiss him.

"Put me down," he said.

"Rough day?"

"Everyone's still taller than me."

"Well, there's not much you can do about that, is there?" Jemima said, stirring the soup.

Timothy cocked one eyebrow. "Isn't there?"

Jemima put down the spoon.

"Timothy . . ."

"Call the doctor, Jemima. Make an appointment."

During the operation Timothy gripped Jemima's hand, weeping and terrified. Her face was calm and pale green in the fluorescent light. The surgeons wore masks and spoke quietly and mechanically. Timothy could only see their eyes.

He heard one of them say, "She was crazy to agree to this."

Six weeks later, Jemima pulled her skirt up over her knees.

"The doctor says the casts can come off soon," she said, looking down at her bandaged legs.

"Good," Timothy said, and kissed the top of her head. Joe Prince looked in from the living room.

"Need a hand, Tiny Tim?"

"I need a smaller kitchen, jackass."

"You'll never win that argument," said Prince, and he looked sadly at Jemima. "How's it going, shorty?" he said gently.

Jemima looked back at him, her wide brown eyes slowly filling with anger.

CHECK MATE

(From Broken Pencil #23)

zoe whittall

i.

Judy will not wear this sweater again, the flawless one with the grey sleeves and black torso. Perfect thumb holes are worn in around the wrists. Familiar.

She wore it today and she began to choke on the bus, ready to die.

She coughed up the hard, red candy, expelling it onto graffiti written on the silver back of the bus seat. It said: "Save yourself first," and "I Love You."

Now the sweater is bad luck. Judy tossed it on top of the kitchen garbage before she brought it out. Her husband didn't notice.

ii.

She passed the funeral parlour on Marlon Road, the one between her house and her job at Stedmans Department Store. The undertaker outside was smoking, looked at her longer than he should, as if to say, "You're next, baby."

He watched her ass as she sashayed back home to call in sick. Bad luck. Stares ruin everything. Judy rolls pennies on the plastic tablecloth.

iii.

In the support group, there was a guy who chewed his own skin. There was a girl who fell a lot. There was a woman that Judy knew, just knew, wasn't going to make it.

The therapist told Judy she was making progress, even though she had never spoken, just smiled.

iv.

When Judy got home she checked the pilot light again. Again. Again. Again. She noticed a hole in her left sock.

v.

Obsessed, prepossessed, infatuated, fixated, besotted, gripped, held, monomaniacal. A visionary.

vi.

Her husband never ever worried. About anything. Sometimes when he was broke he would sigh a little bit. "Nothing to get all tense about, Jude," he said as he washed the carrots and set them aside. He rubbed a long one against the square metal grater. She knew he wasn't worried about death. Disease. The possibility of both. Just the shreds of orange falling into the ceramic bowl. Sometimes, this fact made Judy dream about chewing wine glasses.

vii.

Judy played harmonica in the window. The lady downstairs in the yard looked up. Her eyes were just like penny whistles.

viii.

Judy said "heaven forbid" whenever she thought about having sex with everyone on the bus. The old man, the girl with braces. She couldn't stop. She said "heaven forbid" without thinking she was saying it. It just came.

ix.

Fatalistic, skeptical, negative, dubious, abrogating, neutralizing, pessimistic.

x.

The doctor said: "People with your condition either kill themselves or go on medication."

She took the scrip into the candy store. She bought red licorice and felt lighter.

xi.

Judy's mother telephoned every Monday night after bingo.

"How are you, sweetheart?"

"Nothing to complain about, you know, same old."

xii.

He fucked her and she wanted to punch him in the head. She squeezed hard around him. She came hard, thinking he looked like a cowboy from the old Western she watched the night before, when she couldn't fall asleep. She loved him completely, for his ability to just live.

xiii.

Judy remembered when God was a petal pulled in want. A first, second, third chew. When it was God(.) not God(?). The brackets are new.

GIRAFFES AND EVERYTHING

(From Broken Pencil #30)

joey comeau

George woke up and remembered that he remembered giraffes existed.

It had come to him the night before, at the office Christmas party, on his sixth drink, an image of faded orange and white. He spent the rest of the party interrupting conversations to tell his co-workers "I can't believe I forgot about them. The necks, and the spots, and everything. The little tails."

He moved from circle to circle, not hearing their snickers behind him, his mind flooded with the grainy video of those public television programs he'd seen as a child, long faces with nubby protrusions on top. Long tongues snaking out for leaves. How could he have forgotten such long tongues?

Having forgotten giraffes for so long was an embarrassment of the type you had to purge by telling as many people as possible, the type you had to reduce to a joke as quickly as you could. George made his way to where his friend Matt was chatting up a girl. The girl watched him approach. She was swaying a bit, drunk, though her drink was perfectly steady.

Matt looked up and smiled when he saw George. They'd shared an office for six months, something like three years ago. The younger man kept a map of the solar system above his desk, detailed, covered with distances, temperatures, masses. Numbers and charts filled the void between planets. The temperature of Venus was circled with a red marker. George tried to imagine Matt ever forgetting something as important as giraffes.

"You came!" Matt said. "I knew you would." He turned to the girl. "This is George," he said.

George smiled and put his hand out. She probably remembered giraffes too, he thought. She couldn't be more than twenty. She probably still lived at home with her parents, maybe lined her room with zoo wallpaper, giraffes and lions. Her shelves would hold teddy bears. They would be soft like the skin just down from her shoulder, where her breast met her body. That spot was hidden now, under her shirt, but George knew it was there. Soft. He realized he'd had too much to drink and he was staring. She shook the hand politely, looking past him at the crowd, bored.

"Listen," Matt said, leaning closer to George. "There's a promotion coming up, and I'm going to drop your name. You're overdue." As he said it, George felt the faint stirrings of anger. He'd been passed over twice now, in favour of Matt. The only reason Matt was in a position to "drop his name" was because he'd taken promotions that should have gone to George. Still, the feeling passed quickly, and he pulled Matt close. He raised his voice above some braying woman across the room, and he said, "Do you remember giraffes?"

Matt shook his head.

"What?" he said, like George was joking.

"Giraffes!" George said, louder. "With the long necks and the awkward knees? Do you remember them?"

Matt laughed again, and nodded.

"Giraffes!" Matt said. "Of course. Mary in Human Resources is obsessed with them. Her office is full of books and those cheesy inspirational posters. 'Reach for the sky!'"

George tried to think of where Mary's office was. He was sure he'd been there. Up on the nineteenth floor, probably, with the other executives. Someone had abandoned their drink on the table between Matt and the girl, and George picked it up. Coconut.

"Can you show me her office?" he said, and Matt looked back at the girl. He grinned.

"Sure," he said to George. To the girl he said something that George couldn't hear, then kissed her on the neck. George started for the elevators, not looking back to make sure they were following.

Lying in bed the next morning, George tried to piece together the rest of the night. He rolled over and he shook his wife's shoulder. She said something into the pillow.

"What time did I get in?" he said. "From the party last night."

She pulled the blanket up and turned deeper into the pillow.

He remembered standing in Mary's office, the light coming from a little table lamp, giving the room a warm feel. Where had Matt and the girl been?

He remembered the elevator ride up. He stood to one side, pressed as far against the wall as he could while Matt and the girl went at it, pulling at each other's clothes, their kisses mashing their faces together. He looked at his feet, and he ran his hands along the seams of his pockets.

When the elevator opened on the nineteenth floor, George stepped out and held the door. Matt pointed up the hall.

"At the end, there," he said, and he took the girl's hand, led her the opposite way, fumbled keys from his pocket.

George watched them go. The girl pulled her shirt up as they reached Matt's office. Matt fought with the lock, and in the split second before they went inside George could see her naked back, spotted and dark in the hallway. Then the door was closed, and the frosted glass was yellow with the light beyond.

George found his way to Mary's office, the hallway only half familiar in the darkness. Her door was locked, and George pressed his face against the cold glass, trying to make out the office inside. He hadn't been in Mary's inner office during the interview. He had never even met Mary. The secretary had interviewed him at the desk in the outer office. There hadn't been any giraffe posters there. He would have seen them. They would have reminded him earlier that giraffes existed.

He tried the door again and it was still locked. There was a big brown smudge in the office behind the frosted glass, the secretary's desk. George turned and made his way back down the hallway to where Matt and the girl were. As he came around the corner, he could see that the light was still on. George steadied himself against the wall. Matt would have something to drink in his office, he thought.

But there were sounds coming from the room, and shapes just beyond the glass. There was music playing, and the girl was saying "yes," over and over. George stopped with his hand on the doorknob, and thought about knocking. He could just turn around and get back on the elevator. There were drinks at the party downstairs, and they were free, but he didn't feel like seeing those people now. He was tired.

If he knocked, Matt and the girl might hurry into their clothes. They might give him a drink if there was anything in the office. But more likely they would just tell him to get lost. He'd end up standing in the hallway just like this, ashamed. He began to turn the knob anyway. Who cared what they thought. He needed a drink.

But the shapes moved closer, and then the girl was up against the frosted glass, mashed into focus against the white, her breasts outlined perfectly, flat and out of shape. The two figures were moving rhythmically against the door. He could see her mouth move with every "yes" and he could see Matt behind her, a dark pink shadow. If someone came along now, someone else from the party, they would think George was a pervert standing in the hall like this. And if he could see her, couldn't she see him? George stepped back. He should just turn around and get on the elevator.

Instead he reached out and put his hand against the glass where her breast was. He imagined he could feel the warmth. One day she would forget about giraffes, or anteaters, or gazelles. He let his fingers linger against the door, and then turned around and walked to the Human Resources office.

He kicked the frosted glass of Mary's door and it fell around his leg. The sound was a quiet crack. He pulled the big chunks of glass free, and reached through to unlock the knob. The outer office was just as he remembered it, plain and beige. It was a bit more sinister in the darkness. The walls of her inner office were decorated with pictures of giraffes, like Matt had said, giraffes pulling leaves from trees, giraffes with their tongues reaching out, twisting. There were some tribal-looking giraffe statues in the corners, and the shelves were lined with little giraffe knick-knacks and books.

This was someone who thought about giraffes every day, who took pride in her love for the slender animal. When she got presents from co-workers, they knew to get her giraffe-themed gifts. George wondered how many of the knick-knacks were gifts from his own coworkers. He wondered if Mary from Human Resources kept something to drink in her desk. He looked. There was a bottle of gin in the bottom right drawer.

While he drank he rifled through her things. None of the papers on the desk was interesting. They were only personnel reports and job applications. He turned on her computer, hoping to find his own personnel report, but it asked him for a password. He tried "giraffe" and was denied. He knew what the report would say, anyway. He was useful in his current position, and that position alone. He'd reached the top of his personal corporate ladder. There wasn't anything interesting on the computer.

George stood, and looked around the room for something to pick up.

The wooden giraffe sculpture was heavy in his hand, like a club. He swung it a couple of times in the air, getting the feel of the weight, and

he looked around at the dark office for something to break. Mary from Human Resources didn't forget things like giraffes. She surrounded herself with them.

George tried to put the statue through the computer monitor, but it was one of those new flat screen things, and the picture just cracked and bent in on itself. There was no tube to explode and it was unsatisfying. It just made him angry. He pounded on the monitor with the heavy wooden giraffe, little shards of the screen falling across the table and to the carpet. He pulled the computer itself out from under her desk and started hammering the side of it, trying to break through the metal casing with the idiotic long-necked conversation piece. He dented the machine quite badly, and pulled all the cords out of the back.

He busted every light and pulled down the giraffe posters, hoping to tear them up, but they were mounted against some sort of wood. He managed to break one of them in two, propping it against the wall and stomping on it. He swung the giraffe in wide arcs, sweeping knick-knacks to the floor and breaking as many as he could. It wasn't until he began pounding the giraffe on the big plate window that he realized the girl was standing in the doorway, smiling at him.

"Do you need any help?" she said, crossing to pick up another of the heavy giraffes from the corner. She joined him at the window, took a step forward, brought the giraffe down over her head and put a good crack into the reinforced glass. "My name's Julia," she said, lifting the giraffe above her head again. "Matt passed out on his desk."

George nodded and pointed at the bottle of gin. He took a bit of satisfaction in Matt's failure, but he couldn't let it distract him. He didn't want to lose his momentum. He wanted to break through the glass, to let the cold air into the office. He wanted to throw these knick-knacks and expensive statues down into the courtyard below.

"There's gin there," he said. "Help yourself. It's not mine." And he hit the window again, as hard as he could. Julia set the giraffe down again and took a drink. After a couple swings, he needed to rest. "Do you work in the building?" he said. "Or are you a friend of Matt's from somewhere else?"

"I'm an accountant," she said, and she leaned closer to George. "But really I'm just biding my time." She winked, and George smiled. "I just met Matt at the party." She lifted the giraffe again. "He seems sort of boring." Her giraffe punched a hole right through the glass, and fresh air suddenly swept into the room. She stepped forward so that her face was near the hole. George did too.

"He is," George said, taking a deep breath, letting the cold air fill his lungs. The wind was sweet against his face, and she slid her hand into his. They looked out at the offices in the next building.

She let go of his hand and went to the desk for another drink. George stayed at the window, looking out at all the other offices. How many of them had animal posters on their walls, giraffes or ducks, or baboons? George wondered if there were any other animals he'd forgotten.

Julia took his hand again from behind.

"This," she gestured around at the damage. She kicked the giraffe at her feet. "This was nice," she said.

"Help me with this stuff," George replied, indicating the scattered curios and figurines all over the floor. He scooped up a group of little stone giraffe carvings, and carried them to the window. They fell away into the darkness.

The two worked quickly, stopping only to bash the hole a little wider, so they could throw the posters out as well. The last to go were the giraffe sculptures, and they let them fall headfirst, spinning slowly. Watching them fall was like watching the ball drop at Times Square, New Year's Eve. It was like watching a penny fall into a well. He wanted to close his eyes and make a wish.

LAST WINTER HERE

(From Broken Pencil *#39;*
Semi-Finalist in the First Annual Indie Writers Deathmatch)

emma healey

curtains

I take an English lit class once a week in this room. It's a class that everyone says is important, and good, and useful, and for those reasons, it's hard to concentrate on anything the teacher says. It's harder still to listen. I do a lot of half-looking, where I stare out the window, but don't take in the scenery. The first time I actually looked, I saw snow dust on power lines, office towers, and parked cars. I had to turn away and regroup. Now I avoid eye contact with that window. Sometimes our gazes meet, and I feel guilty and strange.

five blocks

I walk home the way you'd read a book. Left to right, or it doesn't make sense.

If you'd like, you can come home with me and read my street like a page. The cars and the wind are like commas, gulps of air between run-on sentences. The dance you do passing strangers on the sidewalk is made of verbs and adjectives. Start and stop. Eventually you'll get there.

slush

I hate the winter. I hate the cold, I hate the snow that turns to grey slush so quick, I hate the smokers huddling in doorways, I hate visible exhaust and breath, I hate the dry. I love the trees, how they tear the edges off the sky like pulling a page out of a notebook, all ragged and torn. I love skating. I love quiet. But I hate winter.

Today when I came home, my father was sitting at the kitchen table, staring at a large cardboard box I didn't recognize. He was half-smiling. "What is that?" I asked, knowing he wanted me to. He took the things out of the box.

It looked wrong standing there on our kitchen table, shiny, and smooth, and mechanical. Its body tilted towards our faces like it was asking a question. It made me nervous for some reason I didn't fully understand. I looked at the side of the box.

"Seasonal Affective Disorder Therapy Lamp?"

My father smiled again, really.

"It's going to make me marginally happier," he said.

the problem with st. george subway station

Is all the green. I get distracted so easily. Everyone moving and talking, stomping the slush off their boots. Everyone so sure where they're going, pissed off and pushing. The fluorescent lights that make you look tired. Sometimes I just stand and watch, and wait for things to calm down. I'm always late for everything.

contemporary studies in vocal cadence

I like this class, but the teacher speaks in italics. She sounds like a full symphony orchestra. All swells, emphasis, everything a beginning or a short, plucky aside. It's wonderful and exhausting. It becomes hard to tell where you're really supposed to be paying attention, to tell what's really important. I end up listening for the art in her lessons, for the patterns. I notate her speeches in the margins of my textbook, the markings rising up and down through definitions and diagrams, taking up space.

the agony

Of not kissing him. On the subway. The boy. Me in my stupid fucking trapper hat my mom bought me from the Bay for $16.99, and my giant backpack, my giant flashing neon sign that says "HIGH SCHOOL, HIGH

SCHOOL," and him all university coffee-shop cool, half-smiling the whole ride there, six stops, everyone else frowning. I sneak a glance behind myself, twisting. He is reading philosophy and I am reading his eyes. That half-smile, and if I could be half as good as Plato. The beautiful brown curly hair. The headphones around the neck. When I am older I will know better, and when I was younger I knew less than this. We are at Bathurst. I am getting desperate. If he looks up at me before we get there, if the two tight-lipped, angry-faced, cold-hearted, fur-coated women crossing their arms over my view of him (get away) will move, if he will turn that same near-smile to me, if I can make out what's on that button on his jacket, I will kiss him. I will. I swear under my breath and try to attract his attention with my feet rooted to the spot. I don't want to talk, I whisper, nearly, hoping he'll get it.

seconds

I think about time a lot. I find myself wanting to turn off all the clocks in my house, to stop everyone's watches just to see what would happen, but it would be so hard. In my household there is never a lack of time. We have clocks everywhere. Bedrooms, bathroom, living room. Five in the kitchen. It gets crowded sometimes, all these numbers, and there's a sort of secret code you have to learn if you want to get anywhere on time. The clock in the bathroom is six minutes fast on purpose, the one in the kitchen always inexplicably three minutes slow, no matter how much resetting we do.

Outside the house it's worse. The air is crowded with minutes. Parking meters, pay phones, iPods, watches. The clocks in my school are all out of sync with each other. Mandatory math class lasts five years and art's over before you can take out your paintbrushes. You spend the day in class, exhausted from calculating the differences, from anticipating, and then you get home. It's different there. The clocks make it safe. They mean the house never gets that wind-tunnel feeling buildings can when you're alone. You can always flick a switch, or cast a glance, and you are anchored, a part of the world, running late, but still running.

INTO COLLAPSES
(From Broken Pencil #13)
robert benvie

Apparently, kids are skateboarding, playing video games, having sex.

An informal study was presented on television depicting *The Greatest Atrocities of Modern Times.* An array of bar graphs gave further insight as to the criteria which determined the study's selection, i.e. geographic extent of havoc wreaked, estimated rate of accidental casualty versus meditated torture ritual, blitzkrieg versus sustained political terrorism, ethnic vendetta, ecological devastation, generational repercussions, etc. The bars in the graphs looked like rainbows of teeth, filed to squared planes.

10/08/88. BOY, 14, DIES IN AUTO ACCIDENT. Insert black-and-white photo of two policemen in long coats, lurking sombrely around a severely damaged Ford Taurus wagon. Surfaces are slick with rain. Dots of ink confirm nightmarish possibilities. Look closely: a shred of torn material is trapped in a bend of metal, a sleeve of sweatshirt, an outline of a logo. A region of a gurgling skull, shakily penned.

Two kids are sitting on a curb. The sun above is slowly burning the backs of their necks and the ridges of their noses a bold pink. A third kid approaches on a brand new skateboard, his face glowing with pride. Lance Mountain deck, brand new, unscuffed. There is a discussion. Minutes later, the newcomer exits, near teary. The seated two snicker, watching him go.

3:30 A.M. The Commodore 64's screen depicts a crude computer-rendering of something flesh-coloured, something vaguely rodlike, moving into, then out of, something resembling a dark puddle. German text flows along the bottom of the screen in binary stutters. The boy in front of the computer giggles, jiggles joystick, then yawns.

Eventually all the coffins in the graveyard across from the radio building downtown will have to be dug up and reburied, so they are saying. A complete re-plotting. At the current rate of soil erosion and deterioration of the crest of its marshy slope, an already problematic quantity, the entire cemetery will eventually collapse, so they tell me, falling into the adjacent gorge, which is currently occupied by train tracks. They say utmost respect will be assured for the wishes of all parties. Measures are being undertaken to prevent an uproar. People are very sensitive in matters of exposure.

Two boys are skateboarding in the hospital parking lot. As of the Previous evening, one of them has just lost his virginity. The other has been preparing to lose his own status thereof by practising donning a Durex Sheik Sensi-Thin Lubricated condom, then slipping it off, while he watches television.

There is no grudge here.

One of the boys had a letter published in *Thrasher* magazine's "Mail Drop" letters column this month, the May '88 issue, expressing his disgust with the police in his community. He recounted his own run-ins with law-enforcement officials, as well as relaying the sordid tale of his cousin's current incarceration (possession), a degree of sentence made harsher for his "History of Disobedience" in dealing with local officials, particularly in defiance of legislation forbidding skateboarding, or similar recreational activity, on private or semi-private property. The author of the letter managed to express genuinely emotional ruefulness and desperation in the letter's brief and decidedly terse prose; the letter was quite eloquent for a kid.

Both of the boys have stickers on their decks declaring: "SKATEBOARDING IS NOT A CRIME."

"Insert quasi-fascist quote here."

News breaks and diminishes. Time favours achievement, distinction, bravado. Atrocity. Haywire. In the drunk tank they were ordered to take the shoelaces out of their shoes, and their belts out of their belt loops. The two young guys were nervous, trapped behind those bars with a crew of growling drunks, but everybody seemed to accept their communally sour fates, and most of them just quietly slept it off.

A decal wore a skull, a rib cage, a lesion. Pus, celebrated. Tissue, glorified. Borders of neon pink and neon green trailed in flames around skateboard wheels, sizzling. Scabs waited to be picked. Bones toppled into a bulldozer's maw. Days went by, years.

"Punch line."

Apparently, "atrocity" means "large-scale loss."

We all had terrible haircuts that made us feel better about ourselves. In our youth the sun went ignored, things went assimilated to the Now. Some of us were too fat to be elegant; some of us were too pale to be bold. Some people fell off the conveyor belt before deciding whether they even wanted to be manufactured.

Everything was unfixed.

FOUR STORIES

(From Broken Pencil *#6)*
geoffrey brown

killers

They killed him after dark. Night had its advantages. So they waited until dark. There were two of them who killed. It took the two of them to kill. The two of them took turns. First one of them killed. Then the other. The killing happened quickly. It was over quickly. The body lay unmoving. The killers stood above it. They picked up the body. They put it in a bag. They took the bag outside. They went back in and wiped the floor. The body they disposed of. The body and the bag. Then they went and bought another bag. They took turns paying for the bags. First one of them paid for a bag. Then the other.

piano lesson

"Follow me," my father says. He pushes back his chair and stands.
   My mother doesn't move. She is on the sofa.
   My father taps his foot. His hands are on his hips. He stands above us.
   "Come on," my father says.
   My mother shakes her head. She looks away. Outside it is dark.
   My father says, "Let's go." He takes a step towards me.
   My mother shuts her eyes.

knowledge

Suddenly he knew.
   He sat up.

My God, he thought.
He went downstairs. The house was dark.
He checked the windows. Both the doors.
He went upstairs. Got into bed. He closed his eyes.

noise

My mother was speaking.
"Listen," I said. I held up my hand.
But there was nothing to hear. I knew there was nothing to hear. I knew.
My mother was waiting.
I lowered my hand. Nodded my head.
My mother continued.
I let her go on.

AMSTERDAM AT MIDNIGHT

(From Broken Pencil *#39;*
winner of the First Annual Broken Pencil Indie Writers Deathmatch)

graham parke

Can't sleep. Again. After several hours of restless tossing and turning I decide to head out, my mind dull, my eyes burning. I can't help but wonder how long this can go on, if not sleeping night after night can cause brain damage, irreversible health problems. I wonder what it will do to my hair, to my eyes, to my skin, if this doesn't end soon. The night is wet, cold, and I'm not wearing enough clothing, but I don't want to go back, so I walk on, along the canal, to the centre of Amsterdam. There, I'll find some life, some pale reflection of society, albeit distilled, and raw, and craving things mostly illegal. I pass a group of teenagers trying to get high on their last crumbs of weed, and a suit about to reverse his oversized SUV into one of the tiny parking slots along the canal. It's starting to come down hard and I hear little over the hiss of the rain on the water. There are thoughts churning away at the back of my mind, but they're slow, and unpronounced, and I can't really make them out. I know I must be the one thinking them, but right now, it doesn't really feel that way. I pull up my collar, keep my eyes on the ground, walk on. When I reach Rembrandt's Square, the downpour seems suddenly ineffectual; the rain's no match for the coloured light streaming from the pubs and the arcade, and the drum 'n' bass helps cancel out the discomfort. I'm still getting wet, still freezing, but somehow I don't feel it as much. Sensory overload superimposed on thought deprivation. I keep walking.

A homeless guy pulls on my jacket and asks me for a cigarette. I don't have one, don't smoke, and I tell him so. He doesn't let go, wants to know about my cash situation, specifically, if I have any change to spare. I tell him I can give him a few Euros if he lets go. He says it's a deal. It's a deal if

I take my Euros and get him some smokes from the machine in the arcade. I give him a look. He asks if I think it's easy getting this spot right in front of the club, right where the wallets are pulled out to spill the big bucks, the paper cash. He glances over his shoulder. Homeless people sit scattered around the square, their positions now looking less random. He tells me he's been waiting for this spot for five weeks and he can't move. They may seem slow, he says, they may seem harmless, but they're vultures, predators. I look again, note the hungry expressions, the snide glances. My coat is heavy and cold with rain. I go to the arcade to get the smokes. It's the least I can do, and right now I'm all about doing the least I can do.

You'd think that without sleep you'd eventually get to a point where you just roll back your eyes and pass out, problem solved. But that's not the case. It just doesn't work that way. Somehow you keep moving, running on fumes, zoning out a few minutes at a time, just long enough and often enough to keep you going. You're alive, but not really. You're awake, but not all there. It's true what they say: when you never sleep you're also never quite awake. Not really. The worst of both worlds.

Inside a club I wander aimlessly until some girl catches my eye. I stare at her, trying to work out why I'm staring at her. Not an easy task. At first glance she's exactly not my type: tattoos down her left arm, long white hair—not blond, not imitation blond, but white—wearing a skirt that's way too short and smoking a cigarette. She takes long, slow drags, pulls the cigarette away between fingers with shiny purple nails. All of it conspires to make her a complete turnoff, but it somehow fails. Totally trashy, but still I can't take my eyes off her, and for an instant, just a second, she looks at me with this dark, brooding gaze, a look just a few muscle twitches shy of a smirk, and all sorts of things stir inside me. I try to ignore her and I tell myself it's the beer, not this girl. It's the long sleepless nights. It's the bad, pulsating light, the fact that I haven't had sex in weeks. But her eyes are cool and thrilling and when she disappears into the crowd I head back to the bar to order something stronger, a whiskey-orange juice, then head up to the balcony to scan the dance floor.

I usually start my sleepless nights by ordering some drinks in this twenty-four-hour place, this shrine to red and blue plastic that's bathed in bright fluorescence. I'm not really sure why I go there or how long I stay, but I'm there a lot lately. I sit, and zone out, and try to smile when the waitress comes over, pad in hand, rings under eyes, hair out of whack. You can always tell she'd have no trouble sleeping. She'd fall asleep right on your

table if they'd let her. Maybe that's why I go there: to see how the rest of the world struggles during my ghosting hours.

She asks me what I want, but what I want she cannot bring me, so I order a beer or a shake (never a Coke, never coffee). I tell her not to hurry. I tell her to take her sweet time, I'm not going.anywhere. She'll shrug and walk off, and my gaze will wander, moving over the other patrons, all bathed in this unholy fluorescence.

A few nights ago, as I sat there gazing, this girl by the window stood out. She was sitting alone, nursing a shake, holding a single red rose. She was plain-looking, but in a good way, if there is such a thing, and she smiled amiably at nothing and no one, at the world in general. A guy in coveralls came in and sat down at the table next to mine, opening a paper and calling for the breakfast menu. This guy had no sleeping problems. This guy wasn't there to kill time. He was night shift, supposed to be there, awake at that hour, and I bet he'd never had problems sleeping during the day either. The girl with the rose went over to his table and introduced herself, asked him if he was Marcel. The guy said he might be, told her to sit down, asked her who was asking. She sat and told him she was his blind date. If he was Marcel. He smiled, said he was.

On the dance floor I coast along on the beat, moving with the crowd as it expands and shrinks, throbs and pulsates, a gigantic multi-faceted heart of which I'm a mere cell, one insignificant little element of a giant muscle. Only part of what I do is the result of conscious effort, the rest is automatic response, much like the way I spend my days at work. When I think about it, I'm the opposite of a sleepwalker; I'm a wake-walker, though only barely so. I look like I'm alive, but most of the time I'm an empty shell. I keep the lights on, but I'm not often home. I coast and sway in the heat until I lose all orientation, all concept of space and time, until I finally find tattoo girl, dancing her heart out in the crowd, and I smile when she spots me and comes over, dancing away the distance between us. The words Totally Trashy leave my mind and instead I see this young, vibrant, mysterious female. Someone who knows more about the night and about life than I'll ever want to know. I move with her and keep my mind blank. No judgments. No thoughts at all.

I really can't remember when it first started, how it first started, but for as far back as I can recall, I haven't been sleeping. I know sleep exists, but it's a strange and intangible thing that mostly happens to other people. I can't imagine what an hour of deep, uninterrupted sleep might feel like, never mind a full night's worth. It's been that long. That far back. The midnight walks are relatively new though, a thing of the last two or three months. They don't happen every night, but they happen most nights and they happen more and more often. I don't know of any great problem that's keeping me awake—if there is, if there ever was, it's long since forgotten. The main problem I have now, the only problem in fact, is the not sleeping. Apart from killing the real me, the person I can almost remember being, it's also killing all sense of taste, smell, and colour. It's leaving me with nothing but dull impressions.

One moment I'm dancing with her, or what passes for dancing, the crowd being so close and loud and tangled, the next moment she's gone. My throat's dry and hoarse. In the sweltering heat under the laser show the alcohol is starting to give me a buzz and I decide to ignore the implied rejection and go after her, find my tattooed vixen, and get her to have a drink with me. As I'm about to move away, something holds me back, locks up my legs. I look down, there she is, and already she's undoing my buttons, and already she's taking hold of me, and already I can feel her warm breath on my skin. With a muted sense of excitement I'm suddenly aware of the reverberating bass. I alternate between looking down and glancing around, wondering if anyone sees us, notices what's going on. Later, standing at the bar, ordering anything without caffeine, she looks at me and asks how it was. I nod, and then she looks down at nothing and says that now it's my turn.

I saw her again, a few days ago. Again in the diner, the bright, fluorescent shrine to red and blue plastic, and she looked vaguely familiar. I couldn't place her until I spotted the flower, the single red rose she kept under her table, out of sight, invisible until she got up to meet her guy. There was a little confusion when she sat at his table, a little hiccup in the fluidity of her movements, and, although this time they were out of earshot, I could follow the exchange easily. A blind date, she was saying. A planned meeting. She showed him the rose. Was his name Tom? (Or Marcel, or Freddy, or whatever?) Quick flash, his eyes scanned the diner. Thinking, Can I pretend to be Marcel? Do I want to pretend to be Marcel? If I pretend to be Marcel, can I get us out of here before the real Marcel shows up? She smiled. He smiled. He wanted to know if she'd leave with him, go somewhere else for a drink, and she had no problem with that.

Tattoo girl asks me for a twenty, and when I want to know what it's for she smiles and says I'll find out soon enough, then she disappears in the direction of the restrooms. I assume she's going to get some viciously ribbed rubbers with hot, tasty, gel. I realize this isn't the case when I find her again an hour later, lying on top of some guy on a couch in the foyer, sleeping off the drinks I got her. I can't really tell which one of the two is more out of it, but it's clear they're together; they're wearing the same lame ring—eagle on a skull—and their tattoos, in that shade of red that never quite works well in tattoos, match. Suddenly I'm sick of this scene, this club, or as sick as I have the energy to be, and I decide to forget about the twenty, the girl, and the rings, and get some fresh air.

Sleeping pills don't help. They just make you more lethargic, deepen your daze for a couple of hours. It's more like a self-inflicted prison than a cure. Hypnosis doesn't help either, nor does acupuncture, the obligatory glasses of warm milk—with or without the honey. Water with valerian, doing more sports, depriving yourself of oxygen, and a hundred or so other tricks: no go. Sleep will not be tricked, not mine anyway, and I passed the phase of trying to guide the river where it won't go such a long time ago I can hardly remember all the insane things I tried.

I'm walking down a narrow alley when the smell of piss and stale beer jars me awake, and I look up to see that daytime has finally arrived. The sky burns with a hopeful mix of magenta and bright blue, but I feel anything but hopeful. Seems I've been wandering the streets for a while, although my memory cannot tell me anything about leaving the club or what I might have done since. The alcohol has burned off, and my daze is back to its old level of dull half-wakefulness. Eyes burning, body heavy as lead, I navigate around a pool of vomit and turn into Kalver Street, step over a body lying there, half dressed, passed out, and I note that this guy looks like the guy who took my wallet last week. I'm not too sure though, so I only kick him in the crotch lightly, then walk on. I pass a tribe of street cleaners and sense my mind cycling back down to low-power consumption. I can almost feel it slip away into non-thought, into non-being, but the effect is only really noticeable the few seconds after it returns, like now, as I touch cold metal, and open the door to a place that serves an early breakfast.

It's too late to go home and too early to go to work, so I sit and wait, nursing something I don't remember ordering. It takes me a while to realize she's also here, sitting by the window, casing the place. I take another sip, not sure what I'm tasting, and watch her get up and stroll through the diner, holding the flower, the single red rose, like a shield, like a torch. I glance about, but there's no one in sight, no eligible bachelors, just some junkies by the slot machine and an old guy in a dirty coat licking the Styrofoam casing of a long-departed burger. When I look back, she's sitting across from me. She's sitting at my table and asks me my name. She doesn't give it to me, doesn't give me the name of the date she's waiting for, just wants me to tell her mine. She looks at me with red-rimmed eyes, blinking slowly. The door opens and a small group of people shuffles in, dark, harrowed faces. The faces of the desperate. I'm not sure why they seem familiar, why I think I know them. I look back at the girl and it occurs to me there never were any blind dates. Not a single one. Just a girl with a rose selecting guys and getting them to pick her up. A double bluff. A little switcheroo. But me, I get no name, no hook for reeling her in. She stares at me, and waits, and I don't get to say I'm Marcel.

I ask her, "Why don't you tell me my name?" My voice comes from far away and I'm not sure she hears me, she seems busy studying my face, looking into me, looking through me. She says, "You're one of us." A statement, not a question. "I've seen you around. Yesterday, last week, a month ago. You go to all our places. The places we go when there's nowhere left to go."

I take another sip. I'm drinking a shake, strawberry maybe, or raspberry; it's hard to tell when your taste buds are in limbo.

"You're new," she says, "but you already have the look. You've given up trying to control it, trying to force it. Now you're like us, you follow the flow."

She's talking about sleep, about the absence of it. She knows. She has it too. I've seen her too often, too late at night, too early in the morning, for her to be talking about anything else.

"There's no cure," she says, casually squashing the final remnants of hope I didn't know I had, "but," she says, "there is a way to cope." She puts down the rose to take a sip of my shake. She says, "There's a way to survive, a way to build a life around this problem." She gives me an encouraging smile, looks deep into me, says, "Isn't that what life really is?"

She's right. I look around at the dark, harrowed faces, feel my shoulders relax. They don't look so desperate now, so lost. And I realize this must be her. This must be the girl who'll teach me about the night. The one who will tell me what I need to know.

BEAVERLAND

(From Broken Pencil #36)

david burke

Funny that, with all the girl trouble, Ben should find himself underneath a moose rack staring at a long, pointed antler and the pink cotton of a dangling pair of panties.

He's at a lodge north of the city, hours from home, and he tugs his ball cap over his eyes as girl-laughter floats by. He has no idea, really, how he got here, but across the gap between two small cottages, he spots a naked woman, skin a violet white, chased after by a naked man, patches of dark hair scattered across his back. Her breasts bob as he snaps a towel at her shrieking body.

Ben shakes his head and walks across the lot, then enters the lodge, a tall log cabin leaning precariously to one side.

At first glance the room looks empty. Brown bristol-board walls define the room, a makeshift bar by the looks of the dim lights and the smell of damp pretzels and beer. On the room's low ceiling is a collection of hats from fishing camps and lodges, while the walls are plastered with pictures of mustachioed, flannel-jacketed men hoisting guns above the steaming carcasses of deer.

From behind the bar, where he sits on a stool, a fat man greets Ben. His fat arms are folded across a fat stomach. He is wearing a T-shirt, Molson, yellowed from sweat and work.

"I take it you saw the panties hanging out front," the fat man says.

"Yeah," Ben shrugs, his hands in the pockets of his knee-torn jeans.

"I better grab a pool cue to get those down," he says. "Or I suppose I could tell customers I shot the moose just like that, with the panties on his head."

The man swallows what's left of a beer and wipes the bar with a rag, then leans back on his stool and unleashes a big belly laugh. Ben is blown back by the sheer volume of it, and jumps when the man smacks the television, balanced on the edge of the bar, spouting grainy scores and highlights.

"What did you say your name was?" the fat man says, wiping a tear from his eye.

Ben tells him.

"Nice to meet you," he says, extending a thick hand across the counter. "I'm Jim Bower. This is my place."

"Nice," says Ben, looking awkwardly around. In one corner is a pool table, the fabric torn and frayed, and in the other is a stage bordered by mirrors and a ceiling supported by a gleaming brass pole. The surrounding tables are littered with empties and overflowing ashtrays.

"We don't usually let your type hang around here," Jim Bower says. "Young folks like yourself, I mean."

"Sorry to bother," Ben says.

"What are you doing in these parts?"

"I don't know," Ben says, and he doesn't. "Just kind of ended up here, I guess."

"I understand. Heading north?"

"Yeah," Ben says.

"Can't do that for long, you know. Road turns west just a few hours from here."

Ben shrugs. He figured it went north forever, until he'd see polar bears drifting on ice floes beside the highway.

"I got a telephone," Jim Bower says, tapping an old rotary phone on the counter. "You want to call your people? Let 'em know where you're at?"

Ben considers, but shakes his head.

"What are we talking about then. Girl trouble?"

Ben doesn't know anymore. There was a girl, Laura. He borrowed his father's truck to go for a drive and to clear his head. When he hit the highway he followed it north.

"Yeah," Ben says. "Something like that."

"Wish I could help you there," Jim says. "I'm surrounded by women, and between you and me, I can't figure out a damn one of 'em."

Ben laughs a little as Jim Bower chuckles loudly, wiping his mouth with the back of his hand.

"Well, it's getting late. I take it you'll need a place to sleep."

"I didn't mean to bother," Ben says. "I was just curious . . ."

"We get a lot of those."

"I was going to keep on driving . . ." Ben says, and he was, but after hours and countless miles, a sign lured him off the highway, and a pair of pink panties convinced him to stay.

"I've got something to show you," Jim Bower says, stepping awkwardly off his stool.

"No, really . . ." Ben says.

"Come," Jim Bower says, motioning with his thick hand. "I insist."

Ben follows Jim Bower behind the bar, through a greasy kitchen, the walls lined with deep fryers, the floor littered with French fries, and out a back door. There is a golf cart waiting under a tree. Jim Bower sits behind the wheel, the golf cart leaning under his weight.

"I don't get around like I used to," Jim says, patting the vinyl seat beside him. "Hop on."

They drive along brick pathways, the *whirr* of the golf cart and the roll of the tires sounding against the log cabin walls, some cabins wild with music and laughter, some quiet, the lights turned off and red curtains hanging in the windows.

The path leads past the cottages, where they drive the length of a long dock thrust into the river, small aluminum boats in the dark water on each side. There are beer bottles and wine glasses tossed about the boat hulls, along with tackle boxes, a spool of line, and a can of worms. Ben also spots what he thinks is a scattered box of condoms.

They sit in the golf cart at the end of the dock. The night is cool and brilliant.

"Let me tell you a story," Jim Bower says, leaning over the edge of the steering wheel. "You know anything about hunting?"

"Not really," Ben says, his fingers picking at a piece of stuffing bursting from the seam of the vinyl seat.

"Ah," Jim says. "A city boy. Anyway, these two guys are sitting up in a tree stand, waiting for a bear to walk by. Good pals, these two, work at the lumber mill, and when they're not working they go hunting. They're up there all day, and they don't see squat. You follow?"

"Yeah," says Ben, looking beside him at Jim Bower's belly hanging over his blue jeans, his boot dangling over the dash while a golf ball circles in a cup holder.

"So the one guy decides that his friend has been talking too much, scaring all the bears away. He's always been a bit of a talker, this other guy, and his friend means to fire a shot to shut him up. A joke, you know? But his hands are cold, and he's drunk, and he misses."

Jim throws back a slug of beer, then runs a fat finger over the mouth of the can.

"Shoots his friend's head clear off," he mumbles.

Ben imagines a body smeared with dirt and blood, covered by leaves, and picked at by animals. He imagines a man with no head.

"That's terrible," he says.

"Tell me about it," says Jim Bower.

"So what happened?" Ben says, tucking his hands under the seat of his jeans.

"The guy doesn't know what to do," Jim Bower continues, "so he crawls down from his tree stand and runs. Now meanwhile there's a big manhunt. Search planes and helicopters flying overhead. Search teams and dog teams trampling through the bush. They look for two weeks, but the guy was a survivalist. He carried his gun and killed partridge until he ran out of shells. Then he fed himself on ants and tree bark, and once in a while he cornered a fish in the shallows and ate that, too."

"They ever find him?"

"Sure did. One day he just walked out of the bush."

"Just walked out?"

"Just walked out," Jim says. "Want to know what made him surrender? I'll give you one guess, and it wasn't guilt."

Ben thinks for a while, but nothing comes to mind.

"What was it?" he says.

"Bugs," Jim Bower says.

"Bugs?" Ben says.

"Bugs," Jim Bower says. "The guy could have lived out there all winter, if he had to. But this was prime bug season, and he couldn't stand 'em. Bugs drove him nuts."

"Huh," Ben says. He can imagine the black flies and mosquitoes crawling under the man's sweaty collar, the sound of their swarm, and the frantic slapping. He knows how confused the mind can get. "This guy was a customer of yours?"

"No," Jim Bower says, his eyes frozen on his hands, hanging like meat hooks around the steering wheel. "He was a friend."

They are silent, Ben staring into the black water at his side while Jim Bower takes a long pull from his beer and leans back in his seat. He throws

the can at the far side of the river, but the can, emptied of its weight, flutters and falls, landing with a cold clank in the bottom of a boat.

"Am I gettin' through to you?" he says.

"What do you mean?" Ben says.

"I guess not," Jim Bower says, shifting the cart into reverse and spiralling down the dock. "Come on. The tour continues."

They drive down the pathway until it spits them onto a dirt road, and they drive to the edge of the forest where a pile of rusted machinery and mangled aluminum canoes sits, encroached by a pile of leaves and overgrowing weeds.

"The end of the line," Jim says with a smile.

They turn around, and as they head back towards the lodge they spot a woman, despite the fall cold, stumbling barefoot in the grass. Ben notices through the moon's half-light that she is wearing a pink bra, but nothing else. The white globes of her buttocks shake as she walks.

"Traci!" Jim Bower says, squealing the cart to a stop. "Good to see you. Say, you wouldn't happen to be the owner of those panties hanging on the moose antlers, would you?"

"I don't know whose those are," Traci says in a smoky voice, her speech gurgling with drunkenness. "Who's the young stud?"

"This is Ben," Jim Bower says, reaching to pat him on the shoulder. "He's lost."

Traci stumbles around the cart. "Little man," she whispers, "I know exactly what you're looking for," and pinches his arm between two pink fingernails before slipping into the dark.

"That's Traci," Jim Bower says as he steps on the gas. "She's in Cabin 14, for future reference."

Ben follows Jim Bower back through the kitchen and into the bar. He has seen all the cabins, all the boats, the lodge, and the boathouse, and much of the grounds, and he has listened to Jim Bower tell him, when he first began this business, how he tried to make a living as an honest fishing and hunting lodge, but that didn't work, so he added some spice. He added the girls.

"Business has been booming ever since," he says.

"What about the name?" Ben asks. "Beaverland?"

"It was always called that," says Jim Bower.

Jim reaches into the fridge, pulls out a beer, and flicks off the television's frosty reception. "I've done a little running myself, you know," he says, half out of breath and leaning against the bar, wiping it dry with a towel. Ben sits on a stool across from him, his fingernails sinking into the wood underneath the countertop, picking away slivers. "I came out here on a night like this. Back then, I wasn't much older than you."

Ben stuffs his hands in his pockets. His eyes wander to a yellowed clipping above the bar, the headline MANHUNT in black letters, and a picture of a field full of uniforms, police dogs digging their noses into the grass, a helicopter hovering above a ragged forest of pines.

"You need money?" Jim says, leaning on the counter.

Ben shrugs.

"I could give you a job, you know. Since you're up here. What do you think of coming to work for me?"

"Doing what?" Ben asks.

"I need someone to help winterize the cabins, take care of the plumbing, haul the boats out of the water."

Ben looks at his hands, velvet smooth and ivory white. He doesn't know anything about that stuff, but making money is never a bad idea.

"And once winter hits," Jim Bower continues, "I need someone to help me tend the place for all the snowmobiles coming through. You ever shovel snow off a roof? It can get pretty thick come February."

Ben shivers at the thought of a winter up here, but he says, "Sounds pretty good," and the words surprise his mouth.

"It's settled then," Jim Bower says. "You start tonight."

"Tonight?"

"We don't waste any time up here, son. You gotta earn your keep."

Ben watches Jim Bower pull a strip of paper from a notepad and grab a pencil off the bar. He jots down a few instructions, then folds the paper and hands it to Ben.

"That should keep you busy."

Ben glances at the paper, then stuffs it in his pocket the way you do when taking cash, without counting, from a friend who owes you.

"You'll be staying in Cabin 14," Jim says, and nods towards the door.

Ben gets the hint, and his boot heels click as he steps outside. He walks across the grass and over the gravel lot. The truck is quiet under the trees.

He sits in the cab and turns the key. The truck coughs to a start and settles into a familiar rumble between his shoulders, the rumble that began the moment he started the truck in his driveway, and followed him all the way here. But why here? Is he really staying? Can he go without seeing Laura again, and without her forgiving him?

Cabin 14 is just around the corner. He looks back at the neon lights of the lodge, then digs into his pocket. He unfolds the slip of paper and reads the message under the dashboard lights:

There are two kinds of people here, kid. Those who were born up here, and those who are running.

Ben drops the paper to the floor, puts the truck in drive and heads for the road.

SUMMER

(From Broken Pencil *#14)*
golda fried

Summer did more than anyone I knew and she had been doing it for a very long time. She had a yellow kitchen. She dyed her hair. She had a friend who painted shoes.

There was a tree outside her yard, and I stood outside with her boyfriend Duane, and she could tell me things about the tree.

Duane and I were like sacks of potatoes looking at the tree while Summer jumped on her bike and went to get her laundry.

Summer had a room with four armchairs all around, and sitting in there always felt like we were sitting in her. Duane, you are always sitting in my section of the house, she'd say.

Summer got her and Duane coffees and croissants from the Italian bakery up the street before Duane was up from his bed.

And I'd be nervous. Nervous that I didn't have any breakfast rituals. Nervous that my job was the rest of my life.

When Duane and her first started dating, even before she moved in, Duane would make the coffee.

Summer spent her money on cabs, shoes, and perfume, and her friend Chisele made the look on Summer's face seem as if Chisele had made all the cabs, shoes, and perfume disappear.

Summer had long bottles of wine with me, or long cups of tea, but phone calls would be under a minute. And I'd always hang up going, what's going on? How blue is her mood? Is she going to find the time to paint?

Duane is okay. He wears shades in sunlight. He can talk to me about her and know what's going on while most guys are clueless. We worked near each other, and he knew where to get his lunch and be satisfied, whereas I would rather forgo the long lunch lines altogether and be a lost soul.

All those girls in the bar who buzz around musicians and are worth anything know more than I do about cooking, sewing, and laundry. Especially Summer. Don't be fooled by their liberated drinking.

Summer is sick of it and the only thing left to do is dream. Lying in bed doing nothing, being still in moments. And I know she won't like it. Her mind will still be on that bike of hers. But that's the idea.

RETARD

(From Broken Pencil *#12)*
grant buday

We stared at that empty seat. Then we stared at the guy next to it. Everything about him said one thing: *retard*. His sweaty head, his hands stuck to his thighs, the way he sat still as a stump. And he was next to the only empty seat on the bus.

It was August. Sunday. Hot. More people squeezed on. That seat stayed empty. No one wanted to sit next to a retard. Especially a big one. You gotta be careful around the big ones 'cause they're strong. When I worked in the mental hospital there was a retard named Conrad. Every morning he made me sit on his back while he did push-ups. He could do thirty-five push-ups with me on his back. I'd sit there going up-and-down, up-and-down, keeping count for him.

Everyone on the bus was sweating. The retard wasn't, even though he wore a yellow ski jacket zipped to his throat. Maybe it was his meds. You could feel people eyeing that seat and deciding no way. You'd be trapped between him and the window. He'd have you prisoner. What if there was an accident? Or some immigrant with a gun started shooting? You'd never get out. And even if nothing went wrong, you'd have to breathe his air, air that had been in his lungs. Like most retards, he breathed through his mouth. At the hospital I heard how Mongoloids have such long tongues they can stick them up their own noses.

No one took the seat. The guy kept offering it though. He was polite. At every stop he said, "Free seat, please, free seat."

Old ladies lugging four bags of groceries pretended not to hear. A pregnant woman lied and said, "I'm only going one stop." People ignored him, made like they were fascinated by the ads. Read the *Province*.

Cheques Cashed. Chew Trident. Helene would have sat down next to him, no problem. That's how she was.

Every time new people got on, the retard swung his legs into the aisle like he was opening a gate. "Free seat, please, free seat." He had a monotone voice, like a recording. And he didn't get insulted when no one wanted to sit by him. He was too dumb. He just swung his feet back in, put his hands on his thighs, and stared ahead as if the windshield was a TV. His hands looked like albino starfish stuck to his legs.

I was on my way home from visiting my friend Edward. He'd had a stroke. I always thought what a weird word that was: stroke. I mean, you stroke a cat, you stroke your dick, the guy at the back of the canoes shouts "Stroke! Stroke!" through a megaphone. Heart attack made more sense. But Edward told me a stroke was worse than a heart attack. His whole right side was paralyzed. He laughed and said he was now a southpaw. That was another one I never understood: southpaw. It's like it means people always stand with their right arm to the north and left to the south. I don't know. I saw a show on left-handed people. There's proportionately twice as many lefties in jail as right-handed people. Plus they die younger because of accidents, and they're more likely to be queer. Leonardo da Vinci and Michelangelo were both left-handed queers. I learned that on PBS. Helene liked PBS.

The bus wobbled its way along Hastings Street, past that Pink Pearl dim sum place, then the Glenhaven Memorial Chapel. That's where Helene's Uncle Victor died. Went in to arrange his mother's funeral and had a heart attack. Keeled over and hit his head on a coffin.

My hand was going numb from gripping the pole. Whenever I have to hold onto the pole, I always hunt for a cool spot where no one's been touching it, because people's hands teem with bacteria. That's the word the guy on TV used: teem. He was a biologist. He said there's more bacteria on your palm than in your mouth. So doing mouth-to-mouth is cleaner than licking someone's hand.

Before leaving the hospital today, I went to the can and scrubbed my hands with soap and water. It was because Edward shook my hand when I arrived, shook it again when I left, and all during the visit covered his mouth with that same hand and coughed into it.

We turned right onto Commercial Drive, and the bus's rods dropped from the overhead power lines. Everyone groaned except the retard. He just sat there like he didn't mind, looking straight ahead at the windshield like he was watching cartoons. People walking past looked in at us. I remember how at the hospital some guys all they did was walk up and down the hall. Psychiatrists say walking relaxes retards and crazy people. Something about the motion. We walked them in the mornings and we walked them in the evenings, like they were dogs. Other than that they watched TV. The driver couldn't get the rods hooked up and everyone started getting antsy. The guy standing in front of me had a bald spot shaved in his hair, and stitches. I counted seven stitches. It was like Frankenstein. I looked at the ads. "Cancer Can Be Beaten." "Make a Will." "Visit Cuba." Helene always wanted to go to Cuba.

The driver climbed back in and everyone felt relieved. We plowed our way up Commercial to Broadway, where a blind woman got on.

It's hard not to stare at a blind person. It's like when someone's asleep, you get to watch without being watched back. The blind woman didn't wear glasses. Her eyelids looked like warts. The retard said, "Free seat, please, free seat." We all watched the old lady follow his voice, her hand moving from one seat back to the next, her white cane tapping the rubber floor like the feeler of some big bug. She slipped past the retard's knees without even touching him. Like she was only faking being blind. She arranged her purse and her cane, then turned her head to the right like she was looking out the window. A blind woman.

Lately they've been rerunning that show about the blind detective. Even the porn channel's been playing reruns. I wonder what it'd be like to watch blind people hump. Or retards. Some show I saw said retards are horny. I wonder what it'd be like to be blind, left-handed, retarded, and queer. Sometimes I think Edward is queer. He asked how Helene was.

The last time I saw Helene we were finalizing the divorce. She'd lost sixty-three pounds and was getting remarried—get this—to a Moroccan named Iqbal. I warned her about Moroccans. I told her how I'd seen a show about them. She got pissed off and said I was prejudiced. The show said Moroccans had different attitudes about women. They interviewed some Irish woman who'd married a Moroccan and had to smuggle herself out of the country in a shipping container because she was a prisoner in the house. And even when she did get to go out she had to have a chaperone and wear a veil. They showed a street scene in Morocco. The women looked like beekeepers. I told Helene be careful, that even though we were washed up I still loved her.

At Kingsway a bunch of people got off the bus. Then at Thirty-third I got a seat, one of the singles on the left side. Those are the best. You don't get stuck next to anyone. By Forty-first the bus was almost empty and I started to relax.

Despite the divorce, I was thinking, who knows, maybe me and Helene still had a chance. People change. That's what they said on this show. People change. The show said that without the belief in change we'd be reduced to Asiatic standards of fatefulness and apathy. Those were the words, fatefulness and apathy. It was our belief in self improvement that made the West superior. Besides telling Helene be careful, I told her I'd changed. I said how I'd been developing an appreciation for *Jeopardy*, answering the questions and everything, because it's good when two people in love love the same show. It's good. It's something to share.

By the time we hit Forty-ninth and the top of the hill it was just me, the blind lady, and the retard, all staring out that window, and you know it was kind of nice. I mean I figured that ride could just go on and on, because moving like that was soothing, you relaxed, you forgot yourself.

THINGS I DON'T REMEMBER

(From Broken Pencil #37*)*

sandra alland

Hospital grass isn't like real grass. It has no smell and it's full of cigarette butts. But that's where I'm sitting because I'm too young to go inside.

My grandmother's in the hospital because she has cancer. None of the adults tell me that, they just say, "Grandma's sick." Then they point up high to a form in a window and say, "Wave hello." I think I see her, but can't be sure. I don't remember her face like I used to. I do remember her voice because her ghost talks to me whenever I come here.

"It's booby cancer," my brother said a week ago, pinching mine hard. My brother is four years older and knows things. "She'll be haunting you soon," he added with a freaky smile.

I chew on some tasteless grass and wonder if she's got booby cancer because she's French. The French movies on TV are always about boobs. But Grandma never speaks French and neither does my mom, so I think maybe in Cornwall French means something different. I wouldn't know because I don't remember Cornwall either.

My mother's inside, and I know she's crying though I can't see her. She's been crying a lot lately, even when I don't eat my dinner, which is really no big deal. Mom thinks I'm not eating because I'm sad, but she's wrong. I am sad, because my mother's always in the hospital and never with me, but that's not why I don't eat.

My best friend is Jody Sumi. She's also my next-door neighbour, so I go see her every day. We're always stuffing our faces with rice balls covered in seaweed. I especially like the ones with egg in them, though any kind of seaweed will do. I like seaweed because it reminds me of mermaids, and I'm pretty sure that's what they eat.

I don't know why I'm so into mermaids, seeing as I'm terrified of water. Maybe it's because Jody's into them, and I'm into Jody. She has shiny black hair and her dad lets her drink from his beer bottle.

"Tais-toi, ma p'tite."

That's my grandmother's ghost talking French in my head. I don't know how she got to be a ghost before she's dead, but Grandma always seems to

do whatever she wants. I also don't know how I understand French.

"Ribbit, ribbit," I answer, imitating my father. Grandma goes quiet and I know she's mad. To change the subject, I pick up a pop can and wave it at Dad, who's pacing in front of the hospital entrance.

"Don't play with garbage," he growls. Then he goes back to pacing. I start to worry about my mother. I want her to come out. Why can't she just talk to Grandma's ghost like I do?

"Touche-pas le nez, p'tite. Tu n'es pas un cochon."

I take my finger out of my nose. Grandma's ghost rarely has anything nice to say, but this time I listen since I was rude about the frog noises. "Grandma," I ask, "why do you have booby cancer?"

"On parle pas de telles choses."

There are very few things Grandma's ghost does like to talk about. Mostly she just likes to tell me to be quiet. She's into silence. Sometimes I think that's why she got cancer—every time she wanted to say something important or French, she just tucked it in her bra like my mother does with money, and all those unsaid words started to eat away at her boob. Mom says words are powerful things.

"Tu dois la protéger, p'tite. Chaque jour, les fleurs meurent dans sa coeur."

Whenever Grandma's ghost says too much for her own liking, she starts to make bad French poetry. I have no idea what she means by it, but I do like rhyming.

I watch my mother as she comes out of the hospital. She doesn't look like she needs protecting, though she does look smaller. I run to her and smush my face between her boobs, being careful to check for any unsaid words stuck to her bra. I don't find any, but somehow I know they're there.

Mom goes over to Dad, and I'm left with Grandma's poetry. The real Grandma, or someone that might be her, is standing at the window up high.

"Ne mange pas de la beurre. C'est l'heure. T'es la soeur."

My brother suddenly appears from nowhere. He has Dad's necklace and starts waving it frantically in front of my face. "I'm a part-time hypnotist," he grins. He's always a part-time something. "Follow the medallion with your eyes and you'll forget all of this." As always, I do as he says.

PARADE

(From Broken Pencil *#34)*
sarah gordon

We had a parade today. A big fucking dog and pony show for the Governor General. The old bag has the nerve to be fifteen minutes late. She wastes the country's money on upgrading herself from first class to first-class bitch and then has the nerve to be late. She thinks she's, like, Queen Canada. She doesn't know that it's actually kinda hard to stand perfectly still for so long. And that it's fucking hot out there when the sun's beating down on our suits, and all we wanna do is scratch our sweaty balls like the monkeys we are. We got nothing else to do when standing there except swell on how much it sucks. Well, this one time the CO's daughter was there 'cause he was getting an award or something, getting another plaque for the wall, and, God bless her, she was wearing a skirt and sitting in such a way that we all got a nice view of her spread, little lace panties and all. But that was a rare treat. It still comes up at parties. Some of us like to think she did it on purpose and some of us like to think it was a just a lovely accident. The only parade I ever really like is November 11. Here's the thing about Remembrance Day. We're all well turned out. But it means something, for once. Fresh haircuts. Shined boots. Pressed uniform. White gloves and a smudgeless winter sky. Blank, and pure, you know? The gunshots go off so nice and clear they crack the shell right off your heart. And we're so still we really feel the charge in those rounds, and the sound of the horn, and the pride puffing out in our chests, and the respect. Respect for ourselves, and respect for the row of old vets parked across from us in their wheelchairs, plaid blankets over their legs, such skinny old legs. And then the bagpipes start up and I think we all get convinced, I mean totally convinced—for at least the space of that song—that joining the forces really meant something. That we're important, part of a big thing, like history or something. Then we all go to the mess, and get drunk on free beer and moose juice. And it gets me kinda stirred up, and I start having thoughts. Like maybe if there is a God, his voice sounds like those bagpipes. But then I remember hearing Flanagan talk about how bad the inside of those bags actually stink, with all that old spit in them. And how he threw up on there once when he drank too much at a funeral, and he still smells it waft out from time to time.

FLAME RETARDED

(From Broken Pencil #37)

kate story

Flame Retarded, Quality Costumes, Colourful Masks with Wide-Vision Eye-Holes, Brite for Nite!!!

I squished my nose against the grimy glass. I wanted it, the ballerina outfit with the white tutu. In my family we got costumes Mom made, or one of a series of ancient devil costumes passed down from our vast array of older cousins, all of whom apparently wished to go out on Hallowe'en dressed as Satan. But this year, it was ballerina or bust.

I was going out that Halloween night with Lisa "Where's-the-Loot-Bag" Cooper. She was so named because at my fifth birthday party, as soon as she walked through the door, she shrieked in her nasal voice, "Where's the loot bags? Where's the loot bags?" She didn't stop until my mother said, "Here's your damn loot-bag, Lisa-Where's-the-Loot-Bag Cooper, for the love of Christ!" The name stuck. Lisa was a skinny little kid with a head of stiff red hair. I've always had a thing for redheads. Lisa-Where's-the Loot-Bag Cooper was my first crush, grade one, and grade two, and grade three. It probably would have continued if she hadn't failed grade three, staying behind while I moved on to other grades and redheads.

Lisa was going out this year as a princess. She'd described her costume to me: "It's all white, and long like a bride, and there's a cloak, and a diamond crown!" White and long like a bride—I couldn't walk next to her as a tattered, grubby devil. I was afraid to ask my mother, yet something about Lisa's lust for loot must have rubbed off on me for I took my courage in hand and I nagged. I nagged until my mother said, "Stop nagging!" and then I whined, and I whined until even I was sick of it, and finally (in a towering rage that did nothing to dampen my utter triumphant joy at getting my sticky hands on that cheap white netting) my mother stormed into the Arcade and bought me "that damn ballerina outfit." Lisa's hair was bright like copper and it stuck out in all directions. She'd look beautiful in a diamond crown. We would look wonderful, the princess and the dancer, together.

Yes, I've always had a thing for redheads. My second redhead was Beverly: Beverly of ballet class, Beverly of the long red hair. Thick, so thick that her braid was three inches across, and long, so long it went all the way down to her waist. Beverly was a beautiful dancer, but cursed with short legs and big tits; even at the age of twelve it was obvious she wasn't going to have a career in ballet. Even so, she always wore her hair pulled back tight into a bun as if she was about to spring into a tutu and practise Swan Lake. Beverly was suicidal and used to run away from home. She'd call me from phone booths: "I'm going to kill myself. I really mean it this time. I don't know where I am. My mother doesn't know I've left the house. I'm going to throw myself in front of a car," and then she'd hang up. I'd sit by the phone in an agony, waiting for her next call. "I'm going to do it now. As soon as a truck goes by." I'd walk for hours in the Newfoundland winter night, looking for her; once she'd walked halfway to Cape Spear before I got to her and coaxed her all the way down Blackhead Road to my house. Our mothers called what we did "sleepovers." I'd chase her all over town, pluck her from the brink of death, and then we'd go to her house or mine and drink hot chocolate. We'd give each other massages and she'd take her hair out of its bun, and then we'd lie next to each other. I'd be stretched out there on the mattress next to her listening to her breath, and burning up inside.

But before that, before outgrowing Halloween and taking real ballet classes, and flirting with real anorexia, and pointe shoes, there was Lisa and the Brite for Nite costume. I walked to the bridge that separated her road from mine, clutching an empty bag for candy, heart pounding. She was already there waiting for me, a white blob in the twilight. I have to say that her costume was, as far as princesses went, a disappointment. It was pretty much the same as mine, except her skirt was longer and she had a cheap tiara on her head, almost lost in her hair. Of course I had my magic wand, and in a burst of genius, a little bag of sparkles that I could throw into the air.

"Hi," she said when she saw me.

I took a deep breath, and wished hard, and looked at her again, and because I wanted it enough she was a princess, and I was a ballerina, and we were beautiful, despite our toques and woolen socks.

We hit every house along the Waterford River between her place and our school. It was a long stretch, maybe a mile, with a cold wind, but we were determined. (She wasn't Where's-the-Loot-Bag for nothing.) We got pretty close to the school, and then Lisa said in her nasal voice, "Hey, I wonder if the perv is around?" and I said, "Naw, b'y," and she said in sepulchral tones (with nasal overlay), "How do you know? I bet he loves Halloween. I bet it's his favourite night!" and I said, "Yeah, he dresses up as the Perv!" and this wasn't very funny, but we laughed, staggering along in each other's arms. And we were indeed close to the school, and there was indeed a perv, and I can't speak as to what his favourite night may have been, but a night when children roam unattended surely couldn't be too far down his list. He was an old man—in his forties, ancient. He used to hang around in the small clump of trees we called "The Woods," at the top of the hill above our elementary school, and flash little girls. We'd shriek and run away.

It was dark and I spun along the sidewalk ahead of Lisa, waving my wand in the air. I was trying to do pirouettes, only I didn't know what pirouettes were yet; this was before Beverly and the ballet classes. And I was trying to be enchanting, and I remember a strange feeling in my six-year-old body, because I was trying to appear enchanting. You couldn't be enchanting in a devil costume with a fraying forked tail. But this year I was a ballerina. And I remember feeling a bit sick, and strange, and at the same time very excited. "I'm dancing, I'm dancing! I'm a beautiful dancer!" I hummed to myself under my breath. "I'm a beautiful dancer!" And I waved my wand, and spun my plastic bag full of candy, and I hopped up and down. And I sang a little song, and spun some more, and then I looked behind me, and the sidewalk was empty; that is to say, there was no one on it except me.

Years later I would be walking along that same stretch of sidewalk alone, only this time it would be a New Year's Eve night, that Halloween of young adulthood. And I'd be dressed in sparkles then too, gold pants, with shine on my décolletage and a good pair of shoes. And I'd be coming home from the house of a red-haired star, well, star in the local sense of the word, a star and a redhead; could I ask for more? I was a good girl, good enough to leave when his girlfriend phoned, and I was always so good about it, even when he wouldn't fuck me so he could save himself for her. I'd laughed and spun around, right out the door for him; I could fake a pirouette by then. He had red hair and I burned for him, flame retarded.

And I stood there on that same sidewalk when I was six, and the sidewalk was empty of Lisa and of anyone, and I said, tentatively, "Lisa?" And then she screamed. I knew it was her, even though I couldn't see her, the scream came off the side of the road, in some trees. And I said, "Get off it, that's not funny!" and I started backing away from the scream, and then she screamed again, and I turned and ran away up the road, then spun and ran towards her, then away, then towards, back and forth like a little scared mouse. And then I heard rustling in the bushes, and a grunting noise, and a sob, sort of choked off. And I'll never know why, but I charged into the bushes where the noises were coming from  and saw him there in his awful dark coat, and Lisa was under him, only I couldn't see her face, just a bit of whiteness that was her costume, and he was jerking at her in this awful way. And I shrieked, and I hit his back with my little plastic magic wand. And then I spun around, and I hit him again, not exactly pirouetting, because I hadn't learned that yet.

"Get it right, Joan," the ballet teacher would say to me. "Turn! Turn!" Beverly had so much hair that she had to use those giant metal hairpins to fasten it up in a massive sleek ruby bun, and in the recital we spun around and around, only I could never quite do it, and the pins started coming loose from Beverly's hair, and they shot around the stage—*ping! ping!*—like tiny missiles, like bullets, and the rest of us tried to keep dancing, but they were shooting out at a furious rate now, pinging and zinging, and people in the audience started ducking, then a woman cried out, and there was a great roar, and confusion, and people were flinging themselves into the aisles, one dancer screamed as a metal pin pierced her white-feathered breast. Blood blossomed around it and she fainted. We other dancers fled, the audience trampled each other in their panic, and at the centre of it all was Beverly, spinning, spinning, and the light on her grew whiter and brighter, metal shot out from her hair like steel hornets, and she glowed, seemed to rise from the ground in her spinning, a vortex of light and weaponry until her hair finally came loose, and spread around her shining red like ruby jewels, like fire, like blood, and joy, and she spun up and through the roof of the Arts and Culture Centre, blood angel ascending to heaven.

Years later it all got written about in the newspaper—not Beverly the Blood Angel, that was too strange and too wonderful, and those who had been there could never agree on what had happened. What got written up was the Perv and all us girls at the school, and there was an interview with Lisa's mother wherein she wept and said she grew up back when you really didn't talk about those things; I mean, we just didn't know about those things. And after failing grade three Lisa and I sort of lost track of each other, but the newspaper article—my mother showed it to me—went on and on with the usual story: how she got sullen, and difficult, and stopped doing well in school. And then she started doing drugs, and had an abusive boyfriend, and left home, and her mother didn't know where she was. And my mother was very grave as she showed me this, and she wanted to talk about it. She said she hadn't realized . . . had it . . . had I . . . was that why . . . ?

"Why what?" I said.

And that was the end of that.

Years later as I walked along that sidewalk, bleeding, it was still dark and I couldn't remember exactly where it had happened. Was it here? Or here? Or those bushes in there? It being New Year's Eve in St. John's there were three different cabbies who slowed down and offered me a ride home. "No thanks, I don't mind the walk." I need to walk off my sweet-temper, it's making me sick.

"If it's a question of money, me luv, don't worry; hop in, I've made enough tonight."

"Aw, thanks, but I'm nearly home." I'd never be able to find the place again, so much had grown over it, it'd been years and I still hadn't learned to pirouette, had, in fact, given up trying.

But once, one Halloween night, I'd danced around Lisa and the man. I'd spun with my wand and my tutu. I'd thrown sparkles. I didn't know then that those would be the best spins I'd ever do. The perv ran away. Lisa sat up. We walked home together. We didn't talk. We were covered in sparkles. We shone.

RATS, HOMOSEX, SAUNAS, AND SIMON

(From Broken Pencil *#26)*

josh byer

My friend Simon Simpson had decided not to be a homosexual. He was sixteen years old, and lived in a jungle of duplexes located in Ottawa South. It was the Deborah Street area, a collection of badly cracked roads and mean kids who drank Malibu rum out of Coca-Cola bottles. Those mean kids were real bastards. This story is not about them.

Simon's neighbor, Stan, was a similarly impoverished young man. He was a big, fat, doughy kid who was not jolly.

Stan had introduced Simon to the casual, nobody-has-to-know, teenage blow job. So that was Simon's thing for a while, until he discovered that it was "gay." In the summer of 1994, Simon was in violent withdrawal from his participation in homosex.

A week after he decided not to be "gay," he set Stan's house on fire with a bottle of Zippo lighter fluid, and a roll of toilet paper. The house did not burn down. All the toilet paper did was burn toilet-paper shaped marks into the paint job.

His parents, staunch and strict career aggressives, grounded Simon for six months and would not allow him any social contact. In retaliation, he sold his mother's microwave at a pawn shop for sixty dollars. Then he came to live with my family.

We didn't have a spare room, so he set up an army cot in our broken sauna. By the end of the summer, Simon and I had jury-rigged the sauna machine and got it sort of working again. Then, we invited a bunch of girls over. Well, two girls, sisters, who lived down the block and were conservative agnostics. One of them suffered from chronic acne, and the other was pretty in a Candace Cameron kind of way.

We had a sauna party in Simon's bedroom. Everything was steamy and fine. All the posters slowly peeled off his walls. His sheets gradually became red hot and soaked. Then the floor flooded.

It cost seven hundred dollars to fix all the water damage. Simon gave my folks the sixty microwave bucks at dinner that night. I acted like a complete ass and revelled in the irony. "You're taking stolen money, you bastards!" I yelled at my parents. I wasn't in my right mind.

I had just discovered water-drunkenness, which is caused by an over-consumption of H_2O. A four-litre bottle of Evian, which my mother loved to buy, would get you right and royal zipped-out if you could drink it in ten minutes.

The only drawback was the constant peeing, but Simon and I had secret plans to buy Depends adult diapers, and walk around town listening to the satisfied crinkling noise while we pissed ourselves to utopia.

"Lay off that goddamned water!" my father yelled. I told him water was necessary for human survival. He took Simon's sixty bucks and left the table.

The next morning, my mother told us that for the rest of the summer, we couldn't spend time in the house during the day. 8 A.M. to 5 P.M. were to become the vagrancy hours. My folks figured if they restricted our time in the house, they could limit the liability for the amount of damage caused to their property.

So Simon and I wandered the streets of suburbia, past pool parties and yups washing their Honda CRXs, past the park where they handed out limeade beverages to poor people, through the random placement of plywood fences, finally finding privacy in a large, grassy field on the edge of a triplex housing development.

The field was thirty acres wide. It had been zoned for housing twenty years prior. The city had come in and laid storm sewers down, but then ran out of funds, and abandoned the housing project altogether.

So what you had was a big field, with endless kilometres of sewers underneath, and a bunch of trees and bulrushes up top. We stole a crowbar and some flares from a parked caboose in a CN Rail yard, pried open an overgrown manhole cover, and descended into our own personal labyrinth. I felt just like David Bowie.

The tunnels stretched on forever. Eventually, if you followed them east, they'd lead to the street sewers, and you could go anywhere in the city with street sewers.

There were rats. Simon the not-gay attacked rats with two lit train flares once and got bit. We were too scared to go to a doctor, in fear that he would narc us out to my water-damaged parents. Simon coasted out the rest of August, wondering if he would fall victim to rabies, or herpes, or whatever disease that you catch from rats.

We found all kinds of things in those sewers. Someone had set up a home in a cubbyhole, where water couldn't flow. There was a cot and a poster of Jane Fonda on the wall. It was old, maybe from the 1970s.

I told Simon if we got kicked out of my house, then we'd have to come live here. He nodded and tore the Jane Fonda poster off the wall. He still has it, even today, framed and in the kitchen of his half-a-million-dollar condo. But I digress.

We found a dead dog, still wearing his collar. Simon wanted to find the owner and take them their dog-corpse, so they could have closure. I strongly argued against it, because the dog was very, very deceased and slowly falling apart.

Simon was intense and offended, so I told him he was acting rat-bite crazy. He told me I was being homophobic. I told him that he had told me that he wasn't homosexual, so I couldn't be homophobic. He told me to shut up.

One day in August, before it was all done and Simon went home and I went back to school, we decided to take one last venture—to go as far as we possibly could through the tunnels. Our previous record had been three kilometres, coming up in Ottawa East, near Jojo's, a pub that served minors if you knocked on the back door and drank in the storage room.

So this time we went past Jojo's. Past the abandoned cot. Past the dead dog. And we found a small tree, alive and green, not a ray of light or sunshine in sight. It was growing in a pile of dirt-mud in the middle of the sewer. It was impossible.

We climbed up and out, and never went back.

YES MAN

(From Broken Pencil #41)

charlie anders

Juan put a Flintstones toothbrush up his ass in the parking lot behind the Westview Mall in daylight because some boys told him to. They didn't force him to do it; he just liked to obey. Nobody ever gave Juan an order he disobeyed, as far as I know. He had a beautiful sleek body that healed quick. The mall cops arrested Juan, but not the other boys; he still had gravel on his knees when I came to get him, a bruised candy-apple look on his face.

Juan never went looking for people to boss him. It just happened. He gave off a vibe. He'd be in the drugstore buying toilet paper and vitamins, and a little old lady would ask him to grab something off the top shelf for her. Something about his readiness to jump at the task tempted people to see how far they could go. Maybe they got frustrated when they couldn't find his limits. It was like finding out the ocean had no bottom. People took it as a challenge.

That old drugstore woman started out asking for help reaching the suppositories, and ended up with Juan's tongue in her ass in the back of her Chevy Citation. Juan carried her bags out to her car for her, and then she kept trying to find something he'd refuse to do.

We timed how long he could stand on his head (fifty-seven seconds), and how much water he could hold in his ass (almost the whole contents of two rinsed-out Big Gulp containers). We found a glory hole in the fifth floor men's room at J. Presley Department Store, and made Juan put himself through it and stand there for an hour, no matter what happened. Many people think they're submissive, but really they just like being the centre of attention. When you meet a real submissive, like

Juan, it's like finding a double eagle silver dollar or something. Juan could be your party's centrepiece—an ice sculpture, an angel made out of Crisco. He only got more lovely and pristine as we abased him.

Everybody loved Juan: the cops, his co-workers at Trend Analytics, his public defender, our fellow human chess pieces, his cellmates. And of course we all loved him. Juan was maybe the only really nice person I've ever met, not in a manipulative or give-to-get way, but from his heart. Juan and I were both white pawns, our headgear custom-fitted to our heads. If you're going to stand out in the middle of a field of grass and gravel squares for a few hours every Sunday wearing a big globe helmet, you want it to be exactly the same size as your head. Juan always looked peaceful, staying exactly inside the lines of his grass space, not talking like the rest of us, but waiting for instructions from the loudspeaker.

We tried to get Juan to teach us, not how to be wide open, but how to broadcast it. But it wasn't something he could teach. It just happened. It wasn't just his eagerness, but his beauty and quickness to figure out what you wanted, and guess what you might want next.

How had a man gotten a master's degree in computer science and a decent job, when he had "use me" written on his forehead? We asked Juan, and he said it had to do with context. At work or school, nobody would ever tell him to do anything inappropriate. Unpleasant, sure, all the time—but not inappropriate.

We thought maybe Juan was some kind of sage. Actually, we couldn't agree amongst ourselves, between "sage" or "wild he-nymph." And then we weren't sure what the difference was between those two things. We agreed though that Juan had a limit somewhere. We just might not be mean enough to find it.

A guy pretended to castrate him—a teeny teeny guillotine, like you'd use to behead cigars, had its blade positioned to strike Juan's cock from the record—Juan not even tied up. We always said Juan was a cheap date at a play party because the words "don't budge" were inescapable bondage to him. The guy, who had a trucker outfit and handlebar 'stache but actually sold bongs, put a blindfold on Juan and then took guillotine away. Smacked Juan's cock root with a ruler, then put a soft dildo in Juan's mouth and told him he was sucking his own cock. We weren't there, but we imagined Juan making little slop-pop noises with his mouth.

What if we were all like Juan? Would the human chess game turn into group sex on the checkered field, or would we just stand there waiting for instructions, the way we already did? A good human chess piece has a super imagination. We would have gone nuts, standing out there for hours, if we couldn't visualize the big picture. Or make up stories in our heads about the war we were helping to fight.

Juan called in sick at work because an Elk Lodge had him in their basement, dusting all their ceremonial hats while they took turns plugging his holes.

What would happen, we wondered, when Juan was older and less pretty? Would people still approach him randomly to serve them? If they stopped, then would he just shrug and carry on with his life, or would he spend the rest of his days looking until he found someone?

We would never stop using Juan, we swore on our satin chess-piece robes. We would keep probing and commanding him long after we'd all lost our teeth and had two hip replacements each. We competed to see who could come up with the most time-consuming task for Juan, and I won with the full-body tongue bath I made him give me. A human body is bigger than you'd give it credit.

The person who found Juan's limit was not one of us, he was not even anybody we would want to know. He was a sanctimonious jerk who drew those little religious comic-book pamphlets—in the style of Jack Chick—where people try video games, or Christian Science, and the next thing you know, they're turning on kebab spits that unravel their intestines each time around. One of those angry closet cases.

In the end, it wasn't any particular action that Juan didn't like, it was a person. Before Robert, Juan had never met someone he didn't like. He was the Will Rogers of sex slaves. Maybe that was why people liked taking advantage of him so much, you could tell he liked you from the way his eyes widened, the little nod when you'd just given him some extra horrendous task.

Robert Daly would work for forty-eight hours non-stop on one of his comics, snarfing caffeinated Penguin mints by the handful, not eating or bathing. At the end of one of those stints, he wouldn't be able to sleep until he'd messed up a cute boy. Before he met Juan, he had a few hustlers on speed dial on his cell (labelled things like "Domino's Pizza," so when he was really sleep-deprived he'd call them up and try to order a meat lover's classic from them).

But then he met Juan. And every few weeks, he'd call Juan up at three in the morning or afternoon, and demand that he come over immediately.

Juan would rush over, strip, and bend over the drawing table. Daly would whack at him with a long thick brush, hitting the table instead of Juan about half the time. This went on for an hour or two, while Daly screamed at Juan about his disgusting faggot ass. Then Daly would ram his cock into Juan's ass, cum in a few seconds, and pass out. Juan would dress and let himself out.

Maybe six months of this, and then one day Juan went all Bartleby the Scrivener. He was at the park, flying a long, fancy dragon kite, with a twenty-foot tail that looked like it was threading the clouds. His phone rang and Daly's name popped up. Juan didn't pick up. He missed the second call too.

The third time, Juan looked at his phone, heard the buzzer insisting, and picked up. Daly told him to get his fucken faggot ass over there, and Juan bit his lip. "I don't know," he said. He looked up at his kite, and thought about how long it would take to get it down safely, roll up the fancy tail, get it into storage. "I can be there in about an hour," he said.

Now, Daly said.

Juan said he would do his best. He scratched his head, then started to bring the kite down. He got to Daly's house in about forty-five minutes, then fidgeted instead of undressing. Finally he looked at Daly's eyes, which didn't look back at him, and said he didn't think he could do this anymore. He said it was nothing personal, which was a lie. Daly screamed, tried to push Juan down onto the table. Juan shoved back. Daly fell onto his sofa. Juan went home and took a bath. A couple days later, he gave pedicures to five members of the same women's glee club, and then went down on them.

Some time after that, our White Overlord took an interest in Juan. She kept slipping Juan forward whenever she had no more urgent move to make. Juan made his way halfway across, then into Black (gravel) territory. By the time anybody noticed, he'd gotten four squares from the other end of the field.

We all started rooting in silence for him to get to that last square, to trade his round hat for a big crinkly inverted cone-shaped crown. The next few moves, Juan stayed where he was, then he got another square closer. Nobody said anything or even breathed, we all just looked at him, biting our tongues. Only Juan kept his face totally relaxed and empty. Totally patient and up for whatever. Watching the birds chase each other from one tree to the other, at the north border of the chess grid.

PARKING HER CAR IN MICHIGAN THEATRE

(From Broken Pencil *#22)*

jake kennedy

There is the girl named Daisy and she has that very own car thing going on. She parks it in the Michigan Theatre, and some kids playing basketball bounce their basketball towards that car. They don't care about community feeling, and they only want a look at Daisy's muffin. The parking lot and that basketball net are all contained under the vaulted ceiling of the Michigan Theatre, which is ornate, but wartorn. Daisy has that movie star personality in effect and she puts on big sunglasses. Errand time.

What makes Daisy so special? Her story is interesting not only because her car is one of those new VW Bugs, but because her car is painted like a vagina, complete with labia and clitoris (right at the top of the hood). Pubic hair is courtesy of a modified welcome mat on the roof. Hoo-cha. It is not illegal to have your car in the general shape or idea of a vagina, but you can see why the boys throw their ball towards it and want a show. Police officers are perplexed by the car. They like to circle it and lower their sunglasses. Heh, they chirp, and then look around. The car is only one example, or only the most outward expression, of Daisy's specialness.

This is Michigan.

Daisy is of average height and has average eyes. She has the exact body shape that she always wanted.

Her job involves an assembly line and the sorting of decals for car windshields. That's her day job. Daisy is told by the foreman, every day, that he has never seen a hairdo in the shape of a man's genitals before. That's really something, he says. Work faster. Well, that's just Daisy doing her wild-girl best.

She has a house with a driveway in which she parks her vagina car. The front of the house is special and worth talking about because the house is painted like a giant, yet very attractive, asshole. The front door basically representing the anus. Opens and closes. Daisy's house has been in the paper, and she gets a lot of trick-or-treaters. They are surprised to find that Daisy hands out simple orange and brown toffees wrapped in their regular waxed paper covers. The kids smell those treats.

That Daisy does not live alone is proven by her having secured herself a dog long ago. A dog that is black, brown, and white, and which very much resembles a cat. It's a girl dog, of sorts. But Daisy has outfitted said mutt with a small hat in the form of a woman's breasts—taking the girlishness and felinity of the dog to an altogether different realm. It is very intriguing and right in line with the Daisy chic.

Her errand over, Daisy, and her hair, and her big purse, get in the famous car. The basketball boys are gone. Daisy drives out of the old Michigan Theatre. Daisy has left the dog in the car all afternoon, but the dog is just mostly happy to see Daisy. It sits in the front seat of the VW with its booby headgear. It looks around for other dogs out there.

PANTIES

(From Broken Pencil #39;
Finalist in the First Annual Indie Writers Deathmatch)

greg kearney

All my favourite panties, ruined. I pull one pair after another out
of the washing machine. They're streaked and spattered with blue
dye. They're rags now. Silk uselessness. It must have been Karl. He's
hated me from day one. He knows he can really get to me via my
panties. If we didn't need the rental income I'd throw all his shit onto
the sidewalk.

You can wear mine, Mama says when I bring my ratty panties
upstairs. I'm 240 pounds, forty-one-inch waist. Mama means well,
but she doesn't really understand. I can't just snake my way into any
old pair of panties. I'm meticulous when I cross-dress. I have very
high panty standards.

Karl will get his. When I'm feeling vengeful there is really nothing I
won't do to undo my foe.

I need to call Louise. But Mama is on the phone. Mama has a new
beau. A younger man. He's sixty-six, she's sixty-eight. She met him at
her till at Wal-Mart. He's ex-military. He was over for lunch on Sunday.
He asked me what I did for a living. I told him I was a bacteriologist. He
asked me if that involved inspecting dirt. I said yes, sort of. He
seemed impressed. He has a glass eye. Mama really likes him. She likes
commanding, haunted men.

Karl's rusty Fifth Avenue pulls into the driveway. I watch him through
the kitchen window. He gets out with groceries. Soon he'll be frying up
some pungent, unlikely pig part for supper. The stench will drift and
settle in our living room. But that's okay. That's fine. Pig tongue stench
is incidental, at this point.

Louise is outraged to hear about my panty tragedy. She says it's a hate crime. She gives me five new pairs of panties, and throws in a gorgeous Cleopatra wig, on the house.

Louise is my girlfriend of six years. She owns and runs the Closet, a clothing store that serves the transvestite and cross-dressing communities. She, herself, is a big woman—six-foot-one, 180 pounds—so most of her own clothing comes from the Closet.

I love Louise very much. Her long arms, huge hands, her plush physique hinting at itself through her countless, dramatic caftans—she reminds me of a vast, gliding bird from dinosaur times. Beautiful.

Our sex has never been very inspired. Louise is into "transcendent encounters," which typically involve the two of us spooning in bed while she sings softly something by Joan Armatrading. Then I go to the bathroom and beat off in my panties.

I've tried to spice things up. Dirty talk, strap-ons. Once I told Louise to say "fuck me!" while we were fucking. Louise said it all cautious, almost in the form of a question: "Uh, fuck me? Fuck me." She sounded like she was ordering in a French restaurant and wasn't entirely sure if "fuck me" was an entrée or an appetizer. Finally, Louise said that sex games were disingenuous. And that was that.

She does let me dress up though. But then she'll say things like, "Behold, woman!" which is empowering, I guess, but not very sexy, or even accurate. I'm not a woman. I don't want to be a woman. I don't have a female alter ego. I just like to dress up. I'm pretty simple. I like a good barbecue. I drink Export.

But Louise is just great. Besides clothes, she makes pretty little fans out of this porous sort of paper. She paints detailed, surreal images all over them. A naked lady diving into a pot of stew. Blue roses with serpent stems.

She gave one to Mama awhile ago. Mama said it was the prettiest thing she'd ever seen, and wasn't there so much ugliness in the world? Then Mama started crying and lamenting the plight of my auntie Helen, who went to Puerto Vallarta in 1986 and awoke one night in her hotel room to find the concierge trying to do her up the ass. Auntie Helen has never been the same.

I remember how Louise listened so patiently as Mama rambled on. I'm not a patient person. I sigh theatrically if I get stuck behind an elderly person on the sidewalk. Then I'll feel so guilty, I'll empty my wallet into a homeless person's lap. Even if they don't ask.

I try on the wig in Louise's big, gilded showroom mirror. I look like a middle-aged man in a wig. Louise says I evoke a forties movie goddess. I roll my eyes. I don't know how to accept compliments.

I have to work on that. That, and patience. But how do you work on such things? Find some expensive shaman to give you a healing enema?

I'm a scientist through and through. I can only go about things deductively. I have no imagination. Louise once asked me what my wildest dream was. I  told her about this dream I once had where the fridge was in the living room.

Saul called me "his lady" today, Mama says in between coughing fits. She looks so happy. He wants to take her dancing at Spurs, the Western bar. But she worries that she'll look foolish, with her oxygen tank.

She asks me what she should call Saul. I say she should call Saul "Saul." She says maybe she should call Saul "her man." I say that if she calls him "her man," she'll sound like a twenty-year-old black woman. Mama laughs. Mama coughs, and coughs, and coughs.

I could go into his apartment and pour water on his DVD player. I could piss on his mattress—he'll think it's his cat. I could confront him face to face. With a big knife.

Just as I'm contemplating ways of making him suffer, a knock on our side door. It's him. Smiling, holding a box of something.

Ho, Mrs. Dennis, he says. My sister made a whole big bunch of (a long German word I've never heard and can't spell), so I give some to you. You will like it.

Mama opens the box. I peer around her. Sticky buns of some sort, with beige gunk drizzled all over them.

Don't those look yummy, Mama says. Thank you. What are they called again?

He says the long German word again.

Well, Karl, I'm sure we'll just gobble them right up. We both love sweet things.

Good thing, he says. And hello there to you, he says to me.

I nod. His subterfuge is so transparent. Mama thanks him again as he backs away, smiling and waving.

Wasn't that nice of Karl, Mama says. She brings one to her mouth.

Don't eat it! I scream. Who knows what it's laced with.

That's just silly, Mama says. This isn't some spy novel. They're sticky buns!

Nice. You're on his team. Really nice.

What team? You mean, for curling? Did you sign me up for curling? You know I can't curl anymore.

Mama's pie-faced bafflement. Her dyed red head. I storm down the stairs and pound on Karl's door. He answers, cradling his ratty cat, still smiling.

Ho! You eat them up already?

No. I need to speak with you.

Sure. Just let me put my Malta down.

He drops the cat, which makes a short shriek as it lands, like it's in great pain.

Have you been tampering with my laundry?

Tampering? I—you know I don't like your wash machine. I go to that one around the corner.

No. I mean—did you touch my laundry?

He cocks his head.

What? No. I been at work since five this morning.

That is true. He has been gone all day. I never thought of that. But! He might've snuck back to destroy my panties. It's possible.

Well, I have a load of laundry—of very special, private laundry—that has been ruined with blue dye. My mother can't go down stairs, so she didn't do it. I can only deduce that—

How did they get ruined?

Like I said. Blue dye.

That's not good. I once took a suit to dry cleaners, and it come back, and it smell like shit. Do your laundry smell like shit?

No.

You want me to have look at wash machine?

No. Just. Never mind. Thank you.

Okay then, Gary. You like the (endless, cacophonous German word), I get you a recipe.

I go back upstairs. Storm past Mama. Ooh, you almost knocked me into the coffee maker, she says.

I don't know why I continue to live in this horrible house. I make seventy grand a year. I've always maintained that I'm here to tend to my ailing mother. But that's not true. I don't especially like Mama, and I mostly just let her flounder. Once every few months I change her bedsheets for her.

I call Louise again. She's breathless when she enters.

Why are you out of breath?

I was dancing.

I don't hear any music.

So?

I love Louise. But she is unbearable, and I hate talking to her.

I don't think it was Karl.

Who destroyed your intimate apparel?

It wasn't Karl. It couldn't be Mama. That means that someone—

You. Oh, lovelight. You destroyed your own intimate apparel, and you've blocked it out. You're in so much pain.

I am not. I did not.

Yes, you did, lovelight.

Stop calling me lovelight. You went to community college, for Christ's sake. I'm very happy. Very, very happy!

All your rage would dissipate if you would just identify and name your female side.

We've been through this. It's not relevant.

Oh, love. What about "Portia"? Let's call you Portia. Or Joni. Or—

I hang up on Louise. I did not wreck my own panties and then suppress the memory. I'm not that kind of person. I do not have a spooky, prismatic personality. No. If I wrecked my panties, I'd remember it.

I sit on the edge of my bed. Run my fingers through the white fake fur throw. I am not going to pass out.

It must be Mama's new boyfriend. Mama is enacting a vendetta through her new boyfriend. Sending him downstairs to fuck with my panties.

I'll have to watch her like a hawk, 'round the clock. I may have to take a sabbatical from the lab. Maybe I should hide her oxygen tank. Let her gasp and bob for a bit. Then she'll know precisely how it feels, to be deprived of something essential like air. Or panties.

HANDS HELD
AT RELIGIOUS ANGLES

(From Broken Pencil *#28)*
kevin spenst

Tiny deposits of magic were contained in the tears of fairies, and it was for this reason that any single zone bus transfer blessed by those tears would be transformed into a multi-zone pass. That is, of course, if you believed in fairies.

Tony stood by the bus stop with his hands jammed in his pockets. Apart from the pimples and the blood coursing through his veins there were few differences between the lanky, blank-faced boy and the bus stop itself. Loose change jingled in either his right or left pocket.

Hearing the strange sound of tinkling, Tony looked down at his feet. A fairy was supping on the petals of a buttercup. An idea brought some unattractive intelligence to Tony's face.

"Excuse me. Mightn't you have the time?" he asked the fairy with clumsy formality.

"Three-thirty. I think the next bus should be by in an hour," she responded through a mouthful of yellow.

Tony wracked his brains for the language used in fables of fairies and other such nonsensical stories. "Is this not a day sky-heated to inspire perspiration from the pores?"

"Uhhh, yeah, I guess."

"What it is I mean to say is that the sun brings to mind my father, for I am his son."

"Yeah."

"My father was divested of a huge sum of money . . . once upon a time. One afternoon while he was golfing, the beast that he rode upon across the greens bit a small man in the head. The man was cunning, and claimed that he was vacationing from his vocation of the monkhood, and that the head-chomp would delay his returnance to his monastery. In court this so-called monk held his hands up like in our classical paintings of saints or crossing guards. In short, he walked away with my father's fortunes."

"Weird."

"Oh, but I wish I were enabled to retain this change in my pocket. It would help my father back upon his feet, knees, and upper torso."

"Um, yeah . . . okay . . . well, good luck with that," the fairy said as she wiped her yellow mouth on her sleeve. "Just hang in there and I've got one piece of advice for ya."

As she floated away on her gossamer wings she gave him her middle fairy finger.

SICKNESS

(From Broken Pencil #39
Semi-Finalist in the First Annual Indie Writers Deathmatch)
jessica faulds

After he graduated from high school, receiving honours and an award for home economics, Teddy Pommeroy fell prey to a series of unsentimental diseases. It was never brain cancer, polio, athlete's foot, arthritis, dyslexia, diabetes, or any other condition with a website, a celebrity spokesperson, and a tin can with a slot in its lid at the front till of the 7-Eleven. None of his afflictions could be linked to bravery, or masculinity, or sex appeal. His scars did not curve over his most flattering bone structures, but instead pointed to clusters of moles, and cellulite, and spider veins. He suffered memory loss, but only insofar as it caused him to lose his keys, forget acquaintances' names, and buy milk every time he went to the supermarket. The glorious emptiness of the amnesiac would never be his. Oh, for the joy of perpetual absence, he wrote in his journal. Oh, for a moment's fuck all!

Such glamour was out of his grasp. He instead had to settle for the irritable bowel, enlarged kidneys, pear-shaped skull, furry tongue, oral thrush, squeaky lungs, enlarged goiter, and flatulence. He contracted syphilis, though he had never before even held a girl's hand, except for in social dance at school, when Olga Popov, the second-most beautiful girl in his class, had pressed her palm directly into his as they danced the schottische. The girls had an ongoing competition to see who could be the first to give their partner an erection through nothing but hand-to-hand contact. Olga had hardly begun to swirl her fingers over Teddy's wrist when David Glass ran from the room, hands over the front of his shorts. Later he told Teddy that his dance partner, Sara Peterson, had licked his palm, and Teddy then told Olga, and Olga called Sara a whore, and overturned her lunch tray in the cafeteria.

Several years later, Teddy was the only virgin syphilitic at the sexual health clinic. He was too embarrassed to admit it, but he was sure the doctors knew. During a routine check, a male nurse informed him that his testicles had yet to fully descend.

At times, it was all too much. He decided that he must kill himself, but when he tried, his veins sunk deeper into his fishy-yellow skin, and no amount of jabbing with a penknife could find them. When he tried to swallow pills, his throat closed. His nooses were consistently unreliable. He once began to climb the stairwell of the apartment building he'd moved into after graduation, intending to fling himself from the roof, but his Achilles tendon snapped on the seventh storey. A sudden attack of laryngitis kept anyone from hearing his screams.

It is not often that one finds the word "miracle" embedded in the newsprint of a reputable paper, except for in interviews with the mothers of heart transplant recipients, who, it must be noted, are generally under considerable strain. Nevertheless, there it was: "Real live unicorn performs miracle healings!" In the classifieds, of course, one of thousands of starred, bolded, and underlined captions. Testimonies followed: Cured my ringworm! Quit smoking! Helped me get over my ex-wife! Fifty dollars— cash only.

Unicorns, also, are rarely found in the paper.

He circled the ad with a red felt-tipped pen, and stared at it as he rubbed aloe into the eczema in the crooks of his elbows.

Teddy called in sick to work. He worked at a phone research lab, telephoning people and trying to get them to answer questions about their diet. Often the calls became confusing, going something like this:

— Hello?

— Hello, ma'am, my name is Teddy, and I'm—

— Hello?

— Hello. Can you hear me? My name is Teddy. I'm calling to see if you would like to participate in a phone survey.

— A what?

— A survey. A phone survey. About healthy eating. We're conducting a brief survey on behalf of the Initiative for Healthy—

— Do you know who I am?

— He did not know who she was.

— No, I don't. Your phone number was randomly selected by—

— I'm Norma MacEwan, and I'm eighty-one years old, and my husband is dead.

She sounded defiant. Not sad at all. Sometimes people cried on the phone, but this was not one of those calls. The woman's voice was crisp and dry.

— Oh, I see, said Teddy, who did not see at all, and was beginning to have an ache in his ear from his telephone headset.

— That's right.

— Oh. Well then.

— Thank you, she said, and hung up.

He usually made about three hundred calls in a day, and completed anywhere from two to seven surveys. He made $56 a day, minus five that he spent on lunch. That left enough for one miracle healing, with a dollar left over.

He called in sick.

— Diarrhea again? said the sympathetic receptionist.

He blushed uselessly into the phone.

— No, just a headache. A bad headache. A migraine.

— He faked a cough, then realized there was no reason he should be coughing, and tried to turn it into a simple throat-clearing.

— Well, I'll see you tomorrow then.

He took a tab of Bromazepam to calm his nerves, put new arch-support pads into his orthopedic shoes, and then walked to the bus, which cost two dollars, which brought the day's expenses to $57—more than a day's wages. In his bag he had brought his medications, a sweater, and a banana for the unicorn because he had no apples. He got off at a cul-de-sac of beige houses with two-door garages, and walked along a curving sidewalk until he reached a house whose address matched the one on the ad. He had not been expecting a house. He had thought it would be a dark shop, a musty set of stairs leading down into an earthy cavern filled with the clanking of iron. He had not expected vinyl sideboards. Is it legal to run a business from your suburban home? Is a unicorn a business? He knocked on the door.

It was answered by a white-bearded man who was wearing yellow rubber gloves and who introduced himself as Yorick.

— Thank God, said Yorick, opening the screen door. You the plumber?

Teddy, confused, shook his head and held out the ad.

— Oh, right. I prefer it if you make an appointment next time. There's a phone number in the paper. You got fifty bucks?

Teddy held out the bill. Yorick shook off a glove, took the bill, examined it, and tucked it into the waistband of his pants.

— Come with me.

Yorick led Teddy around the house to the backyard where there was a blue-and-white striped circus tent.

— She's in there, he said, and turned back towards the house.

Teddy stopped him.

— Wait, how does it work? What do I do?

— It will come to you.

Teddy nodded. Of course. How new age. He entered.

It was a goat. A goat with its horns somehow twined together in the centre of its forehead, making one thick horn. A goat wearing a golden cape. A goat. A rope was tied around its neck, and fastened to a wooden pin that had been hammered into the ground. Once more: a goat.

Teddy went out of the tent and found Yorick on his back porch fooling with the barbecue.

— That's a goat, he said.

— It's a unicorn, Yorick said.— I made her myself, raised her from a kid. It's a surgical procedure, passed down secret through the generations. My father taught it to me.

Teddy began to mumble, another of his afflictions. Chronic mumbling, his speech pathologist had said.

— But . . . the paper said . . . a miracle.

— I see, said Yorick, affronted.— If I create a unicorn myself, then she's not a miracle. A unicorn is only a miracle if she flies down from a golden cloud. I suppose you think that triple bypass surgery also isn't a miracle.

He placed his palm flat against the front of his shirt where surely a white scar lurked beneath. He was a very large man.

— No, no, I'm sorry, said Teddy.

— I tell you, this unicorn cures!

— I'm sorry. I'll try again.

Teddy returned to the tent. The unicorn lay on the ground, twisting its head, trying to free its horn from the rope and the cape in which it had become entangled. It was hilarious and depressing. Teddy tried to help it, but when he approached, it backed away, snuffling loudly, afraid of his

touch. He held up his palms to show he meant no harm, but this sort of human signal means nothing to unicorns.

He inched closer, and the unicorn continued to snuffle and began to stamp her feet. The place where the rope was around her neck was rubbed raw, pink, and wet. Teddy backed away and the unicorn became still, so he was able to look at her more closely. There were also sores along her back legs, bald patches that looked like half-cooked meat, and the fur around her anus was reddish and dirty. Her eyes leaked thick green tears, and the corners of her mouth bled. The unicorn stared at him angrily, and he knew what to do. It came to him.

He took the banana and three tabs of Bromazepam out of his bag, then reconsidered. Four tabs. He peeled the banana. The stem snapped cleanly, and he did not end up grinding the banana to mush as he pulled away the skin. He placed a Bromazepam on his finger and then pushed his finger into the fruit. He did this four times until there were four pills inside of the banana, and then he crouched down and tossed the banana in front of the unicorn, who ate it, became drowsy, and fell asleep.

Teddy removed the rope from around the unicorn's neck. She was drooling a green liquid threaded with blood. He wrapped his sweater around her and attempted to lift her, but she was too heavy, and so he simply dragged the sweater along the ground with her on it. He lifted up the wall of the tent, ran from the yard while Yorick was leaning over his propane tank, and hailed a cab.

At first the unicorn did not take well to living in an apartment building. She pulled out strings from the green shag carpet and ate them, and then defecated cotton balls into the corners of the rooms. She generally avoided Teddy and slept in the broom closet. Teddy placed straw in a mixing bowl for her, but she would not eat if he was nearby. At night he could hear her snuffling. He named her Trixie.

She was still dirty, and she smelled like dry rot, and so after two weeks of gentle avoidance, he threw a towel over her and wrestled her into the bath. She flailed, kicking him in the jaw. He pushed her roughly against the side of the tub with one hand, and turned on the tap with the other, and when the water hit her, she stopped struggling. He loosened his hold. Warm water sprayed onto the front of his shirt as he lathered her with baby shampoo, and she stayed still, if only from fear. He gently dribbled water from his hand over the sores on her legs. When he was done, he rubbed her softly with a towel. Then he chopped up a carrot and put it in a bowl, and she let him sit near her as she ate it.

They began to watch movies together. *Blade Runner, Das Einhorn, Legend*. They had to turn off *The Last Unicorn* halfway through because it was too frightening. As the red bull charged towards the unicorns onscreen, Trixie leaned involuntarily into Teddy's side, and the place where they touched radiated warmth. He fed her some popcorn.

He bought lemon oil and polished her horn. It gradually softened and began to gently glow. She made a sound when she was warm and happy, a deep hum. He took to reading aloud before he went to sleep, and often she came into his room to listen, sprawling along the foot of his bed. She hummed her deep hum, and he recited "The Lion and the Unicorn," altering the words so that the lion no longer beat the unicorn all around the town.

One night she fell asleep on his bed, and he covered her with a blanket. She still smelled faintly of rot, but it was masked by shampoo. She'd been having baths regularly. Teddy rubbed her horn with his thumb, and fell asleep clutching it gently.

He woke up in a dream. He was lying in a patch of muddy grass in a makeshift canvas hut. Outside the hut it was raining, and he could hear men laughing. He moved to get up and see what was happening, but he was pulled back by a rope around his neck, tied to a stake in the ground. A voice called outside.

— All right, you! Next!

There was the sound of chain clinking, and then two men entered. The first was tall and blond. He wore a handsome suit and a gold band on his ring finger. As he walked into the tent Teddy saw that he had a limp, a twisted stagger with every second step, his ankle bent sideways. The second man was Yorick. The blond man handed Yorick a bill, and Yorick went back outside.

— Twenty minutes, he called over his shoulder, and left.

The blond man knelt in front of Teddy, and looked into his face. He reached out for the horn that grew from Teddy's forehead, took it in his hand, felt for cracks with his nail. He rubbed the horn. He moved his hand up and down its shaft. Then he yanked it to the ground.

Teddy's neck twisted. The man held the horn to the ground and manoeuvred himself so that he was behind Teddy. He loosened his tie. The man grabbed Teddy's back legs and pulled them apart. His breath was thick and heavy. He leaned his weight against Teddy's back as he undid his belt. Teddy snuffled into the dirt. The man clenched his fist tight on a handful of Teddy's fur and moaned, shaky quiet moans as he thrust forward again and again, each time pulling back hard on the horn. Teddy was torn apart. Then the man dressed himself, combed his hair, and walked out of the tent, his stroll smooth and uninjured.

Teddy woke. Trixie was looking at him, crusted moisture around her eyes. He began to cry. When he was done, he sighed heavily, and his lungs did not squeak.

Trixie slept on his bed from then on. Each night was a different dream of a different man with a different sickness. Each night he cried until his pillow was soaked with greenish tears, until he was limp and ragged, and everything, every ache and pain drained from him. He sobbed and clenched the pillow, and Trixie snuffled, and groaned, and rolled on the foot of the bed. He slept with his mouth wide open and woke up new. His skull shrank, his tongue smoothed, his bowels began to contract normally. The rot smell left Trixie, and the sores on her legs began to grow over with fluffy white fur. After a year, the dreams decreased in frequency, and in another six months they stopped entirely. There were no men left. Trixie's horn fell off one evening in the bath, and Teddy threw it in the compost. He slept entire nights without even the shadow of a dream. He became a *supervisor* at his job, and she became a goat. And so they were healed.

DANDRUFF

(From Broken Pencil #22)
joel schneier

I wake up in bed, sit up, and see that I have been sleeping on a large pile of dandruff. I think I'll stop sleeping from now on.

I have had dandruff for twenty-three years. I've tried every single shampoo on the market. I even tried to make my own shampoo once before figuring out that I needed to know way too much stuff to accomplish that.

Over the years, dandruff has become a very dear friend of mine. Together, we walk down the shampoo aisle in the local grocery store. There are hundreds of different bottles that promise to add bounce, or volume, or curls, or smell, or charisma, but none will successfully prevent my dandruff.

I'm not actually going to buy shampoo. I've tried them all. I just want to check the aisle to see if there are any new ones. The bottles are stacked in alphabetical order according to the name of the scientist who designed their formula.

Instead of successfully passing Dr. Zwiliger's patented formula shampoo guaranteed to prevent any sort of vermin from nesting, I bump into a rather large fellow. I'm so shocked that I fall down. The rather large fellow turns his head, looks down at me, and says, "You've got some dandruff there."

I stand up again. "I'm aware of that. Thanks."

With a nonchalant look, I walk away from the aisle and the fellow. In the produce section, I pick up a honeydew and squeeze it to see if it's ripe.

"You have a really bad dandruff problem." It's the rather large fellow again. He startles me so much that I drop the melon. It joins my dandruff, which has been slowly drifting down to the floor all this time.

"Do you mind?" I say, angrily.

"About your dandruff problem? No. But I figure you do."

I turn around and walk away, but he follows me.

"I can help you," he says.

"Right," I say. I've heard it all before.

"This is the real thing," he says.

I stop walking. "Look, I've learned to live with my dandruff. It might cause a few embarrassing moments every now and then, but I've moved on."

The rather large fellow reaches into his back pocket, pulls out his wallet, and extracts a picture of himself standing in the middle of a pile of snow. I look a little closer and realize it's not snow.

"It took me five minutes to make that pile," he says. "That's how bad my dandruff used to be. Look at me now."

He runs his hand through his hair and not a single particle of dry skin falls.

Five minutes later, I'm standing in the middle of an empty warehouse with the rather large fellow, a second rather large fellow, and a strange-looking machine that reminds me of an egg-scrambler. The second rather large fellow says, "Hello, my name is Dr. Sarlin. I have been told you have a certain problem you wish to get rid of."

I nod.

"Right, then. This machine will make your dandruff go away."

"How does it work?"

"I wish I knew. I bought it at a yard sale a few years ago in Reno."

"Are there any side effects?"

The doctor and the rather large fellow exchange glances. "Some slight lethargy," says the doctor.

"Then why haven't you mass-marketed it?" I ask. "Why has no one else mass-marketed it?"

"Why would any of the personal hygiene product companies actually market something that works?" asks the doctor, patiently.

"So you're saying that the personal hygiene companies are conspiring?"

"Basically."

"Then how are you any different?"

"I guess you'll find out, won't you?"

I am strapped into the machine and de-dandruffed. Afterwards, we all go out for a drink. At the bar I ask the doctor how much he wants for the procedure. He tells me, "Nothing."

After a few more hours of celebrating the discarding of my dandruff, I head home.

MY LIPS ARE SEALED

(From Broken Pencil #27)
esme keith

I am not at liberty to say any more. This is a private matter and we must respect its confidential nature. And so, while I am sensitive to the frustration you must feel, left in ignorance in a matter that touches you closely, I cannot answer any questions at this time. I have divulged all that I am able to reveal.

I know that all of you—if it happened to you, and I pray God it won't—all of you would want to know that you could rely on my discretion. If you had a problem in your personal life, a problem which interfered somewhat—who knows how deeply or for how long?—with your professional responsibilities, you would want to know that your friends and colleagues, and especially your chief, respected your right to privacy. As Head of Section, it is incumbent upon me especially to be alive to the risks of reckless honesty, even while I keep the tides of information flowing, passing along such details as I deem necessary to you in the performance of your duties.

I am reticent therefore to enlarge upon the specific and current circumstances of our troubled friend and colleague, Russell. In my statement today, over which I laboured long, I endeavoured to weigh Russell's need for privacy against your need for information. It is a difficult balance. But I will reiterate the three points of information to which I believe you are entitled, namely, one) that Russell is embarked on a leave of absence commencing retroactively to Tuesday last; b) that the background to this development is confidential; and thirdly) that Ted will *pro tempe* undertake the responsibilities previously borne by Russell. Here, I think I have well judged that difficult balance, simultaneously informing you and respecting Russell's right to secrecy. Further discussion is unnecessary. It would serve no useful purpose to spend our time recalling Russell's many deficiencies or those endless hints of impending crisis.

So farewell, then, Russell. Our old friend will not be at his desk for a while, for an unspecified and indeterminate period of time. In this difficult time, he has applied for and been granted a leave of absence. It is a personal leave. That means that the reasons for it are not to be made public. I will say no more.

It is not a medical leave of absence. I should emphasize that, in case those many friends of Russell among us are feeling now some anxiety on that head. Our friend Russell is not suffering from problems of health. Or, more exactly, I should say that, if he is experiencing health concerns, he has not brought them forward to the attention of myself or the other members of the Management Committee.

To digress for a moment—and I believe that I may speak my own opinions, without intruding on Russell's right to privacy—I will mention parenthetically, that, in our most recent encounters, Russell did not look like a well man to me. His skin is pasty and his eyes glitter. I will go so far as to publish my impression that at this point in time he may not be completely balanced. In my opinion, he is nurturing an unhealthy state of mind. I felt personally menaced in his company, given his dire situation, and the unreasonable rancour he is nursing against me in particular.

However, these are merely personal reflections, and are by no means to be understood as facts, so to speak. Nor did these reflections contribute to the decision of the committee. His leave was granted solely on the grounds of personal and private issues, which, in the considered opinion of the committee, might, if allowed to range unchecked, have compromised in the future, or might arguably have compromised already, or even might at this moment be, in spite of the timely and proactive response of the Management Committee, in the course currently of compromising the output of this office. I cannot be more specific as, beyond the sensitive nature of Russell's particular case, the proceedings of the Management Committee are privileged.

I will also say, as you have, I'm sure, already guessed, that Russell has not taken a professional leave to pursue an irresistible opportunity. He has not been seconded to the ministry, or awarded a fellowship at a prestigious research institute, or decided that, dammit, he could afford six months in a villa on Corfu, where he could rest, read, finally finish that novel, and try to work things out with Darlene because their marriage is worth saving. No, if such happy news were the cause of his absence, there would be no mystery. I would tell you all. He would tell you all and try to inspire your envy in his bantering, light-hearted way. While the going was good, we could count on Russell to exult in it, and rub our noses in our own puny lives, a habit which, if he recalls it now, I am sure that he regrets in his hour of shame and misery.

I need to direct your attention to the business side of these unsettling events. Although our hearts and our hopes go out to Russell, and to Darlene and the children, we must not be blinded to the business repercussions we may face, and we must therefore take appropriate, corporate action. Over the course of Russell's long history with this institution, he has, as you know, developed a network of acquaintances in the outer world. This will be a time of transition for Russell's many customers and business associates. They may ask difficult questions out of a misplaced sense of personal loyalty to the individual involved. They may subtly make inquiries into procedures. They may demand audits. They may lobby for the opening of confidential company files. They may threaten bombastically the withdrawal of accounts. All this they may do out of goodwill to old associates and the unconscious but irresistible demands of the human animal's social instinct.

We, as an enlightened corporation, salute their motivations. But we must do our job of bringing them back to earth, and reminding them of the day-to-day logistics of living in a dog-eat-dog world. Self-interest and concern for the well-being of our client base both instruct us to keep them on the short and narrow, and to slap down any impertinent interference with the internal workings of this organization. We must do this with the sensitivity and subtlety of the highly trained marketing specialists that we are. We must strive above all else to normalize these strange events, to reassure our customers and clients, and to tell them, truly, that although Russell is not here to look after their many important needs, we are here to service them exactly as he would have done. For the sake of the company, and for our own personal and professional well-being, we must try to behave as if the situation were normal and we are happy.

If I may say, we must do this as well for the peace of mind of Russell himself. At a time when he must surely be tortured by the memory of so many ill-considered acts, we must not fan the flame of self-recrimination by allowing his hijinks to destroy us utterly. For everybody's sake, we must maintain a cheerful facade. It is what Russell would wish.

In a similar manner, I may suggest that, if nosy busybodies approach you, attempting to ferret out the details of the situation, your best response is: "I don't know." This response will also be truthful as, to a man, you are in the dark, lacking all specifics and hard facts in this case. This response should certainly be sufficient for any member of the press who might contact you, at your home after business hours, say, or through a mutual acquaintance, insinuating that he or she is onto a "big story." If anyone approaches you on such a fishing venture, you can tell him with perfect honesty that you know no details of the situation. This is one reason I have deliberately kept all of you on a short leash, informationally speaking, as under these circumstances, you can easily and truthfully testify that you are in a state of ignorance. However, if pressed, or if you find yourself accidentally in possession of real data with regard to the situation, you could, alternately, say, "No comment." This is also an acceptable response.

Matters would, of course, be different if you were approached by an official figure, a court-appointed auditor, say, or some member of the legal system, like a police detective armed with a valid search warrant or subpoena. If this happens, then naturally you would be obliged, by your own conscience as well as by this department's clearly articulated policy of full co-operation with all accredited bureaus, to be as helpful as you could. However, since you do not know the facts, you would probably decide to refer such figures to myself. This would be my preference in the matter: a multitude of perspectives in these events may serve merely to complicate unnecessarily a fairly ordinary and straightforward narrative of greed, incompetence, and loss of nerve. I will remind you again that in referring any such figure to me, you would only be doing what Russell himself would have wished. It is in keeping with his current need for privacy, and his history of zeal in serving the department.

And now, I would like to speak deeply and from the heart, revealing my feelings as one individual on the receiving end of Russell's perverse, selfish, and destructive agenda. I was personally saddened and disappointed by the ingratitude that Russell's alleged crimes imply in his attitude to me. I had hoped that my attention and my guidance might inspire him to a better return. As chief, I must of course accept full responsibility for the actions of my team. And as Russell was a member of my team, no matter how unwillingly I accepted his continued tenure in my department, I must take responsibility for his actions. And I do. The buck stops here. I have therefore been sure to lead the inquiry into his conduct myself and to penalize his actions as I think best.

In all truth, as I wrote in my most recent assessment of Russell's performance, he was an incompetent bozo. I say this fully cognizant of the fact that performance assessments are confidential. But in these special circumstances, I believe that an exception can be made. Russell was a holdover from a different era, an atavistic vestige of a more primitive stage in our corporate evolution. The miracle was that he survived as long as he did. And although familiarity bred reluctant tolerance, we could not, as a forward-thinking organization, forever close our eyes to his egregious want of professional *savoir faire*.

For all his winning ways, there were times when Russell has frankly been an albatross around my neck. I have tolerated him as a gesture of goodwill to an outdated but still powerful hierarchy that rewards cronies and punishes innovation, and in recognition of his ties of blood and friendship with more powerful forces within this organization. But my tolerance was predicated on the certainty that it was only a matter of time before he shot himself in the foot and was heft on his own petard.

If his time has come on my watch, well, so be it. I comfort myself with the knowledge that, in his crisis, I, in my position of chief—with my habits of moderation, reflection, and fairness—stand in a position to limit the damage that Russell may do to either himself or his unit, and to see to it that the guilty are punished and the virtuous rise again in white raiment. I have tried to protect Russell from himself as best I could. And I will certainly protect myself and those among you who are loyal to me in this time of uncertainty.

This is not going to be easy for you. I am sensitive to your discomfort. But from a personal perspective I would like to add that this is difficult for me also. I have never dealt with anything remotely like this before. It is outside my field of experience. But I am getting good advice from the knowledgeable and discreet professionals I have consulted. And although the forces that drove our friend from his familiar and convenient work station are bizarre and grotesque in the extreme, I have to believe that an expert team can help him to pick up the pieces of his shattered world.

To some this will appear paradoxical. Those of us whose thinking is informed by a broad array of familiar quotations may find solace in the following reflections: I must be cruel only to be kind. Love and be silent. But that I am forbid to tell the secrets of his prison house, I would such a tale unfold.

THE SWEET TASTE OF SLAVERY

(From Broken Pencil #30)

christoph meyer

Little Jimmy spent too much time pondering the human condition. At the tender age of ten, he arrived at a decisive and final philosophical conclusion: Humans have free will and it is a horrible curse. In that glorious moment of revelation and understanding he threw back his head, clenched his fists and howled to the heavens, "Freedom is slavery!"

Little Jimmy decided that the best way to live in such a wretched world was as a slave, so he sold himself into slavery to his older sister in exchange for her weekly allowance of five dollars. After pocketing his five bucks, Little Jimmy grovelled at her feet and inquired, "What is your bidding, my master?"

"I don't know. Just get outta here for now. You're, like, creepin' me out."

Confused again over the meaning of life and stricken with existential grief, Little Jimmy wandered the mean city streets searching for something that would give his life purpose. Then he saw a sign! The sign was in front of Ivan's hot-dog stand and it read: "5 foot-long chili-dogs for $5."

As Little Jimmy swallowed the first bite, he thought, "Freedom never tasted so good." By the fifth dog, he was feverishly scribbling on his napkin, outlining a grand, extensive philosophical system that had suddenly become clear in his mind's eye. No longer would he be anybody's slave. He'd pay his sister back the money he owed her. He'd pay her back all right—with interest.

BAND NAMES

(From Broken Pencil #41)

tor lukasik-foss

Gord walked out of the grocery store, felt the wind in his hair, pulled his last joint from his breast pocket, and got another great idea. He smacked his pants to see if there might be a pen or a pencil in his pocket, but there wasn't. He didn't have paper either, but he could have fished around the bag of groceries and used the receipt. If he had a pen. But whatever, he lit up, inhaled, and repeated the idea in his mind until it began to take shape.

Pussy Lingus and Kitty Vulvus: all-girl punk bands. Lead singers have to be hot and raunchy.

It was already a good day. Kathy had left fifty bucks to cover a small grocery list: sausages (or at least good hot dogs), buns, prepared salad greens, and razors. Her morning note, taped as always to the refrigerator where Gord was certain to find it, urged him to take a cab both ways, because of the high humidex and the way it had been wreaking havoc lately with his delicate immune system.

Gord's plan, however, was this: walk the twenty-five minutes to the grocery store, lie to Kathy and tell her they were out of razors, but buy fancy buns, big salads, and all-beef wieners. Maybe a six-pack of butter tarts. It would still look like he spent a majority of the money; therefore she wouldn't ask for her change back. He could either cab back, or buy a gyro for lunch, and keep a cool twenty in his pocket.

Pussy Lingus and Kitty Vulvus: identical twins who hate each other form two identical dirty-girl punk bands. They always seem to be playing at the same club, on the same night, right after each other. Every song the one band plays sounds eerily like a song from the other band. Every show ends in a horrible yet tantalizing girl fight.

Smoking up outside the grocery store at eleven o'clock in the morning delighted Gord to no end, so he made sure to do it brazenly. Pent-up mothers with their toddlers would smell what he was doing and flash angry looks his way. Professional women in nice office clothes would smile from the corners of their mouths, obviously attracted to Gord's rock energy, possibly yearning to escape their lives and have a puff with him.

Pussy Lingus and Kitty Vulvus: the thing could be, I could play bass in both bands. The girls could fight over me. That would be awesome.

He flicked his tiny butt at a passing car.

They knew him by name at the gyro shop. He bought one, extra hot sauce, to eat later, and walked twenty-five minutes home. He was so tired when he got back to the apartment, he had to lie down on the couch and watch two episodes of *Court TV*. The phone rang a couple of times, but he let the machine take it. He fell asleep for fifty minutes.

He dreamt about breasty Japanese women.

Fifty minutes was just enough nap to throw him off his rhythm, but not enough to make him feel like he was going to waste another day. He rubbed his eyes and started a pot of coffee in the kitchen to get rid of the headache he always woke up with. Kathy had told him the headache was because he never drank water. But what the hell does she know. Coffee has water in it.

"Crap," he said aloud. "What the fuck was that idea I had. It was good."

Gord fished out his gyro from the grocery bag, removed it from its foil, and put it in the microwave. Then he walked over to the sun room of the apartment, the one that he and Kathy had been slowly transforming into a home-recording studio. After only a few months, he was able to cobble together a good microphone, drum machine, used portable digital recorder, and a few effects boxes. Kathy sewed a heavy curtain at her mother's house, which was then hung in the door frame to block out noise. Kathy also constructed a large dry-erase marker and corkboard with the title "Gord's Music Epicentre" rendered in heavy-metal calligraphy, flanked by a two angry looking musical notes.

The home studio was overwhelming in its way. His current project, a series of long, complicated instrumentals organized under the title "The Key to All Mythologies," was so sprawling it sometimes sucked all the initiative out of him; there were days he couldn't even look at his instrument, let alone play it.

But today was going to be different. Gord stood in the room, concentrating on the dry-erase bulletin board, which had been organized into three columns: GIGS / PROJECTS / BAND NAMES. The last column was there because he had a knack for thinking up good band names, song titles, and concepts for shows. He tried as often as he could to write his ideas on Post-it notes and stick them up on the board. It was just a matter of time before he would hit upon some idea that would make him boatloads of money.

He stared intently at last week's ideas:

BANDS:
Sweet Lady Wine ('70s hippie rock)
4 Star Motel (any kind of band, any kind of genre)
Unisex Unitard
   (name for a small indie label, could have a great logo)
Clinical Trials (trash-punk, gotta be a girl on drums)
The Creams (retro-glam pop)
Frenulum (prog metal without the goth)
Forgotten Gyros (Mediterranean jazz fusion)

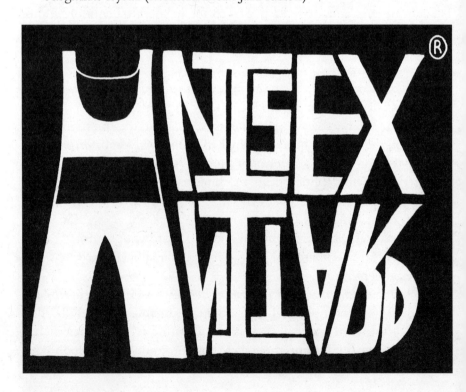

SONGS:
"All My Friends Are Horses"
    (some sort of hideous new country song.)

"Fuck. What the hell was that thing I thought of this morning?"

The microwave dinged. He ate his gyro with two cups of coffee at the kitchen table. Within about twenty minutes he started cramping up. Gord hobbled to the bathroom, and found the near-empty bottle of No Name Pink Liquid Antacid (hidden in the corner of the bathroom medicine case, behind the vitamins, and pregnancy tests, and creams, and jars, and whatnot Kathy had brought home with her last night). He took the bottle, and swigged it down watching more *Court TV*. It was always best to sit still and wait for the pain to pass.

When he woke up the second time, there was a soap opera on the television, which meant it was sometime after three o'clock. But his cramp was gone, so all Gord needed to do was go to the bathroom, and set about his work. The phone rang again, in the middle of his business, so again the machine took it. Gord remembered the phone had been ringing earlier in the day. After washing, he went back into the living room and listened to four new messages:

"Hello Kathy, dear, and hello Gord, it's your mother, I just wanted to say that if we are going to do any scrapbooking this weekend, we'd better switch it from Friday night to Saturday night because your father seems intent on taking me to some infernal boat show. Come for dinner if you're not too busy; tell Gord your father will be doing steaks, so he needn't be frightened of my cooking." (Beep.)

"Hey. Yeah, uh, I hope I got the right number. I'm Lars Henry, I'm looking for Gord Reed. Lou at the Corktown gave me your number 'cause our bassist just fucked off on us, and we got these two label guys coming down to see our show, right? Lou said you were good, and could play from charts, so I was wondering if you might be interested. It's like not a lot of money or anything, but we gotta get someone, right? Let me know, okay? (Beep.)

"Gord, honey, if you're there, pick up . . . if you're not, I hope to God you didn't walk home just to save money. We've talked about that. I don't want you falling asleep with sunstroke again. Not tonight anyway. You know what night it is. And I think I might have a little surprise for ya. Anyway, luv ya."(Beep.)

"Oh, shit, yeah, it's Lars Henry again, I just called like an hour ago. I don't think I left my number. Sorry man. Oh yeah, and the gig is soon, it's a one-hour set, and we do it at the Corktown on July 22. Plus we got a rehearsal tonight, and it'd be great if you could make that too. So call okay? Jesus, oh yeah, the number is 905-525 . . ."

Gord stopped the machine because he had no pen. He fished around in his pants for one, but then he remembered how didn't have one earlier in the morning. He knew who Lars Henry was; he sang for a band called Spliffylis, formerly the Fateless. They were heavy, fast, completely humourless, and really fucking good.

The Four New Messages: Christian a Capella quartet.

His head began to throb. Gord hadn't played a show in maybe a year, not since the last show he played with Maggots in the Meat, the funk-metal outfit that by now would have had its own major label deal if it weren't for the hissy fits of the lead guitarist. Spliffylis seemed like a much more stable entity. Who knows what kind of opportunities this might create.

"July 21. I don't even know when that is."

He walked into the bedroom, to Kathy's oak vanity set. Near the mirror there was a oval wooden box covered in black felt, where Kathy stored a set of expensive ballpoint and calligraphy pens (she often hand-wrote letters). Beside that was a miniature desk calendar. Gord sat down.

There weren't many times when it occurred to him how unlikely a couple he and Kathy really were, and had been for nearly five years now. Ever since the night she waited around for him after a gig. He never asked why someone like her would be spending time at sweaty hard rock shows. He never asked himself why mousy girls in wholesome clothes were such a turn-on. All that ever seemed to matter was that she didn't rag on him, and she was a real tiger in bed. So why ask questions?

He looked at the page of Kathy's desk calendar, and for the first time that day began to formulate an awareness that today was Wednesday, July 19. Wednesday. That's why Kathy sounded excited on the phone. Wednesday was *Navy Crime Unit* night on television. It was usually one of the two times each week they made love. That's why she wanted something good for supper.

"'Pussy Lingus.' Fuck me. That was it. That was totally it. That was the name."

He grabbed one of the good pens from the box. He thought of getting up to write and post his idea immediately on the dry-erase board, but was distracted by Kathy's desk calendar. For a moment, he sat and marvelled at the strange symbology she used on it, the incomprehensible shorthand:

						1
2	3 P due?	4 X	5 X	6 X	7 X	8 X
9 X	10 X	11 X	12 X	13 X	14 X	15 X
16 X	17 X	18 X	19 TEST!	20	21 Prnts.	22
23	24	25	26	27	28 $	29
30	31					

JULY

Then he realized something. If he took this gig with Spliffylis, he would have to bail on Kathy and *Navy Crime Unit* so he could make tonight's rehearsal. But it would also create an opportunity to duck out of Saturday dinner with her parents. Kathy would get sucky about it for sure, but this was a serious opportunity. Gord needed to be serious about this. Spliffylis was a dream band, the sort of outfit to which he could easily take "The Key to All Mythologies" when it was finished. The sort of band that would tour across the country for long periods of time, play big shows, maybe get somewhere.

His stomach gnarled up inside. A smoke would help right now.

He went to the phone machine, retrieved Lars Henry's number and immediately dialled.

"Yeah?"

"Hey, I'm trying to find Lars Henry."

"Yeah."

"It's Gord Reed."

"Oh, hey man. Cool. Thanks for getting back."

"No problem. What's up? You said your bass player fucked off on you?"

"Yeah, well, not really. Not for good. He's getting married on Saturday, so he's kind of, you know, tied up with that."

"No shit."

"Yeah, he's really pissed to miss the gig, but it's the only time these label guys could come out. So we just got to make it happen, you know."

"Huh. So you're not looking for a replacement guy, just someone for the night."

"Yeah, think you can help us out with that?"

"Yeah, I mean, man, I don't know, you know? I got these commitments I gotta sort out first. Is there money?"

"Uh, not really. We're on with three other bands and are splitting the door. I mean I can get you $50 for sure, but you know, not really tons more. Lou kinda said you might just be looking to get out and play, you know?"

"Huh."

"But you'd really be helping us out."

"Yeah, well, okay. Um, let me just see if I can squeeze out of some stuff, and I'll call you right back. If you find someone else in the meantime, that's cool. Otherwise let me see what I can do. I'll make some calls and call you back."

"Yeah?"

"Yeah. I'll call you once I find out for sure. Either way I'll call."

He hung up the phone. Instinctively he fished around in the breast pocket of his shirt, even though he knew he had smoked his last that morning. He then thought about using the twenty in his pants to buy some more No Name Pink Liquid Antacid, because his stomach was acting up again. He might have even been sweating. Something was wrong.

No Name Pink Liquid Antacid: Double NPLA. Power funk, maybe like ten guys in the band. Lead singer should be a rapper. Hot-looking backup singers.

Gord tried in his mind to piece it together. It had started out as such a good day, not like the others. There was all of this good energy. And now it was as if the day had split off into a variety of different strings, and he had to choose which one to follow. Or worse, it had become a kind of math puzzle, something you had to think very clearly about in order to resolve. And as he sat there, he felt the coming moments become more and more important, more critical. He clenched his abdomen.

In the refrigerator, Gord foraged for a cola and found one. He chose cola because the bubbles sometimes helped his stomach to calm down. Even though Kathy always insisted that peppermint tea was the answer.

He went to the home studio and looked at the dry-erase board. Nothing.

He went back to the couch and turned on the television. The only thing on was a woman's talk show. The topic today was "How to Raise Kids and Kick-Start Your Dream Career."

In less than two hours, Kathy would come toddling home. She would bound through the doors and begin to enthusiastically ferret out the details of his day. If he had nothing to say, she would still find a way to be supportive. Or she would segue and suggest that they make supper together, perhaps open a bottle of wine as they worked (although she hadn't been drinking that much these days). Then she would begin to tell him about her "surprise," whatever the hell that was.

There was no way he was going to sub for a band if the pay was shit and it had no promise of leading anywhere. What's the point? Why bother? Still, it would get him out of the house. And fifty bucks is fifty bucks. If he really had guts, he would tell Kathy about the rehearsal tonight, then go somewhere else, maybe the donut shop that sells the two-dollar beers. Get some space. Whatever, it seemed like an impossible decision to make, it seemed as if there was no satisfying answer.

Down the hall, near the door, a row of delicately framed photographs hung clustered together on the wall. Kathy's mother and father, Kathy graduating, Gord and Kathy in a rock club about a month after they met, Gord looking especially jowelly and uncomfortable in a tight suit at Kathy's sister's wedding. And Gord standing with the band he had formed in high school, Broken Ice, a moody black-and-white taken on the floor of an abandoned textile factory. The band name was his idea. It was his idea to have all of their faces buried by shadows.

The Daytime Ladies: all-girl band, must wear business appropriate clothing.

He belched, and then winced. He stared intently at the breasts of the curvy host of the talk show. The answer would come to him. It always did.

SMALL GAME HUNTER

(From Broken Pencil *#38)*

joel katelnikoff

A factory, Saskatoon, 4 P.M. Al forklifts a palette of melamine-coated particleboard onto the Big Saw. The saw cuts each sheet into five-and-a-half-inch strips, which Ryan and Flavius stack on conveyors. Chi feeds the strips through an edgebander, covering the rough edges in white plastic. Dean cuts the strips into lengths with his mitre saw, and Mike drills and dowels these into four-sided boxes. I stand at my station, waiting, staple gun in hand. It's powered by compressed air, which means, in layman's terms, that it can shoot fucking hard and fucking far.

In my peripheral vision, something moves. I turn and fire a dozen staples. After I catch my breath, I check my kill. A grasshopper, stuck to a stack of cardboard sheeting. One staple through its upper back leg and two through its thorax.

I chalk it up under "street cred" on my hip-hop resumé.

I hate every machine in this factory.

When I was in high school, I worked at a grocery store. For fifteen hours a week I was Super Bagger, watching cashiers scan cans, eating expired chips in the back room, and surviving after-hours produce fights. It seemed like a glamorous job when I was seventeen, but at twenty other dreams began to creep in, like making enough money to move out of my mom's house.

Laura helped me get a job in her dad's factory. She told me to wear steel-toed boots to the interview so the foreman could put me on the line right away. The factory was expanding so fast that they'd built a whole new bay just for the Big Saw, which is able to auto-cut strips all day, so long as someone is there to stack the pieces.

The expansion was a local success story. Reporters from STV and the *Star-Phoenix* took notes as Laura's mom christened the Big Saw with a bottle of champagne. Workers cheered, cameras flashed. A hired band played garage rock while the workers danced and drank free beer. I held Laura close, laughing to myself at the thought of a full-time wage.

I'm not laughing anymore. Mike hands me boxes and I staple bottoms onto them. These will become cabinet drawers after I screw on glides, allowing them to smoothly roll in and out.

Staple and screw.

Fuck this drawer. I stapled it too fast and the bottom is sticking out on one side. Now I can't put a glide on it. I could grind it down with a planer, but bashing the shit out of the whole drawer somehow seems more appropriate.

I pretend to know savate, a French martial art I've read about in comic books. I scream "Savate!" while putting my foot through it. I only do this when the drawers are flawed. Some days they all start looking flawed, and I yell, "Savate! Savate! Savate!"

Friday night, after work is done, I hop into my '82 Citation (the Kitty) and head up Thirty-third Street to California Subs, where Gnarly Wayne is cashing out. We drive back to his apartment with a stolen thirty-inch sub, smoke up, open a forty of whiskey, and watch old rap videos on tape.

"Soul Clap" by Showbiz and A.G. comes on. In the video, A.G. repeatedly explains that his initials stand for "A Giant," even though he is clearly only five-foot-three. "Yeah I'm a giant, that's what you'd better say / You don't believe it then yo—check my resumé." We choke and gag at the wonderful awfulness of the line. Wayne begins to draft his own version of A.G.'s resumé. "Name: A Giant. Occupation: Giant. Work experience: Pizza Hut, Giant."

When we were in high school, we dreamed of starting our own rap group, but didn't get further than choosing nicknames. DJ Gnarly Wayne never quite had enough money to buy turntables, so we gradually turned into armchair rappers, now laughing at the same videos we thought were cool ten years ago.

Monday, 6 A.M. I wake up and hop in the Kitty. I go in through the passenger door because the driver's side doesn't open. For awhile I would just jump in through the driver's window, but then I kicked the signal arm off and now the wipers won't stop. I hit Circle Drive and speed up. At eighty, the dashboard heaves in and out like something behind it is trying to kill me.

At work, I staple and screw.

During break, Roy pulls out his scrapbook and shows it around. Polaroids of women passed out on rubber sheets. Everybody in the break room is smoking cigarettes, except the guys who are broke until payday. Sam stuffs a tissue in his ear to sop up the perpetual stream of pus. Nobody knows why his ears leak, and nobody asks. As I sit and speculate, the supervisor says it's time to go back to our stations.

A bee floats by and I fire a quick shot at it. I've captured it alive against a wooden post, a spike neatly piercing each of its wings. I call the nearby guys to check it out, then I give the bee one more staple, point-blank, separating its head cleanly from its body.

I lean over my work table, stapling bottoms onto boxes, screwing glides onto boxes. I'm working in Laura's dad's shitty factory, and she's off at university. Every staple sends a pulse up my arm, travelling out through my shoulder.

At Gnarly Wayne's apartment, he tells me to sit down. "Have you ever heard of MP3.com? People record and upload their own music. I have to warn you, this is really awesome."

He presses a button and a MIDI keyboard demo starts to play. Then I hear the voice of a twelve-year-old named Prozac, talking into a cheap computer microphone, trying to rap. His weak lyrics and poor timing are best summed up by the phrase: "So for now you can listen to my crap / I might be white, but I can still do OK rap."

The musical phenomenon of "OK Rap" changes my life in four phases. First, I feel a sense of shame and disgust over how bad this music is. Prozac is an embarrassment to himself and to all of humanity. I instinctively want to put him out of his misery. As I cover my face in humiliation, Gnarly Wayne laughs like a maniac.

Second: While saw blades shred and clamps capture slabs of medium density fibreboard, OK Rap reaches into the sawdust-parched monotony of my job. Although I know I'm wasting my life in this factory, I hear echoes of Prozac and I can't help but smile.

Third: I start sending Prozac's URL to everyone I can trust. In doing this, I realize there's no turning back; I am abandoning myself to a process of spiritual decay that promises to reconfigure my entire state of being.

Fourth: "Hey Wayne, let's start our own rap group."

And so it is born: the Sons of Prozac. Our mission is to adopt Prozac's persona and parody his music so cruelly that the young man will commit suicide.

"Son of Prozac, the son of the master / You can fuck my mom, but I can fuck her faster."

Worst take equals best take. It's easy to fuck up and quit on a verse, but tough as hell to stumble and still keep going. If we get through it, we use it.

Ideally, Gnarly Wayne and I should be on at least three substances when recording. These are the necessary conditions that allow us to slur our speech, burst out laughing for no apparent reason, and perceive the air turning into water.

At the factory, I write lyrics on order sheets and drawer bottoms, eager to get back to the studio (a computer with a microphone plugged into it) so the Sons of Prozac can record more gold.

After we've recorded six or seven songs, all of which have received minimal attention on MP3.com, I manage to get tickets to an advance screening of *The Blair Witch Project*. The movie is eerily similar to OK Rap: menacing, fear-inspiring, and mind-ruining. That night, when I'm too afraid to turn the lights out, I call Gnarly Wayne and tell him my idea for a new song.

It doesn't take long to write "The Blair Witch Project." We just rip off old Ice-T lyrics and change them to reflect the movie, dropping dope lines like: "What would it sound like if a muthafucka took a laser beam and shot that shit right through a Blair Witch's muthafuckin skull?"

Unsurprisingly, our song called "The Blair Witch Project" shoots up the MP3.com charts when the film tops the box office. For a moment we even surpass the popularity of Ice-T, whose single "Don't Hate the Playa" is three spots below us. So I decide to drop him an email.

> Dear Ice-T,
>
> You should peep our song, "The Blair Witch Project." We're better than you on MP3.com, and we jacked you for your lyrics.
>
> Don't hate the playa hate the game,
>
> Sons of Prozac.

In an intoxicated dreamstate, I imagine hearing the doorbell ring. Ice-T is standing there. He says, "I heard you've been biting my rhymes, motherfucker," pulls out a gun, and levels it at my head. But when he squeezes the trigger, it's a trick gun that turns into a gold microphone. Ice-T wants to rap with me!

The next day I check the Sons of Prozac email.

> Sons of Prozac,
>
> I'm putting together a show in Calgary. A lot of people like your music. Come and rap. I'll take care of your travel and set you up with a place to stay.
>
> Amanda

And just like that, Gnarly Wayne and I have made it. We are actual rap stars, both on the Internet and in reality.

I call him up. "Hey Wayne, we've got a show."

"Oh yeah, what kind of show?"

"The SoP's going to play in Calgary in January."

"Calgary, that's fucked. Why can't they come here to see us, fuckin' lazy motherfuckers."

"Listen. This is our chance. We've made it."

"That is the sound of a non-drunken person. And I hate that. Sons of Prozac is a joke group. We're just pretending to be a twelve-year-old. We just say stupid stuff."

"But people like it in Calgary. I have no idea why, but they like it. Lots of them, I think."

"That's the dumbest shit I've ever heard."

"But Wayne. This is our chance to make a name for ourselves like we always wanted to do in high school, when you were going to buy turntables, but never did. It's like we get a chance to go back in time and change our entire lives. Just think about it. It's not until January."

Three days before the show, I'm sitting on a bus to Calgary. I've booked a couple of sick days at the factory so I can head there early. I'm listening to MC Ren on headphones: "I don't give a fuck if niggas is fightin in the crowd / I only got one concern—that's my vocals pumpin' loud."

I would have taken the Kitty, if I didn't mind driving on the highway with a bent axle. I also could have gotten a ride with Wayne, but he won't be arriving until the night of the show. I want to get to Calgary early, meet the fans, and check out the venue beforehand.

I look out the window and feel the burden of Saskatoon becoming distant. Fence posts speed by so fast that I can barely see them. Trees in the fields fall back slowly, one at a time. The horizon is crisp, but I cannot perceive its movement at all.

Now I'm listening to Pachelbel's Canon in D. Gnarly Wayne and I have agreed to start our show by playing a beautifully orchestrated rendition of it as we walk across the stage, gazing reverently down at every audience member. And then, in one quick and brutal attack, we'll change the beat, assaulting them with sour MIDIs, shameful lyrics, and obscene acts of self-fondling. Calgary is about to learn the true meaning of OK Rap.

The sun is starting to set. I move forward in space and time. I watch the shadows lengthen until there are no shadows.

The Greyhound station is at least twice as big as the one in Saskatoon. Amanda is waiting inside. She's sent me pictures of herself over the Internet, but this is the first time I've seen her in three dimensions. She's about five feet tall and cute, with short-trimmed bangs and arms covered in simple plastic bracelets. She asks, "How was the ride?"

"Seven hours. Long and tiring." I feel alien, exhausted, too stupid to think of anything better to say. Amanda smiles like it doesn't matter.

"Well, you're here now," she says, putting her arms around me. I hug her back.

"Do you want to stop at Taco Bell on the way home?"

"I've never been to one. In Saskatoon, we only have Taco Time."

"Really? Well, you're in for a treat. I'll show you what to order."

She does, and it's great. I mean, not as good as Taco Time, but still fucking good. She talks about the bands she likes, and I talk about the bands I like. I drink Pepsi and she drinks Dr Pepper. It's almost flirtatious, the way she looks up at me as she sips at the straw. After we finish eating, we head back to her place, into the basement.

"Shh. We need to be quiet. My parents are sleeping."

"Yeah?"

"Yeah, and if they ask, you're nineteen. This is my room here, and you can stay in my brother's room, here. He's out of town right now."

Her brother's room is palatial. It's like three or four rooms put together, easily as big as my mom's living room and kitchen. There's a king-sized bed, couches, coffee tables, and a huge entertainment system. I couldn't have asked for a better place to stay.

She folds the couch out and gives me some bedding before heading to her own room. I have an exceptionally good sleep, with utopian visions of Ice-T, Eazy-E, and Schoolly D all pointing gold microphones at me.

The next day, Amanda shows me around her house, introducing me to her mom, grandma, and little sister. She shows me the Au Claire Market and Stephen Avenue, the IMAX theatre, sculptures, foods imported from all over the world, skyscrapers, streetcars, and hobos who say "weed" as we walk by. The Calgary Tower too, and so many other things.

In the evening, some of her friends come over to talk about zines, drums, and ska guitarists. I guess these are the fans I've heard about, but I'm not receiving the type of adulation I expected. Are they aware of the Sons of Prozac at all, or only shitty groups I've never heard of like Reel Big Fish and Gob?

I glance at Amanda and roll my eyes. She smiles like it's the most charming joke of all time. After they go, we hang out in her bedroom and watch *Dead Alive*.

She explains, "This is the goriest movie in the history of cinema."

In the morning, I'm startled to wake up beside her, sleeping peacefully above the covers.

The concert is spread out over two nights, with Sons of Prozac slated to close the show on the second night. We'll be playing right after Moneen at 2 A.M. Saturday. It seems so close now, and Gnarly Wayne and I haven't even discussed what to do for our stage show, aside from Canon in D.

The first night, I investigate our venue: the cement basement of a small hall. There's no stage—just a swarm of punk teens crowded around the musicians. Sound bounces off solid walls. January air pours in. I can see my breath.

Amanda emerges from the black-jacketed mob. I want to ask her why this place is so cold and loud, and why there's no stage. She walks away, yelling, "I've got shit to take care of!"

A girl is throwing fists at random people. Two big guys drag her out screaming. The bathroom is crammed with hoodlums and I've needed to piss for hours. By the time the night is over, I'm practically too numb to realize it.

The next morning, Amanda wakes me up. I stumble around her brother's bedroom for a few minutes, then take a long shower. I do everything as slowly as possible, hoping that it will buy some extra time before the show tonight. When I come upstairs, Amanda's mom has prepared the best breakfast I've ever seen: eggs, toast, sausage, and name-brand orange juice.

Amanda and her sister spike my hair. "You look better this way," they tell me. "Better for the show." I put my toque on to cover it up. For lunch we have Chinese food, and when I get sick Amanda drives me to the drugstore for antacid.

I can feel tonight's show approaching. I'm still cold and my blood isn't circulating. I realize now that I'm totally out of my element here, and I can only hope that I'll feel better when Gnarly Wayne shows up.

At eight o'clock, he pulls into the parking lot of the hall. Bzarhands and Al are with him. I don't even know these guys, but it's a relief to see them. I double-check with Amanda that Sons of Prozac is the last act, then we head to the café across the street to order tea and burgers.

I sigh, "So, we're going to do a show!"

"I guess so!" Gnarly Wayne is working on his burger.

"The venue kinda sucks though."

"Whatever."

We sit around, riffing about the fact that Calgary has a freeway called Deerfoot Trail. We decide that "Deerfoot Trail" is, in fact, an inappropriate name for a freeway. What we talk about instead of the show is excruciating, and the burgers are dry. Still, I try to stretch it out as long as possible. I chew slowly, sip tea, and chain-smoke cigarettes.

When I can't think of any more reasons for staying, we head back across the street, into the hall. This is when Wayne sees the venue for the first time. "Whoa. I thought we were going to have a stage. I didn't know we were going to have to stand in the middle of a bunch of fucking riff-raff."

I say, "Yeah man, don't worry about it," even though I'm worried about it too. Grindcore skinheads smash their hands into drums, and guitar strings, and each other.

"Well, I have no interest listening to this bullshit music," Wayne says. We head out, walk around the parking lot, and sit in the car with the heater turned on. We play our CD of instrumentals and rap along with them. From the back seat, Bzarhands and Al laugh and applaud. We slip up on half of the lines.

Halfway through the CD, Amanda comes out to the car. "Hey, can you guys do your thing right now? Instead of after Moneen?"

It's only ten o'clock. Gnarly Wayne and I look at each other. We get out of the car, walk to the building, through the crowd, to the front of the room.

I hand Amanda our CD and ask her where to find the mics. "Wait," she says. "You didn't tell me you needed a CD player."

"Our music is all recorded. We need a CD player to play it."

She says to me, "Oh god." Then she motions to the crowd and asks, "Does anyone have a Discman?" Nobody does.

Amanda sets up the next act and leads me and Wayne to the parking lot. We speed back to her house, a thirty-minute ride each way.

"I hope those guys have more than an hour of material, or we're going to come back to an empty hall."

When we get back with the CD player, the band is still going and the next group is setting up. So again, Amanda adjusts the schedule, with Sons of Prozac set to close the show.

Gnarly Wayne and I spend hours outside, listening to echoes of the music. My fingers jitter as I light a fresh cigarette off the last. I haven't brought any marijuana with me. Wayne hasn't brought any alcohol. We are in no condition to perform OK Rap. We've never even recorded in such a state. The air has not turned into water, not even close.

Bzarhands and I go in at 2 A.M. to watch Moneen. "The Passing of America" is undeniably moving. The lyrics are passionate, sincere, meaningful. The crowd is in love with them, the way they hold back nothing of themselves. These are very good, very serious musicians.

When they finish their set, the crowd begins to drift up from the basement, into the parking lot, back to their homes. Amanda asks if we still want to play. I head to the car to talk to Gnarly Wayne, who is asleep, or pretending to be.

"You want to go on?"

He sighs, he groans. "If you really want to play this show, I'll do it. If you really want to."

The car ride back to Amanda's is silent. When we're in the basement, she says, "You guys can sleep here." She puts mats and blankets on her bedroom floor, accommodating all of them. She says goodnight, closes the door, and leads me to her brother's room.

I'm lying on the pull-out couch, covered with a blanket, shivering even more than last night. I know that I ruined Amanda's show. Ideally, I'd like to apologize, but I'm afraid I'll start crying. She grabs a videotape and puts it in the VCR.

"Do you want to watch a movie?"

I say nothing.

She puts on *The Rocky Horror Picture Show*.

"This is my brother's. He watches weird stuff." Amanda dims the lights and joins me under the covers.

She runs her small hand over my chest. My stomach is aching. My fingers and toes aren't getting warm. I want to vomit. She unfastens the button on my jeans. Funny, I'm wearing jeans in bed. She pulls at the zipper. She slides her head down under the blanket.

I fucked up Amanda's show. I have failed, I have failed, I have failed. I am pitiful. And the pleasure intensifies the sorrow. My dreams amount to nothing. Anguish. It feels good. Oh yes, good. And here I am inside Amanda's mouth. Fuck, fuck, fucking good, fucking garbage. Fuck, I hate myself, fucking loser, fucking scum.

Amanda spits semen onto my stomach. "What the fuck? Why didn't you tell me you were going to come?" I'm so ashamed that I don't know how to respond. She points me to the bathroom with my jeans around my knees.

The next morning, Gnarly Wayne asks if I'm ready to leave. I don't worry about formality or niceties. I don't even ask Amanda for reimbursement for the bus money. We just go.

On the drive home, we listen to hardcore gangsta rap. Bzarhands sits in the front, even though I'm usually auto-shotgun in Wayne's car. In Drumheller we stop at A&W and eat in silence. I have a chicken burger. My stomach is too weak for ground beef. When we're done eating, I sit in the back again. I'm on my way home.

Monday, Saskatoon, 6 A.M. I'm stapling bottoms onto drawers. Mike has built stacks and stacks while I've been gone, and they're all waiting for me. I shoot staples into boxes. The compressed air gasps with every touch of the trigger. I screw glides onto boxes. Spasms shoot through the muscles in my back and stomach. I move fast, struggling to catch up.

Ryan and Flavius are making a commotion, running around. I keep my head down and focus on the task. There will be time for goofing off Wednesday or Thursday, but not today. I fasten bottoms to drawers so quickly that when I'm out of staples I don't notice for six or seven shots. I attach glides so fast I'm sure that by the end of the day a screw will slip and stab me in the hand.

The guys at the Big Saw are making a lot of noise now. "Hey, Joel, you've got to check this out!" I finish a drawer and set down my tool. As I walk towards the crowd, Flavius and Ryan are both holding staple guns. They take turns calmly firing into a metal wastepaper basket. The guys are laughing. Something in the basket is scuffling around, trying to get out.

SOME OF THIS IS TRUE

(From Broken Pencil *#42)*

janette platana

When we came out of the evening and into the Kinsmen Field House, people were still mostly in their seats. I wanted to be right in front, so I dragged the girl I was with down the aisle. It was as though we were a bathtub plug that had just been pulled: I looked behind, and everyone was draining towards us, carrying us to the edge of the stage.

Big bass notes rolled through like a hearse.

The hall went black suddenly, then the lights came up fast on treble chord chops.

Twelve.

There. Feet planted together, right leg jerking with each chop like he's trying to stomp change out of a hole in his pocket. White shoes, white jeans, black cowboy shirt with the sleeves cut off, white star in a red circle on the black T-shirt underneath.

I nail the first line, right on cue, sing along so that I'm part of the band.

The girl I'm with thrusts her mouth to my ear and screams, "Oh my God, I want to fuck him."

I'm thinking, "I want to *be* him."

The girl next to me got me the ticket to this show. I gave her eleven bucks. She offered the ticket to my cousin, who is an asshole, but he didn't want it. She's seen him pick me up after work and he's given her a ride home a couple times. He flirts like he's got an affliction: "Anything that squats to pee," he tells me, and then he looks at me like I'm going to be next.

I back off for the next line, then come back in on time, every time.

Yesterday, the girl next to me, Paula, came into the tube room. We both work at the Sears Catalogue Warehouse in Regina. My summer job is to stand in front of a rack of pneumatic tubes, open the ones that are coughed into the trough, pop the top, read the order, stuff the order back into the tube; reposition it, lid-first, at the open mouth of the appropriate screaming vacuum that will redirect the order to shoes, housewares, linens, small appliances, ladies clothes, infants', toys, children's, men's, and every other fucking thing. It's hot, it's noisy, it's mindless, it pays more than minimum, and it's mine because my mom used to work in Customer Service (Complaints) before she went on Disability. You have to know someone to work here, even for a summer job.

At the end of yesterday's shift, Paula followed me out to the parking lot. Paula is heavy and tall, narrow and mannish in the hips but with big breasts, so my cousin has his eyes on them when he says to me, "Sit in the back."

He looks at her shirtfront, she smiles, he turns the music up loud. "My blood runs cold! My memory has just been sold! My angel is a cennerfold! My angel is a cennerfold!"

Paula shouts at my cousin. I see her happy mouth moving, but because of the music I can't hear her until my cousin turns off the radio, so then there's the one of those moments when the person is accidentally yelling.

"Tomorrow night in Edmonton!" she suddenly yells. Then, more normal, "Do you wanna go?"

My cousin frowns. "I don't do that punk shit," he says.

"I'll go," I yelp from the back seat.

Paula looks confused, but says, "Okay. We have to get the 9:30 bus," and looks out the passenger side window. My cousin turns the music way up again as we pull out onto Albert Street.

When we get to our house, my mom's house, my cousin parks so close to the garage door that I have to get out and walk around back of the car to get to the front door. My cousin is already opening his door and getting out, and he meets me behind the car. Grabbing me above the elbows, he says, "Gotcha!" like it's a game and he's tickling me or something. He gets his face in close and hisses, "What do you think you're up to?" He pulls his arms in around me fast so my feet leave the ground and my breath leaves my lungs in an ugly grunt. "Your fucking problem," he says, "is you're always trying to be different." Drop. "Don't even think of fucking going."

But I do.

Next morning, at the start of my 7:00 shift, I go to my boss and say, "I've got to leave at nine for a doctor's appointment."

"No way, José," my boss says, not raising his head. His scalp and his hair are the same colour. "You change your shift twenty-four hours in advance. You know that. Besides," he says, now looking at me over the tops of his glasses, keeping his shiny chins pressed into his neck, "Paula from Mail already used that excuse." He stares at my head for a long while, until I unclip my ID badge from my shirt, put it on the counter beside his fat hand, and say, "Alright. I quit." He frowns deeper in surprise, but only snorts as I leave.

By 9:20, I'm in a Greyhound seat beside Paula. She has a mickey of Southern Comfort. She wants to talk about my cousin. The ride is ten and a half hours long. "What's he like?"

"A jerk," I say. "Exactly like a jerk. He listens to shitty music, and drinks beer, and doesn't smoke dope."

"I like his car," she says.

"Uh huh." It's my mom's car, but I don't tell her.

"We went driving around last night," she offers, "after we dropped you off."

"Yeah?"

"Yeah. We drove around for a while, and drank some beer at Wascana Park." She giggles. "After I gave him a blow job."

I already know this.

"Why'd you do that to your head? To your hair?" Paula says.

"I don't know. Felt like it."

"Your cousin is really cool," she says.

I say, "He doesn't like punk rock."

"Neither do I," she says.

"Why'd you buy tickets?" I ask.

"I didn't." My heart skips a beat. "I stole them from my sister. This morning, after your cousin dropped me off. She's going to shit."

I hate this girl. I feel sorry for her sister. But I'm glad I'm going.

"So … let's get drunk!" she says.

"No thanks," I say, turning my head and pushing it down into the chair back, shutting my eyes.

The bass line starts to roll up the song, and a rooster crows three times.

Last night, after my cousin and Paula left to go driving around, I sat with Mom in the living room and watched *Love Boat* on TV. Then I watched *M*A*S*H*. My mom didn't wake up, or come up, or whatever it's called when I kissed her forehead, and checked her IV, and everything. We call it the living room even though she is dying in it, and the hospital bed doesn't leave room for a couch or anything. I sat on a kitchen chair beside the bed, ate some soup, held her hand, put Vaseline on her lips once. I turned her onto her other side, making sure her arm wasn't stuck underneath.

A guitar string hammers Morse code short short short long long long short short short; short short short long long long short short short, just like on the record. Ess oh ess. Ess oh ess.

My mom's hair never did grow back in after the last time. When she was allowed to come home, I don't think anyone expected her to last more than a few weeks. My cousin was still working at his job when he moved in to help out. Now, whenever the hospice nurse comes, she always asks if we want to move my mom into palliative. I always say no and my cousin always says no, but for different reasons.

I hold my mom's hand, listen to her breathing and mine, and think to myself, "What a knob. It's not about going. It's about coming back."

Then it's dark again. The spy-movie guitar riff and a single spot that picks him out. All the lights come on and as the song kicks in he slips the strap over his head and with a straight-arm throw sends the guitar into the dark behind himself, without even looking. A roadie, waiting in the dark, catches it. He grabs the mike, growls, "Driiiiiiive," like it's a threat. Boom boom. "Drive." Boom boom.

When I hear my cousin come in the back door, I turn the TV up really loud. Even so, I can hear my cousin's low voice, and then a higher laughing voice reply. After a while, I go down the dark hallway towards the bathroom. I have to pass my cousin's room, which used to be my mom's, and then mine, and then the bathroom is across from the kitchen, at the back.

The door to my cousin's room is open. They're not in there. I'm walking down the dark hallway. The light from the TV in the living room flickers on the walls so that it's all underwater blue. Everything feels really slow as I get closer to my room. The door is open, and what I see first are the soles of Paula's dirty feet. Her toes are bent under, her heels pointing towards the ceiling, and they rock slightly. Her bum is sort of covered by the short skirt she is wearing, but she has no shirt on, and I can see her breasts swing and then slap, swing and then slap, against my cousin's knees. She's got her arms up on the bed, and he's got her head held down.

My cousin's eyes are aimed right at me, so I stop, and figure out too late that he isn't seeing me. Then he is. His eyes fasten onto me.

Joe Strummer knee-drops to the edge of the stage, falls forward, and grinds the side of his face into the floor, bellows into the mike he's holding down so it will stay still and listen. Already hoarse three songs into the set, voice raw with something more than half grief, he tells it: "My baby drove up in a brand new Cadillaaaac! Yes she did!"

Beside me, Paula is still screaming. "I wanna fuck him! I wanna fuck him!"

"Why don't you just fuck everyone then, you fucking hosebag!" I bawl as loud as I can, hurting my throat. It's like screaming underwater. She smiles big. Mouths back, "Right on!" and gives me two thumbs up, nodding meaningfully with her eyebrows raised, waggling her thumbs in enthusiastic agreement, and I realize she hasn't heard me at all. Then she turns back to the stage. We're both sweaty: where her bare arm slips against mine, it's slick.

I know my cousin sees me because he rams his arms into the mattress of my bed, his hands press onto my old pink towel bedspread, and he locks his elbows. He is pumping so fast, fucking Paula in the face is what he's doing, and he's doing it so fast that his chin points at me as if he is nodding and nodding and nodding, agreeing to something I don't want to know what. Or he is pointing at me, at me, at me: you're next.

I try to stop looking, and I try to make my feet move. For some reason I want to go back to my mom, but when my feet move, they keep taking me down the hall to the bathroom. I go in and lock the door, slide down to the floor with my back against it, sit on the cold tile until it's over.

I sit there on the bathroom floor for a long time. I run a bath, but I don't get in it. I wonder if my mom is okay.

After I figure they've gone, I open the bathroom door, peer out. The hallway is dark. It's quiet. They—he—must have turned the TV off.

And when I get to the living room, I find out why it's so quiet. My mom's not breathing.

Joe Strummer is crawling around on his hands and knees, circling the mike that lies helpless on the stage. He puts his mouth close, so close his lips touch it. "Baby baby won't you hear my plea?" I feel like crying too.

For a long time I sit in the dark living room. She hasn't been on painkillers for a long time. There are none in the house as far as I know. Her IV is still in place. Her face looks calm. I bolt the front door and the back door from the inside, hoping that bastard will stay out all night with Paula. I get into my mom's hospital bed with her, sleep there all night.

In the morning, the house is cold, my mom is cold, and I feel like I'm never going to warm up. Except for me and her, the house is empty. I know she can't feel it, but I tuck the blankets close in around her arms and legs and feet, the bones, bone-thin.

In the bathroom, I use scissors first to get my hair short all over, then use a razor to get down to the skin on the sides. It takes a while, but I get it done eventually. From some angles, it makes me look more like my mom. When I leave the house, it's still early enough to make it to work on time, even though I have to walk

He stays low on the stage. I can almost touch his mohawk curls. His left arm is jackknifed up, choking the mike stand. We are so close, when he whips himself back up to standing; the sweat from his face and hair splashes my fingertips.

He leaps for the mike. "She ain't coming back!"

Squeezed in beside me, Paula seems to sober up enough to notice where we are, and starts to dance up and down, or is danced by the press of the crowd around her.

"She ain't coming back!"

I'm bobbing my head so hard my neck hurts. I wish I could raise myself up a little higher so Joe could see my Brigade Rosse shirt. I am happy.

"She ain't never coming back!"

I know I am not Joe Strummer. He is the frontman of the only band that matters, and I am a teenage girl from Saskatchewan.

Feedback cuts above our heads in the Kinsmen Field House like a bullwhip, and lasts as long as the pain of that might.

Packed tight on the floor, the stage edge cuts under my arms as I reach. Joe Strummer turns his head as though to listen to something, mouths "fuck" to a roadie, or to Mick, or who? Nods at what he hears, nods at Mick, at the drummer, and then at Paul, who is all long legs, biceps, black leather and bass.

The drummer calls, "One two three four!" Drums and bass crash into each other. The drummer plays like he's sprinting on the spot.

The pressure of the crowd behind us is a live, surging thing. I have to push back. I use my elbows, don't say anything, push again, say, "Hey!"

Instead of more room, I suddenly have less. I am vised between bodies that piston up and down, squeezing me tighter with each pulse. Paula is now somehow five or six people away from me, and, unlikely as it is, this makes me feel scared. I reach my hand out to her. She's yelling straight up into the air. My breath is squeezed from me. I feel my lungs deflate. I can't even yell. My arms are still on the stage, but my vision is going funny.

Joe wails. The guitar keeps lashing feedback. "Hey, hey," cries Joe, then, clang buzz feedback squeal. The music grinds to a halt. "Iss a fucking nuthouse, innit? Stop the show. Turn it off. Aw Chris'."

I think the music has stopped, but I could be going unconscious, or going into a dying dream, because Joe Strummer and a roadie each have one of my arms, and are scraping me over the edge of the stage, my ribs a xylophone, my studded belt very hard into me catches, and for a split moment I am stuck. Then scrape of metal fly and thigh, and my legs don't bend that way, but my ankles and shoe tops scrape over and I am beached onstage.

I try to stumble up, get my feet and knees under me, and a hand is on my arm above the elbow. I reach up, grip. I have hold of Joe Strummer's arm when I look up. He looks right into my eyes and becomes utterly still. Doesn't smile, just looks.

His eyes are narrowed at the corners, smiling there only, clear. His mouth is opened slightly, jaw relaxed, and I can see the tip of his tongue.

He is busy, that's all. Saving people, I think.

Then he smiles with his mouth. Topper counts in "Clampdown" again. The ones who have been hauled to safety onto the stage, stranded punks like me, start to dance, heads banging to the drums and bass, washed by feedback.

Joe Strummer smiles maybe at the white star on my red shirt, at my white peg-leg jeans, at my hair, I don't know what. He pulls me to standing, puts one hand on either side of my head where the skin is still smooth from last night, draws my forehead to his so they rest together, keeps his hands on the sides of my head and shrugs his shoulders so I know to put my hands on his head. I wonder what it must look like from the audience, what we look like with our foreheads together and our mohawks touching. I let my thumb and finger trace the outside edge of his ear from the strangely pointed tip down to the lobe. The subsonic growl rhyme that should come next in the song doesn't, because Joe Strummer is whispering instead, whispering and whispering to me only, so that his breath dries the sweat from our skin. He rolls his forehead against mine, and whispers and breathes, and what he says is so low that I know it will take me a long time after to figure it out, the words he pours off the tip of his tongue and into my ear.

For a moment, he lets his cheek rest in my open palm. Then everything drops out.

Kick snare kick snare kick snare kick snare kick snare kick snare kick snare kick.

Joe's hands let go, and he lunges to the mike. "What are you gonna do now?"

It will probably take years for me to untangle it, his breath a web and the words he whispers, one of which was desire, caught in it. But I do know the thing to do is let my lungs fill with air, and it feels like the first breath I've drawn in twenty-four hours. So I draw another breath. And another. And another.

(NEVER) FADE AWAY

(From Broken Pencil #8)

federico barahona

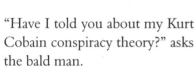

"Have I told you about my Kurt Cobain conspiracy theory?" asks the bald man.

"What?" I ask.

"It was a duck-hunting accident," he answers. "It was a duck-hunting accident, and the media, along with Time Warner, made up this fantastical suicide story to sell CDs. I think Kurt Cobain really meant to go duck hunting the morning he died, so he sat down at home to clean up his rifle, and then boom!"

"That's a good way to put it, I guess."

"So the next thing you know, all the big papers, TV, radio, you name it, are all in on it, getting a piece of the action, of course, and making millions."

"But what about the suicide note?" I ask.

"Fabricated."

"Courtney Love?"

"She wrote the note."

"Courtney?"

"Think about it: nobody ever saw the note besides Courtney. Where would she be if it wasn't for the suicide thing? It's perfect. She's in on it."

"MTV?"

"Yep. They wanted to sell the Unplugged video more than anyone."

"CNN?"

"They bought Time Warner, and Time Warner is the mastermind behind this whole thing, so obviously they are in on it. I hear Oliver

Stone is planning to make a movie about it. He wants Brad Pitt to star as Kurt Cobain."

"Who's going to be Courtney Love?"

"He wants Drew Barrymore, but if he can't get her, he'll go with Madonna. If he can't get her, he'll just go with Courtney Love."

"What if he doesn't get any of them?"

"Then I guess he'll just go with some unknown blond, or a stripper, or he'll just never show her, so it looks like she's always in the next room."

"Oh."

It's the Commodore, you think, but you're not sure. It could also be the Courtney Love lookalikes, or the girl from Cub—you had to say hello to her, you know, just to make it look like you actually know the rich and famous, but you know that you really don't. You are almost certain, however, that the girl from Cub is not rich. She might be famous, but she's not rich. So you're not even sure that your strategy is going to work tonight. Sometimes you get this urge to prove to yourself that you're not so insignificant, and you guess that saying hello to famous people gives you the impression that you are not. But it doesn't always work.

"I'm writing a feature on Kurt Cobain," I say, "how he spoke for an entire generation, but nobody could understand what the hell he was saying."

"You're kidding."

"I'm serious."

"Give it up!"

"What?"

"Why don't you just give it up? Just let him rest."

"I know someone who went as Kurt Cobain for Halloween," I say.

"Oh God."

"She walked around telling people that she was Kurt Cobain's ghost, and how he was sorry that he shot himself because now that Courtney Love bitch is doing it with Billy Joel, and a bunch of other people, and some dogs too, and she's got all the money, and now Kurt is all poor, but he's happy that at least his ghost got to live in Seattle forever—Kurt loved Puget Sound, you know."

"Your friend should go see a shrink."

"No, she shouldn't. It's somebody's way to deal with his death, say goodbye."

"Excuse me," says the big, muscular bouncer, tapping you on the shoulder. "The ladies behind you can't see because you're in the way." You turn around and see three teenage girls who smile at you. You smile back, and then move away. The big, muscular bouncer smiles at you, and pats you on the back.

Then you start to wonder how it is that you ended up feeling this worthless.

"I'm writing a Kurt Cobain feature for *Esquire* magazine."

"Oh," answers the man with the funky goatee who says he had to move from the small town where he grew up because he wanted to find his dream.

"You're not into it, huh?"

"Well, let me put it to you this way: the morning that he died, I woke up, you know, got shaved, got dressed, and then I went downstairs. My sister, who's a little younger than me, you know, she was doing aerobics—she does aerobics every morning, but anyway. I go downstairs, and my sister's doing her aerobics, so she's jumping around, and I go to her, 'Hey, how you doin' sis,' and she's like, 'Oh, that guy from Pearl Jam just blew his head off or something.'"

So this is Courtney Love, you think.

You'd like to think of it as a dress, but it's really a black slip. You know it doesn't really matter, and it's really sort of irrelevant, but you can't help it. Lately all you seem to do is concentrate on the things you know are irrelevant. It's a way to escape, you think to yourself, and that way you get drained by the real issues—you're getting old, you missed your chance to make your mark, you're skiing.

So down the hill you go, your nostrils lead the way as you try to find a way out. You are trying, once more, to ski your way out of this situation. You wanted to be different, but somehow you got lost. You started to dream about guns and suicide. And you started to write about angst and escaping. Yet you knew there was no escape.

SOME DEAD GUYS

(From Broken Pencil #10)

dave hazzan

In 1905, a wave of pogroms spread across the Russian Pale and Abrahim Herzel escaped across Siberia to Japan, where he signed on a freighter to British Columbia and learned to speak Cree, and became a link from the Native Peoples to the authorities in Ottawa, and saved several nations from extinction. Peter Moore was found frozen in the ice on Baffin Island, in his belly the remnants of the other members of the Franklin expedition. At Vimy, Chris Tpeswich was shot. Gilles Lescarbeau spent his days riding the CPR from Halifax to Vancouver and back again, year after year, as the Great Depression continued into its third, fourth, fifth years, and in Regina he was shot in the stomach by the Mounties. At Dieppe, the Allied ships circled the English Channel just out of German Artillery range while the Canadian Infantry stood under the bluff. Then Peter Biscombe took a run for the channel, started swimming across, and a quarter of the way to the ships he turned around, and landed back at the beach, and said that it was too cold. Now he's dead.

CONTRIBUTORS

Sandra Alland is a Scottish-Canadian writer, multimedia artist, performer and activist. She's currently an artist in residence at the Glasgow Museum of Modern Art and Trongate 103. Recently, Edinburgh's Forest Publications published her first chapbook of short fiction, *Here's To Wang*. Sandra has published four other chapbooks and two books of poetry: *Proof of a Tongue* (McGilligan, 2004) and *Blissful Times* (BookThug, 2007). She performs regularly around the UK with the poetry-music-weirdness-fusion band, Zorras. www.blissfultimes.ca

Charlie Anders blogs about science fiction and futurism at io9.com. She's the author of *Choir Boy* and the co-editor of *She's Such A Geek: Women Write About Science, Technology & Other Nerdy Stuff*. Her writing appears in the *McSweeney's Joke Book Of Book Jokes*, *Sex For America*, *ZYZZYVA*, *Pindeldyboz*, *Mother Jones*, the *Wall Street Journal*, *Salon.com*, and many other places. She organizes the award-winning Writers With Drinks reading series, and co-founded *other* magazine.

Federico Barahona lives and works in Vancouver. He is currently completing an MFA in creative writing at the University of British Columbia. He is writing a novel.

Robert Benvie is a writer and musician from Halifax, currently based in Toronto. He is the author of the novel *Safety of War* (Coach House Books, 2004), and is currently rewriting a second novel-in-progress to include more references to Shannon Hoon.

Geoffrey Brown is the author of *Notice* (Gutter Press, 1999) and *Self-Titled* (Coach House Books, 2004).

Grant Buday's story "The Curve of the Earth" won the 2006 *Fiddlehead* Fiction Prize and was selected for the *Journey Prize Anthology*. His story "Marry Me" will be included in the 2009 *Best Canadian Stories* (Oberon Press). He is the author of the novels *White Lung* (Anvil Press, 1999), *A Sack of Teeth* (Raincoast Books, 2002), and *Rootbound* (ECW Press, 2006). His new novel, *Dragonflies*, will be published by Biblioasis. He lives on Mayne Island, British Columbia.

David Burke lives and works in Windsor, Ontario, and was recently published in the *Puritan*, *Front&Centre*, *PRECIPICe*, *Carousel*, *Kiss Machine*, the *Windsor Review*, and *Now*. His story, "Coming Down" was translated into Portuguese and will appear in the next volume of *TransLit*, a journal of comparative literature. He writes stories, novels, and screenplays, and learned to smoke at a very young age.

Josh Byer is a wonderful author and a mediocre gold prospector. He pens fiction and gonzo journalism for *Broken Pencil*, the Canadian University Press, the *Capilano Courier*, *Crank Magazine*, the *Denver Syntax*, *Forget Magazine*, the *Harrow*, McClelland & Stewart, the *Ottawa Citizen*, *Southam News*, the *Surface* (U.K.), *Terminal City*, *Thirst Magazine*, *Trip Magazine*, and Victory Square Publications. Recent awards include a 2005 Journey Prize nomination, a 2006 Praxis Story Editor Internship, and a 2007 writing grant from the Canada Council for the Arts. Josh Byer is now hungry. Josh Byer should stop referring to himself in the third person and make himself a sandwich.

Julia Campbell-Such has published short fiction and poetry in *OnSpec*, *Flushed* and *Kalliope*, as well as *Broken Pencil*. She is also co-founder and fiction editor of *SNAFU Anthology*, and currently in the final throws of a master's degree in Religious Studies at Concordia University in Montreal. Julia specializes in people who believe the world is about to end.

Joey Comeau grew up in Halifax. He has a degree in Linguistics. His fourth book, *Overqualified*, came out with ECW in spring 2009. He can be found online at www.asofterworld.com.

Jessica Faulds lives and drinks in Edmonton, Alberta. She also plays in the band Blind Tiger, Tiger.

Matthew Firth was born and raised in Hamilton. He is the author of three short story collections, most recently, *Suburban Pornography and Other Stories* (Anvil Press, 2006). His short fiction has been published in anthologies, journals, and mags in Canada, the U.K., U.S., Ireland, and Australia. He has been editor and publisher of the lit mag *Front&Centre* since 1998. He founded Black Bile Press in 1993, which has been publishing lit mags and chapbooks ever since. He has worked as a garbageman, gravedigger, variety-store clerk, soup-kitchen cook, asphalt raker, semi-pro lacrosse player, technical writer, and many other jobs. He now lives in Ottawa with his wife and two boys.

Janine Fleri is a writer and filmmaker; born in Vermont to native Long Islanders, she now resides in Queens. Her creative works often explore the topics of desire, physical identity, social anxiety, and clinical touch as inspired by her experiences as a patient of Crohn's Disease. She has contributed content to the La Superette art fair as well as AbecedariumNYC .com, an online exhibition hosted by the New York Public Library.

Golda Fried's first collection of short stories, *Darkness Then A Blown Kiss*, was illustrated by foolish girl comic creator Vesna Mostovac. In 2005, she published a coming-of-age novel, called *Nellcott Is My Darling* about a girl's first year at McGill. It was nominated for the Governor General's Award in Canada. Then in the summer of 2007, she collaborated with Vesta again on *Summer Ink: An illustrated book of letters* presented by *Kiss Machine*.

Sarah Gordon is a Winnipegger, which means she drinks Slurpees even in minus thirty, and owns the first Weakerthans T-shirt. She is also an artist-poet turned soldier turned aspiring nurse. After graduating from art school she joined the army as a field medic. She's now chipping away at a nursing degree. Her prose poetry book, *Rapture Red and Smoke Grey*, was published by Turnstone Press in 2001.

Dave Hazzan lives in Ilsan, South Korea. His first novel, *I Came To in Geumhodong*, came out two years ago.

Emma Healey lives in Toronto. In the past, she has been the playwright-in-residence at the Paprika Theatre Festival, a barista, line-running assistant to many of North America's finest actors, a reliable cat-sitter, a photographer, a reviewer for *Broken Pencil*, and someone who pretends to be sick so medical students can pretend to figure out what's wrong with her. Currently, she writes short stories.

McKinley M. Hellenes, a Vancouver expatriate, lives and writes in Mission, British Columbia, where she listens obsessively to all of Bruce

Springsteen's records (except for *Tunnel of Love*), and watches the skies for signs of extraterrestrial life. Her stories and poems have appeared in magazines and anthologies such as *Broken Pencil*; *Kiss Machine*; *Memewar*; the *Liar*; *Quills*; *Red Light: Superheroes, Saints, and Sluts*; and The Journey Prize Stories Volume 17. To ferret out stories of even lesser renown, you can visit her blog at: www.mckinleymhellenes.wordpress.com. She writes them for you.

Paul Hong lives in Toronto, and is the author *Your Love Is Murder or the Case of the Mangled Pie*. An illustrated version of "Superboy" appears in *Boredom Fighters!* (Tightrope Books, 2008).

Joel Katelnikoff's work has appeared in all fucking kinds of zines and lit mags, including the *Fiddlehead*, *Grain*, the *Malahat Review*, and *Cult of the Dead Cow*. He is the former editor of several top-notch publications, including the *Neo-Comintern Magazine*, and *Qwerty*. During his tenure with the Sons of Prozac, Count K recorded nearly fifty songs, including smash hit singles "The Blair Witch Project," "Cokefest '99," "Drunk 'N' High (Epsilon Mix)," and "This Crack Azz Beat." He currently rules the University of Alberta, where he is crafting a revolutionary dissertation on old-school ASCII zines.

Greg Kearney is the author of the short story collections *Mommy Daddy Baby* and *Pretty*; the latter collection has been rejected by virtually every publishing house that has ever been. He's finishing up a novel, *Violet of Black Lake*.

Esme Keith has published fiction in *Prairie Fire*, *Broken Pencil*, the *Dalhousie Review*, and *Zeugma*. She is currently working on a novel.

Etgar Keret is Israel's most popular writer. His newest collection of short stories is *The Girl on the Fridge* (Farrar, Straus and Giroux, 2008).

Jake Kennedy is a poet and sometime visual artist. With Toronto artist Paola Poletto, he's just finished co-editing a book of graphic poems entitled *Boredom Fighters!* (Tightrope Books, 2008). Jake works at Okanagan College, and lives in Kelowna, British Columbia, with his daughter Rae and partner Marlo. Please email him at the following address and he will send you free things: jakedavidkennedy@gmail.com

Tor Lukasik-Foss is an artist, performer, and writer from Hamilton, Ontario. He writes a column and arts features for *Hamilton Magazine*, and occasionally writes reviews and catalogue essays for obscure arts publications and institutions. He was nominated for a 2008 National Magazine Award. His writing factors heavily in both his visual art and performance work, and he has released three CDs of original music under the stage name "tiny bill cody." He likes to yodel.

Derek McCormack's most recent novel is *The Show That Smells* (ECW Press, 2008). His previous novel, *The Haunted Hillbilly* (ECW Press, 2003), was named a "Book of the Year" by both the *Globe & Mail* and the *Village Voice*, and was nominated for a Lambda Award for Best Gay Fiction. He lives in Toronto.

Karen McElrea's work has appeared in numerous publications, including *Broken Pencil; Grain; Event; Wascana Review*; *Geist*; *Arc*; the *Fieldstone Review*; *Kiss Machine*; *Vallum*; *All Rights Reserved; Zeugma*; *Literary Review of Canada*; *echolocation*; *FreeFall Magazine*; the *Dalhousie Review*; and *Misunderstandings Magazine*; in *Body Language: a Head to Toe Anthology* (Black Moss Press, 2003); and on buses in Winnipeg, where she works as a freelance editor.

Leanna McLennan is originally from the Maritimes, and currently lives and writes in Toronto. She has a Master of Arts in Creative Writing from Concordia University. Her work has been published in the *Antigonish Review*, *Broken Pencil*, *CV2*, the *Fiddlehead*, *Fireweed*, *Matrix*, *Taddle Creek*, and *Third Floor Lounge: An Anthology of Poetry from the Banff Centre for the Arts Writing Studio 2004*. She is currently writing a novel about a young woman who moves to Toronto to become a famous actress, but, instead, finds work as a film extra.

Christoph Meyer lives in the tiny town of Howard, located in Knox County, Ohio, a pleasant rural Midwestern area quaintly infested with Amish. He lives with his wife, Lisa, and five-year-old son Herbie, in a restored 1873 mill. He does the zine *28 Pages Lovingly Bound with Twine*.

Hal Niedzviecki is a writer, culture commentator, and editor whose work challenges preconceptions and confronts readers with the offences of everyday life. He is co-founder of *Broken Pencil*, the magazine of zine culture and the independent arts, and edited the magazine from 1995 to 2002. He is also co-founder of the annual Canzine Festival of Underground Culture. He's the author of articles, novels—most recently *The Program* (Random House, 2005)—and books on culture, like *Hello, I'm Special* (City Lights Publishers, 2006). His latest book is *The Peep Diaries* (City Lights, 2009)

Graham Parke was born in a small town in the Netherlands in 1738. He lived off the land, hunting squirrels and crocodiles, until, in 1799, he finally decided to join society. Society was not pleased. After creating rudimentary working models for an internal combustion engine, a water-powered laser, and a set of surprisingly fuzzy dice, he finally found his true calling; he was to become a scribe. He immediately set upon his new interest with vigor, taking long lunches, sleeping in till all hours of the afternoon, and spending his waking hours lamenting the indescribable hardships of the insanely talented. He also did some writing. His best known efforts to date are: "What I'd like for my birthday—a short list by G. Parke" (1913), and "People I just met—address book entries to add over the weekend" (1965). He's still hoping for that ever elusive big break. Graham Parke has been described as both a humanitarian and a pathological liar. Convincing evidence to support either allegation has yet to be produced.

Janette Platana was born and raised in Saskatchewan, and now lives in Peterborough, Ontario. Her writing has been published in Canada, the United States, and Turkey. She has received funding from the Ontario Arts Council and the Canada Council for the Arts, as well as a fellowship from the Chalmers Arts Foundation. She has been nominated for the K.M. Hunter Award for literature, and has been shortlisted several times for the CBC Literary Awards. She has a collection of short stories and a novel ready for publication, and is working a second novel. Contact her at: JanettePlatana.com, or JPlatana@rocketmail.com

Ethan Rilly is a cartoonist and a policy advisor for the Ontario government, which gets a little weird. His comic book, *Pope Hats*, was nominated for a 2008 Doug Wright Award for Best Emerging Talent, as well as for some other award he didn't win. He will buy you dinner some day. Contact him at: erilly@gmail.com

Ian Rogers is a writer, artist, and photographer. His short fiction has been published or is forthcoming in *Cemetery Dance, Broken Pencil*, and *All Hallows*. His stories have also appeared in several anthologies. Ian lives with his wife in Peterborough, Ontario. For more information, visit: www.ianrogers.ca.

Richard Rosenbaum is a writer from Toronto, sort of. He graduated from the University of Toronto in 2003 with an Honours BA in English and Philosophy, qualifying him either to drive a cab or edit an anthology. He failed his drivers test. His fiction has appeared in *Broken Pencil*, and the Newark-based lit zine the *Juvenilian;* his non-fiction has appeared in a few other places. He is currently associate fiction editor and online fiction editor at *Broken Pencil*, and pursuing a master's degree in the incredibly lucrative field of Communication and Culture. He'll see you in the remainders section of your local bookstore, probably. E-mail him at: richardr@brokenpencil.com.

Martha Schabas holds an MA in Creative Writing from the University of East Anglia where she received the David Higham Literary Award. Her fiction has appeared in several literary publications. She lives in East London and is working on her first novel.

Joel Schneier is a writer, cartoonist, and photographer. He is the creator of NinjaPancakes.com, an offbeat arts and entertainment website, as well as notjoelschneier.com, a writer's blog. Joel grew up outside of Washington, DC, where he started writing when he was sixteen. He lived in Harrisonburg, Virginia, where he graduated from James Madison University and worked for Rosetta Stone, Ltd., then moved to Portland, Oregon, to work as an AmeriCorps VISTA. Joel is currently editing his first novel, and working on his second. He is also right behind you.

Craig Sernotti is a sometimes writer from New Jersey. He edits *THE*, which can be found at: http://welcometoyethe.blogspot.com. That's about it.

Kevin Spenst's prose has appeared in the pages of *Geist*, *Broken Pencil*, and the *Martian Press Review*. He has one collection of short-short stories in print called *Fast Fictions*, which was launched with a fifty-venue, one-day-only reading tour of Vancouver in September 2007. A documentary about the day, entitled *1000 stories*, has since screened at several film festivals in North America. To date, Kevin has written over 1,151 short-short stories, most of which can be found online on various website experiments. Kevinspenst.com is where it all begins.

Kate Story was born and raised in St. John's, Newfoundland, in a house built by her great great grandfather beneath the Southside Hill. Her short fiction has been published in magazines including *Broken Pencil*, *Takeout*, and *Kiss Machine*. Her written performance works have been produced as plays, performance art, and theatre-dance productions in Ontario (Toronto and Peterborough), and Newfoundland and Labrador (St. John's). She has been twice nominated for the Ontario Arts Council's K.M. Hunter Artist Award. Her first novel is *Blasted* (Killick Press, 2008).

Zoe Whittall's first novel, *Bottle Rocket Hearts*, was named a Best Book of 2007 by the *Globe & Mail* and *Quill & Quire*. Her poetry books include *The Best Ten Minutes of Your Life* (McGilligan, 2001), *The Emily Valentine Poems* (Snare Books, 2006), and *Precordial Thump* (Exile Editions, 2008). She lives in Toronto. http://zoewhittall.blogspot.com

Christopher Willard is both a writer and visual artist. His first novel was *Garbage Head* (Véhicule Press, 2006). He has a novella coming out spring 2009. Shorter fiction has recently appeared in *Ars Medica*, *Ranfurly Review*, and *Ukula*. His visual art is represented by Herringer Kiss Gallery, and he is in many collections including the Metropolitan Museum of Art. He currently teaches at the Alberta College of Art + Design.

ABOUT
BROKEN PENCIL

Founded in 1995 and based in Toronto, Ontario, Canada, *Broken Pencil* is a website and a print magazine published four times a year. It is one of the few magazines in the world devoted exclusively to underground culture and the independent arts. A cross between the *Utne Reader,* an underground *Reader's Digest,* and the now defunct *Factsheet Five,* *Broken Pencil* reviews the best zines, books, websites, videos, and artworks from the underground, and reprints the best articles from the alternative press. Also, groundbreaking interviews, original fiction, and commentary on all aspects of the independent arts in Canada and across the world. *Broken Pencil*'s notorious annual fiction contest, the Indie Writers Deathmatch, has attracted controversy since its inception, with hundreds of thousands of votes for readers' favourite story cast from visitors to the contest website.

Broken Pencil is always looking for submissions. To submit artwork or propose an article, email: editor@brokenpencil.com, or write: PO Box 203, Station P, Toronto, Ontario, M5S 2S7, Canada. To submit fiction for our print magazine or website, send stories of 3000 words or less to: fiction@brokenpencil.com.

From the hilarious to the perverse, *Broken Pencil* challenges conformity and demands attention. Everything you need to navigate our culture is available at: www.brokenpencil.com

ACKNOWLEDGMENTS

Thanks to: The Eternal You; Hal Niedzviecki, Lindsay Gibb, Tara Gordon-Flint, and Derek Winkler from *Broken Pencil*; Michael Holmes, Jack David, and Jen Hale from ECW Press; my family and friends who supported and encouraged me in putting together this anthology; all the writers whose work appears in this book, and all the ones whose stories we couldn't fit in (sorry!); and of course all of *Broken Pencil*'s readers and contributors, in perpetuity throughout the universe.